Bright Morning Stars

Bright Morning Stars

A Novel by

Mary Rose O'Reilley

BRIGHT
HORSE
BOOKS

Brighthorse Books
13202 N River Drive
Omaha, NE 68112
brighthorsebooks.com

ISBN: 978-1-944467-14-2

Author Photo © Timothy Aguero Photography for Poetry on Buses
Cover Photo © jaboo2foto

For permission to reproduce selections from this book, contact the editors at info@brighthorsebooks.com. For information about Brighthorse Books and the Brighthorse Prize, visit us on the web at brighthorsebooks.com.

This book is a work of fiction. The characters, incidents, and dialogue are drawn from the author's imagination and are not to be construed as real. Any resemblance to actual events or persons, living or dead, is entirely coincidental.

Brighthorse books are distributed to the trade through Ingram Book Group and its distribution partners. For more information, go to https://ipage.ingramcontent.com/ipage/li001.jsp.

To learn more about Brighthorse Books, go to brighthorsebooks.com.

This book is for Rocky O'Reilley Dias,
Mama J. and Mama B.

PROLOGUE: LUCY

WE'RE FAMOUS, AND I'm dead.

It hasn't slowed me down any.

You were the one who liked to read, and now I see the fun of it: that teeming life, tied off at the end like a parcel ready to mail. But if a reader loves the book, the story goes on and on. So you told me. Behind each leather spine on your bookshelf a room, behind each room a world.

Hamlet is not over.

I am not over.

In my last sketchbook—it lies open under glass at the Art Institute—I drew you over and over with a book in your hands. I drew you down the days we had together, reading to Sylvie, to me, to yourself.

I draw you still, though my work is—shall we say?—ephemeral. I draw your new spectacles, the veins of your hands. If I could, I would sketch the blood coursing through your body.

When Papa taught me to draw, he told me to let *invisible presence* affect the visual surface: what I know is there, but can't see: blood, muscle, spirit. Thus the sketch lives. As long as paper lasts.

I draw you still, and I know you know it. Thus your serenity, so much remarked upon. Your slow walk, as though you moved through a density of many worlds at once. For we are led and kept, we are the hidden part of everything.

This has a weight to it.

PART ONE:
THE WOMAN
WHO LOST HER SKIN

*Northfield State Hospital,
Northfield, Minnesota, 1921*

CHAPTER ONE: LUCY

IT IS APRIL 10, 1921.

How hard is that to remember? Jane Robinson had wanted to know, when she came to get me dressed.

For two weeks, Jane Robinson has quizzed me on dates and names. She knew I was lost and she was determined to throw breadcrumbs on my path, to lead me home. Or somewhere.

As I now know. At the time, it was just another annoyance.

My preferred answer to all questions was "I don't care." The truth was usually "I don't remember."

Jane refused those answers. Sometimes she gave me a little slap. "What's the date? What's my name?"

I could cheat on that one. I read her name off the brass tag over her apron pocket: *Jane Robinson, Nursing Assistant.*

She knew I cheated. It pleased her. I guess it showed I had some brains. Maybe some gumption. "Have some gumption," she would say when I failed her quizzes. "How hard is it to remember the date?"

Very hard.

"How old are you?"

"Very old."

"You're twenty-two. I wish I was twenty-two."

I wished she would quiz me on something I knew.

I still had my grip on the material world. I was—or had been in some other universe—an art student. My eyes still took in details of line and color, face and form. I couldn't reliably recall Jane's name, but I could tell you that her nose turned up slightly, like a pig's, forcing me to stare into her nostrils. I could number the hairs on her chin and tell you they were white and stiff. My imagination had constructed even what I could not see, the shape of her club foot in its leather shoe.

"Where are you?" Jane wanted to know.

"Northfield State Asylum," I mumbled. That I could not forget.

"Where are we going today?" she asked me on the morning of April 10.

At last, *somewhere*. For many days and dates, I had been confined to this ward, this corridor. ("Where are we?" "Admitting and Consultation.")

No one asked me "Why?"

That was the question which, in my own mind, obscured all others.

"We are going to work in the laundry," I said.

Jane Robinson dropped a gray cotton dress over my shift. She bundled up the white nightgown I'd worn in Admitting and Consultation and put it into the basket next to my bed.

"Yes, and after that you're going on the ward. So you won't see me for awhile."

I tried to look bold. Jane had been kind to me, in her way. Now she was full of warnings and advice, like a mother sending her child off to school.

"They'll test you. You must always know the date. But listen, this is the most important thing: you have to get through the day. Today. Especially today. If you don't, they'll wash their hands of you. They haven't got time to fuss. You'll wind up tied to a bed upstairs."

I turned to Jane, my arms extended, displaying my dress. She shrank into herself. Both of us knew she had said too much. Overstepped. I dropped my eyes and tried to look uncomprehending. It was easy. Just let go and lean backwards into the haze lurking always in the corners of the room. Into my terror and memory. Think about Will, the key to our bedroom—where was it?—Mrs. Lerner's knitting. Lean back into the shimmer of Veronal and paraldehyde in the little brown bottles the nurses brought round.

"Max is going to come and get you at quarter-to-ten."

Seeing, perhaps, my apprehension, she went on, "You'll be safe with him. He's one of the ward assistants. They keep order, so no one gets hurt."

I nodded, and looked over her shoulder at my face in a mirror made of polished tin that hung over the washstand.

Order. My eyes, poorly reflected, widened. For the space of a brief hallucination, I stared into the face of a ghost, my dead mother maybe, with her high planed cheeks and the smudges of darkness drawn under them.

Mother-words came to me in my first language and ran off my tongue.

Jane lifted her hand for that little slap. "English! You're in America. They'll think you're talking gibberish. They'll tie you to a chair."

She settled for snapping her fingernail against my cheek-bone. "Say you're sorry."

"I'm sorry." I dropped my eyes from my mother's face.

"Say, *Thank you Miss Robinson for all you've done for me.*"

I repeated the phrase. I flashed back again to my immigrant's childhood, when I parceled out sounds without meaning as a nun tapped restlessly with a ruler on her desk. While I whispered and memorized her hands. Longing only to draw.

Jane Robinson reached under my chin and raised my face to look into her flaring nostrils. "Are you grateful, really?"

I considered, in some moiling part of my consciousness, how she had joined forces with me, setting the two of us apart from "them," who had the power to tie us to furniture. Only months later would it come to me that Jane Robinson had once been a patient herself, "cured" maybe, but what's a woman to do, graduating from an asylum with a club foot and nothing?

The institution, I would learn from my own practical experience, tried hard to smooth the way for those it managed to release into the world.

"Yes," I said. "I'm grateful." My eyes went to a tableau forming in the tin mirror. It had the look of Vermeer, Jane's cap a little askew, her apron a blot of white. All forces concentrated on the *gaze* between—whom? Mother and daughter. Lady and maid? Complicity.

"You're welcome." She gave my chin a little shake and released it. "Is there anything you want before Max comes?"

I caught her gesture toward the chamber pot, but I said, "A pencil."

Dipping her hands now in the washbasin, still cloudy with soap, drying them, she laughed. "Oh, honey, it's going to be a while before they give you anything sharp."

I shrugged. *Charcoal*, I thought.

There was a knock on the door.

"Now, quick, what's your name?"

"Janina Lucy Allen."

From the way Jane's lips tightened, I knew I had got something wrong. But she let it pass. She opened the door, and the light, as it always did, fell in.

There was a short, thin man standing there. I thought of Rumpelstiltskin, with his questions and obscure desire. Max's arms, under rippling muscles, were abundantly tattooed. The hand he thrust out was strong, balancing—I had felt myself beginning to slide—"Well now, young lady, how are you today? And can you tell Max what day it is?"

"Monday," I said. "April 10, 1921."

CHAPTER TWO: LUCY

"*MAX, STAND HER on the easy side of the mangle.*"

I repeat to myself the words I heard Matron say.

I'm trying to locate myself in space (easy side of the mangle) and time (spring? summer?). Five minutes' walk with Max across the grounds from Admitting and Consultation into the humid, heaving enclosure of the laundry has driven all sense from my mind.

No, I cannot tell you the date. I can tell you there is a tall, wide chimney on the building, with a kind of red-and-white brick pattern at its top, and from the chimney rises a blanched column of smoke, bisecting a blue bowl of sky.

It's *morning*. Let it go at that.

Something in my mind flutters like a wounded bat, trying to get home despite damaged equipment.

Although I don't want to go home (do I have a home?). Nor even back to Jane Robinson, who has handed me off to Max.

Max. Max, the laundry attendant, guard, or warden, wears black wool pants and suspenders over a suit of peeping long johns. The underwear looks worn to paper, but fussily clean.

Attendant, guard or warden? I have forgotten, again, where I am, and, above all, *why*.

Prison seems to fit the data.

When the shopkeeper in Northfield caught me pocketing that reel of red darning cotton, Will threatened me with jail. When, another day, the sheriff brought me home, incoherent, from the train station, the front torn out of my dress, Mrs. Lerner offered a dose of salts.

Which of them, in the ensuing weeks, had first spoken the word *asylum*?

English is not my first language, and I don't always bring the perfect weight of connotation to its vocabulary. The word *asylum* filled me with hunger for warmth and safety, sanctuary, rest. Especially after the talk of *jail*, a harsh, clanging word in any tongue. When the uniformed men came for me, I did not struggle.

Besides, Will had given me a bromide.

Let's just say I've landed on the easy side of the mangle. Let's just say it's a laundry room. There are two women to my left, four to my right. We all wear cotton dresses cut to a similar pattern; mine is gray, the women on my left wear faded pink. The other three dresses, glimpsed in a quick sideways glance, come to me as a blur of tiny floral patterns, like those on a flour sack. All of us wear white pinafores. Matron tied one around me when Max brought me to here, to the easy side of the mangle, at midmorning.

Matron: a chubby-faced woman with curly light hair, in that indistinct stage of shift from blond to starry white. She wears a white uniform but no nurse's cap. I suppose that her eyes, which often seek me out, are blue. Blue eyes often reflect a kind of *absence*. I suppose she's Swedish, like so many women in these parts. She sits on a dais at the front of the laundry, watching the action and making things happen if they need to. There is a big white school clock mounted on the wall behind her. I can discern that it is 10:25.

More useful information for the bat in my mind.

The bat struggles for day and date, settles instead on another dim imperative: get through this day.

We mangle-girls stand on a riser and we can see over the top of our monster machine, which is composed of two big padded rollers, each about ten feet long, driven by a noisy engine that makes the laundry an agony to the ears. I can see the women on the hard side of the mangle, doing whatever demanding work they do to keep a stream of material coming at us.

These women are a blur to me at the moment, because tears are running out of my eyes, as they have been, I think, for weeks. My eyes burn all the time from my own body's salt. I won't call it crying, because crying involves some action on a girl's part. These tears are a flood that rises from the plain of my spirit without my volition or control.

Will despised tears. The first time he raised his hand against me, it was because I couldn't stop this tide, which seemed to be pulled out of me by the moon rising up in the northeast window behind our bed.

Possibly I have been weeping since then, since my wedding night. I mean, the weeping has gone on.

"You done this before?" Max had asked, as he anchored me at the mangle.

I shook my head, mute. I know the value of silence.

"Watch what the others do," he said. Then he went back to his place at the door, flexing the apples of muscle in his arms. He'd rolled up his sleeves in the laundry's heat. Later, I will learn he'd been a circus performer in his youth. Some kind of acrobat, a job that required walking on the hands.

How has he come to be here?

How have I come to be here? I am half-asleep or half-drugged. Half who I am, anyway. It's a new habit with me to keep wiping my eyes on my sleeve, taking care to avoid a scrape from the starched white cuffs of my dress.

The laundry room scares me. It's hot, there is danger everywhere. Water cooking in copper boilers. Vats of starch, gently simmering, that could mesmerize you into a trance. An industrial stove with sadirons baking on top. There must be the temptation to throw things you can barely lift.

Hissing and whispering. Sixty or so women doing the work, simmering as well, I suppose.

I am simmering. The tears are perhaps a liquefaction of my rage.

In the periphery of the room, women are busy with more complicated tasks than mangling. They move back and forth from ironing boards to the supply of flat irons. They hang garments on long pipes mounted on carts, which other women take away, out the swinging doors of the laundry through which Max led me at 9:50 a.m. by Matron's clock.

Clearly these women have some status in the place. At the ironing boards, they shake out shirtwaists (who gets to wear those?). They bend over frilly collars. They have freedom to walk from here to there, and to exit. Things I once took for granted.

The frills have been removed from my life.

And the monster presides: the mangle. Here on the easy side, we receive the ironing as it comes through. Handkerchiefs at the moment. What could be simpler? You peel them off the hot cloth roller of the machine. It smells of damp and burning. I like the smell. It has a tang of life. You fold the hankies in half and then in quarters, name tag up. You stack them in the box provided. I mastered this before 10:30, even through a veil of salt.

The riser on the easy side has a shelf, like a prie-dieu. On top of it, we seven women fold hankies rapidly.

I am going to get through this day.

But suddenly, peeling and folding and stacking as fast as I can, I am soaked with sweat and fighting panic. What if I fall behind? What if I stop to cough or use the handkerchief stuck up my sleeve to wipe my nose? The squares of cotton will spin around on another circuit, confounding the women on the other side, the hard side. The cotton will scorch, catch fire maybe.

It emerges as a crisis that my nose is running. I sniff. I feel sick, having taken no breakfast, but I know I must not falter.

I fainted one night, early in my stay on the admitting ward. What a respite—but when I wakened I was on a stone floor that smelled of urine, and someone had stolen the stub of pencil I'd managed to hang on to till then. No one moved me to a soft bed or put a pillow under my head, which ached from the blow to the floor. Around me a forest of legs in white or striped stockings, feet at my eye level clad in black leather shoes, all alike. The other women, attendants and patients, had been exercising when Jane Robinson led me into the room. They'd been shuffling around to music from a gramophone.

I tried to get up, afraid of being shuffled over. Someone offered me a hand and a strong lift. This is what would pass for kindness in my life now, and later I would learn it was no small, no unwelcome, gesture.

That experience has driven the fainting instinct out of me. I stand up to the mangle, take a deep breath of sour air and peel handkerchiefs like crazy.

A sharp kick comes from the woman on my left.

I'd gotten into a sort of dream. Dreaming stops the unhappy thoughts. I was dreaming of something *neutral*: the long field of grass that drops off Summit Avenue into the river valley below, near the art school. I was embodying the field with rabbits and moles and other manageable small life, when I felt a cruel kick to the tender spot just below my ankle bone.

I gasp. The tears spring anew, a sense of injustice floods my mind. Surely I'm bleeding, but I can't let the handkerchiefs go by to check. I seem to feel warm blood spreading across my cotton stocking.

The woman on my left starts to babble in what sounds like a foreign language. Gibberish. Then I realize she is cursing vividly. Her words are English, but none I have ever heard.

"Cunt!"

Well, I have heard that word. But not from a woman.

Suddenly, dizzily, this strikes me funny. I start to laugh. Hysteria rises in my throat, like bile, like reflux.

"Did you crowd her?" whispers the woman on my right, peeling my hankies along with hers. "She can't stand to be crowded."

"I did nothing," I say, tears overriding the giggles. That sense of injustice.

Behind us rises the sharp sound of the kind of handbell teachers keep on their desks. Slam! Slam! Ring! Ring! Ring! *O Spot! Bad Spot! Run, Spot, run!*

Matron's coming. "Silence, ladies."

Someone responding to the bell has shut down the steam apparatus of the mangle, which disengages from its hankies and stops.

One of the upper-class women, the hand ironers, leaves her station and moves in next to me.

This feels like some kind of containment strategy.

Not fair! I have done nothing wrong.

She guides me in and out of the four ladies on my right. Looking wildly around for my footing, I see that, indeed, my ankle bone is rimmed in blood, the stocking torn.

The trustee woman holding tight to my left arm is chuckling softly. "Norah kicks like hell," she says.

Faintness rises again. This time it's pure self-indulgence. I want to sink into the arms of my rescuer and block out the room, the pain, my life.

"Cheer up," she says softly. "Don't you let yourself go." Her voice is not-from-here. A little southern.

Matron's voice barks over a disobedient din arising in the room. It's as though we've all come out of our trances and discovered how hot we are, how angry, how confused. "Annie Leary, take her out. Miss Riordan, replace her on the line. Max."

The guard stands at attention, caressing the truncheon he carries at his belt. Surely he wouldn't use such an implement on the women, I think. I am still struggling for justice.

Merely to take the stick out of its holster, like a husband displaying his wares for the bride: this is enough to make the women whimper and return to work. Matron doesn't even need to leave the platform where she stands, arms folded, looking out at us impassively. Me, as I trot past her, cringing and drowning on the woman called Annie's arm, Matron looks at me with more interest.

I am new. I will change all the equations.

•

Annie leads me past Max and his appraising eye into the long tiled corridor outside the laundry, where there's a lavatory. The minute we're on our own, Annie presses her fingers into my tender shoulder joint. It almost, not quite, hurts. I become focused.

"You stand up straight," she whispers. Her arm is still around my shoulder and, despite her sharp tone, I want her to keep it there. I am hungry for touch.

I pull myself erect. Instinctive obedience to the stronger personality.

"You better stand up for yourself." Annie releases my arm with a light squeeze that might be friendly. I've lost my power to discriminate.

We have come to the washrooms, with their long, barred windows. Sunshine floods in. I instinctively breathe deeply and then exhale.

"That's right," Annie says. She pulls up a small stool from under the line of sinks and sits down. "Peel off that stocking."

Self-consciously I reach up under the gray cotton pique. I try to remember when they took my own clothes away, the clothes Will bought for me. I grope for my garters and roll down the stocking.

Annie sits looking me up and down with a little smirk on her face. But she's taken her own handkerchief out and wet it at the sink. "We need some iodine, but there's none in here."

"Perhaps we could ask Matron," I say in a tone that suggests logic and justice in the world.

Annie snorts. "You just keep away from that woman." She dabs gently at the wound on my ankle—and a small scrape it is after all, despite the blood—taking off my shoe and lifting my foot into her lap.

I lean backward and grab on to a sink for balance.

"Yeah, that Norah can kick," Annie says.

"And curse," I say.

Annie's laugh is a soft, colt-like sound.

"Why does she do it?"

"She just *is*."

Annie rubs the unwounded part of my foot and sets it back down on the cool tiles. For some reason, I feel myself blushing. I take another long breath and let myself feel the April as it enters the lavatory windows. I ponder gratefully the nature of *April*: wind shifting to the south, smell of grass.

"It feels good to be out of that hot room," Annie drawls, standing now.

She reaches under her dress and pulls out a leather pouch.

Jane Robinson has put me in that old kind of slip that has pockets in it you reach from a slit in the dress. Annie wears the same fashion. I guess everything around here is pretty uniform.

From her slip pocket she draws cigarette papers and matches. She tips tobacco out of the pouch, rolls the smoke with one hand and lights it. The windows over the row of sinks are open behind the bars. Annie leans over the spigots to exhale smoke into the world outside.

We hear Max's approaching steps outside the lavatory door, and the rattle of his truncheon on the frame. So that's what he uses it for. "Ladies all right?" he yells.

I turn to Annie in fright.

She reaches out a hand—I can see now that her fingers are stained with nicotine, like a street boy's. They brush my hair's damp fringe, as though we had all the time in the world. "You are such a scared rabbit," she says in a soft voice.

I feel cold now where the heat had risen. *This touching.*

"Want one?" she asks. "I'll roll it for you."

I shift my eyes toward the hall.

She steadfastly refuses to indulge my concern. "Max is not coming into the ladies' *toilette*." She gives the word a little imitation French flip.

22

I don't think it's the right French word, but can't think what they'd say, the French. My mind goes on vacation down the corridors of high school. Sister Antoine's class. *Salle de bain?* No. *Abbatoir?* No.

"Have you ever?" she asks.

"Smoked?"

"Yes."

"Of course." I say.

Incredulous snort. "Where?"

"School," I reply. Mentally I leave French class and walk seven blocks south to the Academy of Art and Design. To Wanda's room. Nips of gin and learning to dance the Black Bottom.

I've impressed Annie at last. "School. College?"

"Art school," I say.

"Art school. I should have known."

"Why should you have known?"

Her face comes close to mine. "You're different."

I hope so, I think. Different from Norah with her string of curses, her evil horse kick. Different from the woman on my left side at the mangle, who smells of vomit, and from the babyish girls with big heads and slanted eyes who carry the baskets to and fro, too incompetent even to mangle the hankies.

"Where you from?" I ask.

She drops her eyes. I hadn't yet learned that questions as simple as that could be intrusive and dangerous.

"Cannon Falls," she says shortly, naming a town not far away. Not far enough south for her accent.

"I married"—I stumble. I had been going to say "a man from Northfield." Northfield is close to Cannon Falls. But that doesn't seem to sum up Will: a man from Northfield.

"His family farmed…" That doesn't work either. Whatever Will is, farming doesn't place him. Will used to call himself, with his little ironic compression of the lips—"a gentleman farmer." I couldn't very well say that.

"…but he did something in the Cities." I have no idea what. Annie ignores my fits and starts, pulling on her cigarette.

"Where is he now, the husband?"

"At his work, I guess. What day is it? Monday. He said he'd come and see me." My words seem to bounce off the tiles, mocking each reasonable statement and making it seem absurd—*work, Monday, he said he'd come and see me…*

Annie does not reply. She nods. Looks out the window. "Can I touch your hair?" she asks suddenly.

I nod, I blush again. Stumbling into the light of this room, I seem to have entered a new dimension of space.

Her fingers, tentative this time. She draws a pin out of my knot of hair. Jane has allowed me three blunt tortoise shell pins. She draws out another, and the third. My hair falls to my waist. "True chestnut," she says.

I smile. She could be talking about a horse.

She thrusts her hand into my hair. I leap back toward the sink. "They'll cut it," she says, not holding on. "Let's run away."

Max's truncheon again. "Ladies!"

"Yup!" she yells, like a boy.

"Leave her alone, if that's what you're up to," Max calls in. "Don't think I won't come in."

"Her ankle is bleeding." Annie calls back. "We need some iodine."

"Come out of there." *Whack.*

I wad up a square of the crackly lavatory paper, stick it to the wound, and pull up my stocking. Annie turns her back this time as I fish for a garter.

Let's run away. What could she possibly be talking about? What world has this invitation come out of? What possibilities? My imagination takes a leap.

I lift my chin and look into her eyes.

"You are a brave girl," she says. "I know you are a brave girl."

•

With Max behind us, humming a bit in his throat, we march

back down the tiles to the laundry. They are white tiles, with squares of green at intervals.

I will come to dream about that pattern because I'll become so accustomed to walking the wards with my eyes cast down. Every ward—I will see a few of them—have the same design. No doubt they were laid to give us a sense of tranquility and order. And they show the dirt, or rather, no dirt. It's the cleanest place you could imagine. No blood on the floor.

"Put her on the hard side," Matron commands as the heat of the laundry room hits us. "She has a high school diploma." Matron's lips draw up over her teeth. Probably she's making fun of me. "Mrs. Leary, opposite her."

We can study each other now across the mangle, Annie and I. She's tall and rangy, with hooded eyes that cut this way and that, never again offering contact but seeming to notice everything in the room. Her thick, yellow hair is bobbed.

Had they cut it? But the bob looks pretty on her.

I try to imitate her technique of look/don't look. Indeed, I waken to the room. *You are a brave girl. I know you are a brave girl.*

The hard side of the mangle is pretty easy, although we're feeding damp dresses now. What apparently takes higher education is lining everything up in a way that promotes the least wrinkling. The patterns pass for interesting. Garments in random flower patterns. We press a field of roses and then one of calendula. Then come the solid grays like mine, the pinks. There is a set with yellow dots and another in pale green—but these are the kitchen staffers' uniforms, it comes to me.

What dress you get, I think, has to do with when you come in, what they're cutting that month. That year.

I feed a new line of smocks into the mangle. The damp dresses—I fantasize—are sad women, fed into the machine. Droopy and wet they go in, stiff and flat they come out, to be shifted onto hangers by Annie and her six companions. The smocks are a strange cut. They hang in a straight line from the shoulders and the sleeves are much longer than they need to be.

I notice that Annie, in my former position, has left enough space between herself and Norah, the kicker, for someone else to stand. She's cosied up against the woman who smells of vomit. I suppose that, in time, one becomes less particular.

I imagine myself hung up by the shoulders on the rack of dresses, wheeled away into the dark.

I am having fun now, watching the play of color and form. As much fun as it's possible to have at that moment.

I am not having fun.

•

The hands of the large white clock that hangs behind Matron now point to 11:30. There's a chicken wire grill over the clock face, in case Norah or someone like Norah begins to throw things. Next to me, a pale young girl with an overlarge head and sparse, light hair shakes out women and feeds them into the machine. When she turns to me, I see that her eyes are strangely colorless and rimmed with wrinkles. She squints as though the light in the room hurts her.

She turns to me as I hear the rattle of carts somewhere outside. "Collation," she says. A quaint word. "Evie," she says.

"No, I'm Lucy," I reply.

"Evie," she repeats stubbornly. I realize she is introducing herself.

"I'm pleased to meet you."

Matron's handbell crashes. "Ladies, no distracting. Here's your coffee anyway."

Max is swinging open the doors to the hallway and a food worker clad in light green pushes in the carts.

I think about how sheep rouse themselves for the feed wagons. Sixty or so women's heads go up, like a flock of Dorsets. The mangle stops mangling. The hand ironers replace their implements. There is a moment of blessed peace. Then the almond-eyed girls begin to chatter and a woman in yellow dots takes one of them out, as

Annie had taken me. We can all see a dark stain of urine down the girl's dress, which is a gray one like mine.

"This isn't anything to wet your pants over." Annie has popped up beside me again.

All the mangle girls are making their way off the platform and heading for the steel carts at the back of the room. We receive our cups of coffee and slices of brown bread smeared with pale margarine. "Sometimes there's jam," Annie tells me.

"Tomato jam," says Evie, the white-haired girl.

I wrinkle my nose, which makes her laugh out of all proportion. I wrinkle it again. She laughs.

We're allowed to talk now. We can sit down on the benches that line the room and act like ordinary women in something like a cafeteria. "Will you have some jam, my dear?" says Evie, as though taking up this very fantasy. "Whoops, there isn't any." She laughs again, a harsh bray.

I long for the coffee Matron promised—have I slept in two weeks?—no. And I must get through the day. But the brown stuff in the heavy white cups turns out to be some hearty grain beverage.

"How's your ankle?" Annie asks.

I haven't thought about it. I have been lost in my story about feeding damp women into the machine. "Fine, I guess."

"Stocking's torn, though." Annie looks down at my feet, which are wrapping and unwrapping themselves around the metal pipe that anchors my bench to the floor as though my shoes have a disembodied will of their own.

She puts her bread into my hands. "I don't want this. You take it."

I'm hungry and grateful.

"That's good. Eat up. You have to eat." She leans in close to me. "You have to control yourself. You have to control your imagination," she whispers. All traces of Southern vanish.

The part of me that isn't occupied with nourishment is trying to figure out the rules of this inverted world I've landed in. I can only compare it to my all-girl high school. Annie is the experienced upperclassman, explaining the rules to me.

It has never occurred to me that I can control my imagination. Or ought to.

I look at her speculatively. Can she read minds? Has she been watching me feed the gray and pink ladies into the mangle, to rise again in uniform wrinkles, each one alike?

"Daydreaming helps, but you can't give in to it. You have to stay on guard."

I think of Norah. But I am not ready to give up my lovely, soft world of—what had the nuns called it?—*woolgathering*.

"What are you in here for, anyway?" This question comes in a whisper. Annie isn't even looking at me now, though there are just the two of us on the bench. The others have gone back to scavenge crumbs at the steel wagons.

This question is out of order; I who know nothing, know that. The nurse who sat with me last night, signing papers that fed me into the maw of the wards while I coveted her pen, had been adamant: "There will be no exchanging of histories."

Though surely she must have known, histories will be all we have. They are our novels and our *Ladies' Home Journal*. We will exchange our stories every time we get a chance to talk. And what will the doctors want from us? Histories, histories.

Nor are the nurses immune from listening.

I will come to know—though I am innocent in this particular moment—that it's our stories make us valuable.

But I'm not ready to offer mine on April 10, 1921. "I-I-I stole things. Kleptomania."

Kleptomania. Annie takes the word like the shiny offering it is. *Kleptomania*.

"It's when—"

"I know what it's when. Why didn't they just send you to the workhouse?"

I lower my eyes.

Annie has a laugh that's low and sugary, like her voice. "Kleptomania!"

This time it's a buzzer that rings, and Matron calls, "Ladies, ladies. Form your lines."

I am still starving. For bread. For Annie's hand on my shoulder. Which she withholds, turning toward the ironer's queue. "And you?"

I want from her. I want.

Her slow smile, turning away. "You are such an amateur," she says softly. "I killed my children." She tosses it off with a detached shrug, the deed of someone on a planet far away.

She has that bad-girl insouciance, like Wanda's.

I don't believe her.

•

I already knew, though I didn't know much, that crazy people lie constantly. It's the very nature of insanity—except for those few whose madness consists of blunt, obnoxious, heedless truth telling—to lie. It makes our histories more intriguing. Each one a work of art. It draws the doctors into our webs, with their pipes and furrowed foreheads.

Lying passes the time.

•

I've just told a whopper, about the stealing. Well, sort of a whopper. A poem about my life and deeds. Similar to the poem beginning "I married..."

When the nurses and aides come to take us back to our wards, I see that Annie is one of the elite. She gets a nurse on either side. And they take her up a different staircase from mine.

Each of us looks back at the other over our shoulders.

CHAPTER THREE

THE NEW NURSE, Mercy Winstead, was making her way across the asylum grounds to her first staff meeting. She was small, childishly proportioned. Lutheran Deaconess School of Nursing had accentuated her look of immaturity by capping her head with an organdy confection better suited to a parlor maid.

Nurse Winstead had mixed feelings about her cap. She loved what it stood for: a life of dedication. Independence. Her own bank account.

She suspected it had been designed by some doctor's jealous wife.

At the moment, its impracticality exasperated her, for the breeze had pulled her hair out of its bun and she was trying surreptitiously to groom. As a recent graduate, she wasn't quite sure what to expect from her cap: certainly not cover from the elements. This was high prairie, with its searing, stunning light and cruel cold.

Just now, its flirtatious, windy spring.

She's fallen a few steps behind her companion, Nurse Edith Malloy, who already has a foot on the brick sidewalk to Unit 1, Admitting and Consultation.

It's a kindness that Malloy does not turn and wait for Mercy to catch up. She must not, of course, use her pocket comb in public, neither must she appear unkempt.

She is the new nurse.

On the last day of the second week of her first job, nervous but resolved, she heads for an important meeting. She will be formally introduced to the senior physicians and ward supervisors. She will give the brief report Nurse Malloy has assigned. She intends to speak frankly and clearly, as she's been taught. People will come to respect her, as her teachers and head nurses always have. Even the doctors, who, like doctors everywhere, will be autocratic and arrogant.

This will all go better if she can get her hair under her cap.

After two weeks on the wards, Mercy has begun to think of the place as a sort of rabbit hole she's fallen down, like Alice in Wonderland. It looks like a hospital: here is the brass door, the smell of disinfectant; she touches her frivolous cap for reassurance. She is a trained nurse, and there are others of her kind striding ahead of her (always, she is last in line). She feels a nurse's pride and picks up her pace.

But so many things are utterly peculiar. She had expected bars on the windows—and found them—but the patients are freer than she could have imagined. Dr. David Grafton, the superintendent, has advanced ideas.

She expected that the patients would exhibit the bad manners and congenital stupidity of the poor.

She knows the poor.

She expected things to be grotesquely strange, because the formal name of this hospital is the State Asylum for the Criminally Insane, Crippled, Feeble-Minded and Indigent. (As if all those people belonged together. It must have been a legislative compromise.) Some of the patients are stupid, but most have seemed clever. The wards are no more peculiar than the indigent wards at Deaconess, but the grotesquerie and—unnervingly—the danger—comes at you out of nowhere when you least expect it.

It's been working on her nerves.

•

At the top of the steps to Admitting and Consultation, Nurse Edith Malloy stops to hold the door for her new probationer. The gesture makes her starched skirts snap, which Mercy Winstead takes for impatience. Nurse Malloy is muscular and tall, especially for an Irishwoman. They head down the long hall, lined with oil paintings of men in aggressive whiskers and photographs of nursing teams, variously capped. Nurse Winstead has trouble matching the other woman's gait. And Nurse Malloy is the sort of tall person who doesn't brake for small persons. Mercy Winstead finds herself skittering along, her dignity assaulted, her hairpins falling out.

Perhaps Nurse Malloy considers short stature to be a sign of congenital incompetence. Eugenics is all the rage in medicine at the moment. Mercy winces before the judgment of a superior physical specimen, aggressively starched.

The scrutiny had started, Mercy believes, on her first day at work. When she tended the woman who lost her skin.

Midway through that initiation, Mercy had had to sit down abruptly on the bathroom bench and put her head between her knees.

"The poor child." Miss Robinson, the aide, came to Mercy's assistance. Miss Robinson was a competent woman whom Mercy intuitively relied on. "She's never seen such a thing."

Edith Malloy had no patience with that, nor for the young nurse's faintness on the bench. "She'll see a lot of things she's never seen," the older woman flung out.

But Malloy had her kind side, and she had relented. "All right then, Nurse? It's your first day isn't it?"

Mercy had forced down the quaver in her voice—she disliked being called a child—and said staunchly. "Perfectly fine. It's just I didn't know what to think. I thought her skin was coming off."

Nurse Malloy's little pink lips had quivered then, "Faith, so did I!"

They turned back to the patient in the tub, a skinny old woman up to her neck in blackening greasy water. The nurses and the aide wore capacious rubber aprons and hoods over their hair. The old woman was docile now. If the strange outfits of her captors worried her she gave no sign.

They must look like firemen, or the department of public works, Mercy thought. She had a gift for putting herself in the position of other people and seeing things through new eyes. That skill was not contributing to her serenity in this assignment. But perhaps it would make her a better nurse.

If it didn't make her as crazy as the woman in the tub, who was tied down in a set of restraints that held her head above the water and kept her from flailing and hitting.

"I'll wash her privates, then," said Miss Robinson, bending to the job.

Mercy watched the aide swing herself briskly around on a crippled foot. She pondered the difficulties of women trying to take care of themselves in this world.

Nurse Malloy had taken on the task of wringing out the pink skin the patient had shed. It proved to be a set of silky drawers exactly the color of the rest of her, filth color. It had been on her body so long it had melded to her contours. The woman was a new admission, which meant she had had to be stripped, bathed and deloused—measures of hygiene that seemed not to have played a part in this patient's previous life. The nurses had peeled off several outer layers and lowered her into the water, the patient kicking and struggling so fiercely that it distracted their attention—til the hot water had melted her underwear off and the silk swelled around her as if she were molting.

"Any more skins on her?" Edith Malloy asked grimly, and the three of them smiled. "Get the mop, Nurse," she'd said to Mercy, and Mercy had mopped till she turned the red of righteousness.

Still, Malloy had judged her. She was on trial.

Another brass entryway, and behind it the convivial buzz of her colleagues gathered around the coffee urn. Again Nurse Malloy has the door. She swings it open and watches Mercy step up, her blue eyes sweeping the younger woman head to toe. *Youth*, she registers with a little sigh. *Red-gold curls and a fetching cap. Ah, bloody hell.*

"There's a lavatory just to your left, if you want to freshen up, Nurse," says Edith Malloy.

CHAPTER FOUR: LUCY

It is April 12, 1921, or is it after midnight, a new day?

I am crazy, disoriented. Miss Robinson warned me not to let this happen.

Nurse Edith Malloy, R.N., is Irish and has a sweet brogue. All the nurses starch their uniforms of course, but she starches hers twice as much as the others. Some people in Minnesota—the Scandinavians and the Germans—say the Irish are dirty, and perhaps Miss Malloy is over-compensating. You can always tell when it is she in the hallway, you hear the *pit-pit-pit* of her starched skirts.

She is leaning over me now, making an unintelligible sound with her lips, the coaxing sound I might make to a lamb I'm bringing on to feed. I loved working the animals on Will's farm, me, the city girl, the art student.

Even as far gone in hysteria as I am at the moment, I notice in the lamplight that the nurse's neck is angrily rashed where her starchy collar rubs.

Poor Miss Malloy, she tries so hard, I think, even through my screaming.

I am not trying hard.

I am giving in to myself.

That is what Will would say. Then he'd slap me, because someone had taught him to deal with female hysteria this way. He'd hit with a kind of sadness in his eyes, as though fate or circumstance had pushed him to an uncongenial alternative.

Other blows of his came from a different, more diabolical

place, but all of them had this air of tragedy, as though he, Will, needed to be comforted for breaking a horse or dog or wife this way.

Will had his dramatic side.

I wait for Miss Malloy to hit me, but she does not. She holds my two hands, though, in a fierce grip. They have been clutching at the bib of her apron. I suppose she thinks I am trying to throttle her. She goes on making kissy noises with her pink lips.

She wears a thin silver watch on a ribbon below a pin engraved *Edith Malloy, R.N.*

As my eyes fasten on the watch, I feel hoarse sounds breaking from my throat again.

The clock's face is not in the right place. It's upside down. Time has run free. Perhaps it is the end of the world, or at least the end of me.

Her grip tightens. "You absolutely must hold still," she says. "The other ladies are waking up. Be quiet now. Tell me about your dream. Whisper."

My hands cease their clutching and relax in hers. She has set her oil lamp on the wicker table next to us, and in its circle of light I'm aware of Dottie in the next bed sitting up and beginning to finger through her short gray hair. A low moan escapes. Her hair is standing on end, as if she has had a fright.

I hear several pairs of footsteps, rubber soled shoes, coming down the corridor. Miss Malloy has some way of summoning help when the clocks begin to run upside down.

If she lightens up on me, I think, I will grab the lamp, throw it on the floor. *Fire, chaos.*

Then I wonder: why do I think these things? Cruel things. Terrible things.

Because I am criminally insane, feeble-minded and indigent.

But remember, Lucy, the young girls with their slanted eyes. Remember the confused old women. How would they escape your fire?

I must keep my conflagrations to myself. Burn alone.

I have lately come to understand that it is because I have some control over my thoughts, even in the grip of hysteria, that I am on Ward 2 North. Nobody on 2 North is, at the moment, tied to her bed. Though all over the ward, women are stirring now and talking. Someone has gotten up and is making her way to the sleeping porch, where four other women's beds are lined up alongside mine. Behind her I sense other presences.

We are rather crowded here in the asylum.

Miss Malloy frees my hands and wipes my forehead with a washcloth that's been hanging on the rail next to my bed beside its towel. "Tell me about your dream."

There are no electric lights in the sleeping hall. But lights flash, now, in the corridor beyond it.

Annie Leary and I are having a picnic in the park, where Minnehaha Creek flows toward its crashing falls. She has brought a feast, and we lay it out on a quilt. In the middle of the quilt is a roast chicken, its legs tied on top of it. There is a wealth of fruit and salad laid around the main dish. We dine on porcelain with silver cutlery and linen napkins. Annie offers me a glass of wine, but I scrupulously decline, as if I am not old enough, though I am twenty-two.

Then she rises and takes a bundle from the picnic basket. I think it is another chicken, but it is a living baby. She swaddles it tightly in a white cloth and bends to show it to me. The baby is serene and beautiful, its eyes closed. It looks like a little Buddha.

How do I know it is alive?

I know it is alive.

In waking life, Annie's hair is cut short. But in the dream her hair is long and golden and braided down her back. She wears a white dress and white stockings and white shoes, like a bride or a girl on her First Communion day. Indeed, Annie, looks young in the dream, hardly into her teens.

She picks up the swaddled baby and takes it down to the shore. There is a boat pulled up on the beach. She lays the baby in the boat

*and, with a quick, ruthless motion, pushes the boat into the current.
I hear the roar of the falls and I begin screaming.*

I hear the roar of the falls, but it is only rain lashing at the
screens, and lightning and wind.

Today has been humid, for spring, weather ever shifting. Now
it breaks.

Nurses and orderlies are running in from everywhere, shut-
ting windows. Nurse Malloy has her lamp in hand again and
she looks at me keenly. "You'll quiet down now, won't you? I
want you to come along with me."

She hands me the cotton chenille robe that's been folded in
my top drawer. Every lady on the ward has a dresser, a pitcher
for water and a washbowl, two towels and a cloth. Our riches.
On other wards, as I will come to learn, there's no crockery.
What if we were to smash it and cut ourselves or someone else
with a shard?

But 2 North is a docile ward, deserving of solid white plates
and cups. I am docile. A docile lady—*lady* is the word everyone
uses here, never *girls*, never last names. This is the superintendent's, Dr. David Grafton's, innovation, as I will be told over and
over, as if I should manifest gratitude. I put on the robe, though
it is still warm in the room. I set my bare feet to the tiles.

"Ladies, go to sleep now," Miss Malloy's voice lilts over the
agitated ward. They are docile. They go back to sleep.

But I will not sleep here on the dormitory porch. I will accompany Miss Malloy into the bright hallway, *pit-pit-pit*. She leads
me to a small room where mine is the only bed. There is a window
in the door, covered with the familiar chicken wire. Up and down
the corridor, I notice other rooms with similar windows and I
sense women behind them, attending.

"Off to bed, now," Miss Malloy calls softly to the hall, to me.
She is like the sleep fairy in some children's book. She stands
beside my cot, turning the wick of her lamp low. She tucks me
under a stiff blanket, no sheet.

I am obedient. I go to sleep.

Just as dawn lights the sky, perhaps around 5:00 a.m., I waken again.

She is not there. The door is closed and I am alone.

CHAPTER FIVE

NURSE MALLOY WAS reporting to the medical committee in her distinctive Dublin accent. It put everything, no matter how disorderly, under a kind of formal constraint.

By custom, the doctors and nurses brought an elevated tone to their discussions, as though calling each other to ever higher standards. Modeling sanity, and themselves as examples of it. This is what Superintendent David Grafton called "a modern therapeutic protocol."

Edith Malloy had gotten a medal for elocution at the Convent of the Sacred Heart, and had a bit of the actress in her. She delivered her reports with authority, inhabiting fully the roll of head nurse. Perhaps even Director of Nursing. (Olivia Passmore, surely a little old for that position, nodded from her corner, a shining example to all the staff. But aging.)

The appearance of a circumspect life, Edith Malloy believed, could be achieved by play-acting. The substance might be more elusive.

"Annie Leary has been caught again with matches, which she can only have gotten from the locked closet in the sterilizing room. This cannot continue."

Nurse Malloy perched a pair of rimless spectacles on her nose and glared around the room. "I cannot emphasize enough the danger of fire."

No disputing that. Five capped heads, the nurses from North, nodded as one.

Dr. Conrad Jessen-Haight struck a match to his shoe and

sucked the flame into his pipe. He was one who frequently spoke about the calming effects of nicotine on demented patients. This was a European idea that found little acceptance on the American prairie. Physicians here might smoke, but they didn't pretend it was good for anyone.

Meeting his pantomime of opposition, Nurse Malloy countered, "She may have tobacco if tobacco she craves, but someone must light her cigarettes and sit with her."

"She shouldn't have tobacco on her person at all," Nurse Lydia Shaeffer put in. She was a pinched, red-faced woman with a punitive nature, who tended to take the most severe view of any situation. "Someone could steal it and eat it. It's a poison, after all."

Heads nodded, some reluctantly. Jessen-Haight, with a nod to David Grafton, spoke up on the benefits of nicotine. "Although I know my position is not universally respected"—he was a young doctor, with a bit of a whine in his voice which made people argue even when they agreed with him—"it must be noted that Leary hasn't had a seizure in over three years."

"*Mrs.* Leary"—the superintendent made his correction gently—"has made significant progress."

The staff nodded and turned to each other with looks of approval. For various reasons—professional pride, Christian charity, a hatred of disorder—they wanted the patients to thrive. Seldom were they able to report that anyone did.

The superintendent always spoke rather diffidently. He went on. "But we cannot with certainty credit that to nicotine. It's an interesting hypothesis." He threw this bone to the younger doctor and fiddled with his own pipe "My concern is how she obtains the matches, and that is something the head nurse on 4 North may want to think about."

4 North housed the habitually violent as well as those patients, like Annie Leary, with a serious criminal history. Lydia Schaeffer was its head nurse. The superintendent's comment implied

a mild criticism of her management, but she regarded Grafton with what affection she was capable of. She was a hard woman, but not one to take offense. She respected authority, became, in Grafton's presence, obsequious.

Now she admired his pale hair, his pleasing profile, eyes cast down on a sheaf of notes. She was attracted to him; what nurse was not? He was one of five or six unmarried males, set amidst some fifty single women. Besides, he was gentle, for a doctor, especially for an alienist. They always had to prove themselves tough as surgeons.

As, in her own way, did she.

His eyes, though… Eyes were said to be the windows of the soul. Nurse Schaeffer had little to say that was original, and she knew it; her expertise was in rules, order and the status quo. Imagination weakened a nurse, she thought.

The superintendent's eyes seemed to mirror no more than one's own face. Miss Schaeffer was pleased with this thought, which seemed to her rarely original. And because she liked him—who did not?—she considered how useful this reflective quality might be to a man in his position.

•

His eyes, though, thought Nurse Mercy Winstead. She was struggling for the tenor of the group. *His eyes are cold.* Blue eyes that looked like chilly sky. Were they blue at all? If he wore a gray weave, they would be gray. But today he wore a blue shirt, neatly pressed in the hospital laundry, and an indigo cravat, ever so slightly artistic. With a gold stickpin.

•

Gold regimental stickpin: Canadian Royal Highlanders. And a pinstriped suitcoat, properly cut, Nurse Malloy observed. She took pleasure knowing that the superintendent valued a proper tailor. As a fellow refugee of the British Empire, Malloy knew that Grafton's quiet manner revealed nothing but boarding school manners. Who he really was—they had worked together for two years—still remained unclear to her. *Still waters*, as Nurse Schaeffer might remark, *run deep*.

What did that mean, exactly? Were the still waters calm, or were they treacherous?

•

"But I forget myself." David Grafton spoke with a self-deprecating smile, "I have not properly welcomed our newcomer, Nurse Mercy Winstead, who graduated from Lutheran Deaconess in Minneapolis last spring. She's been here two weeks now, is that correct?"

Mercy nodded, forcing her eyes to meet the superintendent's eyes, blue at the moment, as they scanned her. She counseled herself not to appear shy.

"And how is your adjustment going?"

Mercy knew he was not inviting a full report, yet felt her treacherous color rise. Her mind had presented her with the story of the woman whose skin fell off. Indeed, the incident had passed into narrative, because she'd written home about it last night. She'd made it seem funny, horrifying as it had been at the time.

But it was not a story that could be tamed to the formality of this conference.

The recollection made her feel guilty, thus the blush. As though she had made some mistake running the patient's bath water. That embarrassing spell of faintness.

Mercy discerned in herself this ribbon of free-floating guilt. She resolved to follow the advice of her first head nurse in the psychiatric rotation: *always observe your own reactions dispassionately. This, young women, is the key to growth.*

And do not speak out of turn.

"Very well, sir." She prudently dropped it at that.

•

Why does the child look so guilty? Dr. David Grafton wondered. *And Malloy, Malloy is smiling.* Must corner her later.

But Olivia Passmore, Director of Nursing, was starting her admission reports. He tried to pay careful attention.

"There were seven new patients coming onto the wards this week. Four up from last year at this time."

Olivia Passmore was a thin and distinguished old campaigner. She wore a black bombazine dress with lace collars and cuffs for staff meeting, as Clara Barton might have done, instead of her nursing whites. She tended to drone her statistics and put everyone into a drowse, however much they respected her. "Spring is late, of course."

•

As if, thought Nurse Edith Malloy, *spring were a reluctant visitor, coming up the drive at all hours.*

Spring, people in Minnesota longed for it, but it made them crazy.

•

Olivia Passmore read: "Janina Lucy Valenta, age 22. This is the name on her commitment order. She wants to be called Lucy Allen. I told you her story two weeks ago. Normal admissions process. Refused nourishment while in seclusion."

"Seclusion" was Dr. Grafton's term for what other facilities called "solitary confinement." New patients were observed in the admissions ward for several weeks after their commitment. They were scrubbed in the tub room, held down for an enema, deloused, sedated, and tied to a bed in restraints. After two days, if the patient showed no signs of mania, she was released from the chemise, as the restraints were benignly called, and mostly kept in bed.

"Because she refused food," Nurse Passmore continued, "she was intubated."

They did not use the word *force-fed*. It had to be all gentleness with Dr. Grafton.

This often meant the staff kept details from him.

•

That pretty, chestnut-haired girl—Grafton recalled he had seen her on the admissions ward, though he had not had time yet for an intake interview. *Curvaceous*, he allowed himself.

Her beauty did not fool him. But in case it should, Nurse Passmore was reading from the commitment orders. "Whoring. Bearing false witness. Manic behavior. Thievery."

The girl was twenty-two. Her story did not yet show on her face and body.

•

"Family?" Grafton wanted to know.

"Immigrant family, Bohemians or some such. She spoke of a husband, however. In fact, as I started to say, she insists on being called Mrs. Allen." Nurse Passmore recalled how Lucy had screamed as they tied her into the chemise, "Will, Will!"

"She wore a wedding ring. But we have no record of that name…"

(The girl had twisted the ring off and thrown it down the tub room drain. It had been the devil to remove it, and now it was wrapped in a piece of surgical tape and locked in her cubby on Ward 2 North.)

"It was a legal commitment and the sheriff brought her here," the Director of Nursing continued. (Wally Norton had stayed for doughnuts and coffee, gossiping about various matters of mutual concern. They were acquaintances from the Northfield Home Mission Society. Nurse Passmore thought he knew more than he was saying about the husband, and that he expected her to keep quiet about whatever hints he couldn't help dropping. Recalling the interview, she unconsciously pursed her lips, as if the perversity of the world would never cease to surprise her. Though it had, long ago.)

•

Whoring, stealing…Why didn't they just send her to the work-house? Grafton wondered. Friends in high places, perhaps. Or enemies. He settled on "friends." It was a model institution, and he ran it.

"Who initiated the commitment?"

Olivia Passmore paged through her notes, slightly flustered. She was past the age when a nurse might have been expected to retire. Lapses of memory made her uneasy. "I, well, this is odd. I don't know. There's only Sheriff Wally Norton's name here."

Had he identified the family at all? She thought not. Just hinted they were *important*.

Grafton said smoothly, politely, "It's unusual that you miss a detail, Nurse."

Olivia Passmore's flush was drenching and darker red than Mercy Winsted's. A blood pressure spike, Grafton feared.

He changed course. "Has any Attending seen her?"

"Preliminary, sir," said Dr. Dominic Kennedy. Another *Boy*, as the superintendent called, to himself, any man who hadn't fought in the recent war. "I suspect a history of sexual interference."

A babble of contention broke out among the junior physicians. Grafton mentally recused himself from it.

Jessen-Haight invoked the writings of the Austrian, Dr. Sigmund Freud, recently published. Dr. Dominic Kennedy leaned in on the side of some other continental genius who disputed Freud.

David Grafton looked from one to the other and then cleared his throat. He wasn't as up-to-date on his medical journals as the younger men. He'd been busy fighting in Europe, he made no apologies for that.

Jessen-Haight would not be silenced. "Thirty percent. *Thirty percent* of these women think they have been sexually violated. It's merely wishful thinking."

All the nurses lowered their eyes. Silence fell like a coat over the room. Grafton thought of the moment between the *thunk* of a shell and its explosion.

Then the Director of Nursing leaned in with the full strength of her moral authority. "For my part, I suspect seventy percent have been, as you say, interfered with."

Mercy Winstead sat up straighter as she listened to Nurse Passmore take on a junior doctor. It amazed her to know this was possible.

Edith Malloy raised her eyes, ashamed to have dropped them, and urged her superior on with a tip of her chin. She loved it when the Director of Nursing came out of her grandmotherly drowse and took the reins. It was stirring. Olivia Passmore had been a bold lass in her time, no doubt.

Nurse Passmore said, "They have been raped by their fathers or brothers or the hired man and they know so little about sexual behavior that they can't tell us the story. They hardly know what has happened to them, except perhaps that they were naughty little girls and needed to be punished."

Mercy Winstead breathed in and out on an audible note. Was this what it was like to listen to Florence Nightingale? And Nurse Passmore had, like the Lady With the Lamp, served on the battle lines. She dared to speak aloud facts of life Nurse Winstead had not even read about in her most advanced textbooks.

"Thank you, Nurse. Shall we let Dr. Kennedy go on?" Grafton offered smoothly. If they continued down this path of debate, he knew, the therapeutic community might fall apart. "What brings you to this conclusion, Dr. Kennedy? Did she claim such a history?"

Kennedy was young, wet. Romantic. He stammered a bit. He could be trusted to back down. "No, ah, no. It's an inference on my part. She is a young woman of some presence and poise. Well-spoken. I can't imagine, somehow, that she would deliver herself to the life she is accused of living without—"

Grafton smiled encouragingly. He was expert, beyond expert, at masking his own feelings.

Nurse Schaeffer cut in. In the two years of Dr. Grafton's regime, she, too, had begun to try out her own voice. "Miss Valenta—or

Mrs. Allen, if we must—was an *art student*," she said, as though diagnosing a psychiatric illness.

Grafton allowed silence to fall again. He thought a bit. Then he said, "Thank you for reminding us of that. Perhaps it suggests a direction for therapy. Nurse Malloy, Lucy Valenta must have access to the art studio, of course."

"Sir." Malloy began writing with her little gold pen.

Grafton continued. "Let's go with a preliminary diagnosis of hysteria. Perhaps, in parenthesis, *dementia praecox-question mark*. And we will call her whatever she likes to be called."

"Miss Winstead," the superintendent said unexpectedly, "what do you think of all this?"

Mercy jumped. "I hardly think, sir—" She began to tread water. Superiors had never before asked for her opinion, they had scolded her for showing the ghost of one, actually. But she must respond.

Nothing rose to her lips. Nothing she dared say.

Grafton shot her what she perceived to be a chilly blue glance. She felt the blood drain from her face. This was more dangerous than a blush.

Nurse Malloy, boldly, kindly, lifted the younger nurse out of the spotlight. "Well, none of us knows, do we?" She put her hand under her apron, where it overlapped Mercy's. She was prepared to pinch the girl, if she threatened to faint again.

•

David Grafton stared out the window.

What innocents these people were, he thought. His staff. There's the girl, ready to pass out. Except for old war horses like Nurse Passmore, they can't talk about seduction, rape, incest, familial violation.

Some were puritanical, some were repressed, all were professionally cautious. Freud had dared to speak the numbers. Freud had been forced to recant. Otherwise he would not be Freud, but some drudge in Vienna working the charity wards.

(Like me, thought Grafton.)

Freud's theories, even expurgated, eroded the foundations of chivalry and the benevolent rule of the Fathers, which made society secure.

He was grateful to Dominic Kennedy for raising the issue, though the Boy spoke, he thought, out of naiveté rather than cynicism. Innocence could, usefully enough, contribute a fresh vision.

On the whole, Grafton respected cynicism. This allied him with Nurse Passmore. She, too, had served under fire in the European war, commanding a brigade of nurses. No one with a memory of the trenches could retain respect for the wisdom of the Fathers.

Or, to be fair, the purity of the Daughters.

He must ask Nurse Passmore how she had handled such matters, sexual matters: for all her sophistication, she ran the nurses' quarters like a convent school.

Beyond the mullioned windows lay the asylum farm, where male patients went about the work most of them were accustomed to. It kept them usefully occupied and helped the institution stay solvent, as the legislature required.

In the barns, animals would, if not firmly tethered, mount each other with abandon, male on male, sire on daughter. And no one thought them *immoral*.

Humans were not all that different, Grafton thought.

But he kept this idea to himself.

To *say* such a thing would be insane.

One of the few things Grafton knew with certainty was that he was not insane. He knew how not to be insane. That's why he was superintendent.

Lonely, perhaps. Close to despair in all weathers.

•

The Director of Nursing cleared her throat and said, "Well." All the others were looking down at the pattern in the carpet, afraid to break the superintendent's concentration. He sometimes went into these little fugues, which reminded Nurse Passmore of battle fatigue. From her side, a preliminary diagnosis.

•

David Grafton came back to himself and smiled encouragingly around the circle. Whatever guilty knowledge hung in the heart, it was appropriate—and healthy—to be kind. He lived by this rule.

•

"What cold eyes he has," Mercy thought. "For a man who speaks gently, he has such cold eyes."

CHAPTER SIX: LUCY

I LISTEN FOR the clank of keys. I hear instead the *pit-pit-pit* of Nurse Malloy's uniform skirts. Has my hearing become preternaturally attuned? I've heard it said that blind people acquire sharper ears.

I feel blind in this dim room. I have become like one of those fish who live fathoms under water, in such eternal night that they lose their eyes.

What the body doesn't need, it sloughs off.

Perhaps I will lose a layer or two.

Perhaps a mind.

I have not lost my mind *yet*.

I did not know this yesterday, or last week, or on the day the sheriff drove me up the winding drive, with its standing guard of poplars, to the admitting ward. I concurred, then, in the opinion that I was mad.

Will had said so.

Mrs. Lerner had nodded.

They had flourished a paper dripping with red wax seals and ribbons which made the same point. It bore an impressive signature, dramatic as John Hancock's, attesting to my insanity.

But here, in this dark room, I have been thinking, remembering, and putting things together.

Will had offered the signed paper—and me—to two men in rusty blue uniforms who had come to stand in our front parlor.

After my husband handed me off, he turned his back and

walked over to the fireplace. He put his elbow on the mantel and his face in his hand.

Hanging between the two officers, still I admired the line of Will's neck where it disappeared into expensive linen. My fingers twitched to sketch.

Mrs. Lerner, in her chair by the fire, kept knitting her veil of lace.

"All right, then," said one of the rusty men. But neither Mrs. Lerner nor Will responded. There was the click of steel needles, their sharp points flashing.

She could do a lot of damage with those, I thought. Back then I was always strategizing about what domestic implements could be converted into instruments of defense.

"All right," the policeman, or whatever he was, said again.

There came a crackle of parchment as he folded the letter and its impressive seals into a leather case. "Will she need restraint, sir?" the officer asked. He had let go of my arm in an experimental way. I tottered.

There I was, on my own parlor carpet, drooping, drowning, looking from Will's profile to Mrs. Lerner's handiwork. Docile. They had given me a sleeping draught or something, I think.

I tried to form words. But my mouth seemed to be full of cotton wool. I croaked something unintelligible to myself.

"Yes," said Will.

"No," said Mrs. Lerner.

•

Now, working this all over in memory, I position myself to the left of the grilled window on my door, where Nurse Malloy will not be able to see me.

I quiet my breathing.

From outside, I hear the stir of other women behind their doors. Someone is sobbing rhythmically, the hiccuping cry of an exhausted infant who has run out of energy to scream. Others are laughing.

Merriment is a prominent feature of asylum life.

My near neighbor scrapes relentlessly metal on metal. Spoon on cup? This has been going on since I came to be locked in here and the sound is agonizing to me. One's senses can be overly keen.

I stand quietly but Malloy keeps still as well. The hunter and the rabbit, I think.

I, for my part, will not break cover. She is afraid that if she enters the room unsure of my location and state of mind, I will jump her and strangle her. Perhaps with my underdrawers. I relish the power.

"Miss Valenta? Are you awake in there?" She raps lightly.

"Good morning, Nurse," I say, polite, though I don't know if it is morning or afternoon. In parochial school, we were trained to stand at our desks in perfect order to greet a visitor. We would chant with one voice, exaggerate each syllable as the principal or the assistant pastor entered, "Good *morning*, Sister Mary Patrick. Good *morning*, Father Lee."

"Will you come here in front of the window, dear, where I can see you," says Nurse Malloy.

It is in my interest to do so. I stand with my hands at my sides, palms out. *I come in peace.*

"That's a good lass." Keys rattle now. Up and down the hall there is a stir and keening.

Yesterday—or was it last week?—a different nurse, Schaeffer—*Annie's nurse*—had come to my window. "Have we learned our lesson, then?" she'd said in her snippy voice. I'd thrown my metal water jug at the grille, rewarded by the shadow of her instinctive dodge.

I think that got me an extra night of punishment.

Nurse Malloy opens the door a foot or so. She smiles in her cordial, nursery way as she glances around the room to catch any trouble I've gotten into.

Nurse Malloy's gaze roves from my nightstand, made of

metal and piped to the floor, its jug in place, to my commode, under my bed where it belongs.

She enters.

Oh, they fooled me. There are two of them. I had discerned only the rattle of Edith Malloy's skirts. But along comes the tiny new nurse, with her gingery soft hair and the pretty orange Bakelite spectacles.

Why the crowd? Perhaps I have become one of the elite, like Annie. Perhaps I have committed some monstrous crime I can't remember and must, according to the By-laws of the State of Minnesota, be accompanied by no fewer than two trained nurses during any transition from hall to hall.

That line of thought tempts me. I feel I am being punished out of proportion to anything I can remember doing. This idea has possessed me for most of the past month but though it seems real to me, I now recognize it as a mad thought.

I am not insane.

I want to greet Nurse Malloy with this insight. They have locked me away in a room of perpetual twilight for how many hours? How many days? I have no idea. I have screamed and moaned and thrown things until suddenly, with the same surprise as Holy Mary Mother of God saw an angel at her bed, I saw—I think I saw—a flash of light. Anyway, words presented themselves to my mind with a kind of aura around them: *I am not insane.*

So my seclusion has not been wasted. I can now, as Annie recommended, try to control my imagination.

I want to tell this news to Nurse Malloy, who always seems kind, though firm. Perhaps she will take my arm, as people do around here, and walk me to the front door, which they never do.

She carries the keys. She has the power.

But Nurse Malloy is suddenly asking me questions I can't answer and I am flustered. "What's my name, dear?"

"Nurse, Nurse"—I sneak a peek at the name on the brass plate that holds her deceptive timepiece. *Edith Malloy, R.N.*

"That's lovely, dear. Good reading. Not everybody around here can read, I'll tell you that." She exchanges a nod with little Nurse Mercy.

Why can I remember Nurse Mercy's name? Perhaps because it's so pretty, so appropriate. I've formed this judgment about her nature though I've only met her once.

"And what is your name, dear?"

"Dear," I echo. Panic rises. I can't remember my name.

It's not as simple as Edith Malloy, R.N. makes out. My names are in flux. Janina Lucy Valenta, Lucy Allen. I've been Lucy Locket, lost her pocket. Will's wife. "I'm Will's wife," I say, settling on that.

What name did she call outside my door? The wrong one. "I'm Mrs. Allen," I assert.

"It says 'Miss' on the form," says Nurse Malloy. "I'm sorry if I made a mistake. We'll call you whatever you like to be called." She exchanges another confirming glance with Nurse Mercy.

Confirming what?

Why don't they believe me? I have a wedding ring. I scratch at the white band of skin on the third finger of my left hand.

They have taken my ring.

Tears well up.

"Don't cry, dear. You're doing so well," says Nurse Malloy. "We're going back to the ward today, and there'll be something special for you."

All up and down the hall, wailing and crying goes up. There has been a listening stillness around the nurses' visit and now all the women moan. They want to go back to the ward. They want something special.

I muster the required gratitude. I pick up my possessions, a wooden comb and a cigar box. I lift the lid and look inside. Empty now.

"Your things are back on the ward," says Nurse Mercy in her perky way.

I remember what was in the box. My three hairpins. Two sanitary towels. Perhaps my wedding ring.

I need the pins. My hair is in mats. They soaped me down with harsh lye soap, and shampooed me from a jar with tag ends of the same gooey bars.

I shake the box again.

There is no wedding ring. Perhaps I imagined having one. But the white band of skin on my finger has a little callous behind the digit. Will had said: *It is a husband and wife who confer the sacrament of marriage on each other.* He'd recited a pertinent line from the *Baltimore Catechism* where it says that.

Baptism is conferred by a priest, Confirmation by a Bishop. But Marriage by a man and woman. That's Catholic theology.

God so loved the world.

Anyway, we visited a judge.

I am making this case to myself, rather as Will did to me on that indecorous ride in his roadster from St. Paul, Minnesota to Decorah, Iowa.

Cold sober, and simply cold, my bare feet on a stone floor, I find something askew with Will's logic.

Even at the time, it didn't ring true, though I deferred to Will—so educated, and—this is odd in a man—religious. He knew the catechism by heart. It was a reason to trust him.

CHAPTER SEVEN

WILL ALLEN STOOD with his hand over his eyes, elbow on the mantel.

The fire was burning down. They would need another log, Nola Lerner thought, to finish the evening unless they were going to go to bed. She could barely make out her knitting pattern. It was simple lace, but her eyes were beginning to fail. She had entered the youth of old age. And after that, she thought bleakly, the age of old age.

Will Allen was striking a pose.

That was her judgment. Soon he would turn and wail, "What have I done?" like some character in a melodrama.

Nola Lerner had had enough of the drama in this house. *Get on with it*, she thought. Do your best. Cut your losses.

That pretty, plump girl had been a dead loss.

Will turned around. He wore a corduroy jacket, belted in the back, and he tucked his hand into the pocket, still posing. "What have I done?" he said.

Did this require a reply? What did he think he had done? Covered his backside. Everyone had to.

"It's all for the best," Nola said. She shook out her lacework and held it up to the lamp.

There. She had purled where she should have knitted. Tomorrow, in a better light, she would have to take the row out. "It will all look better in the morning," she told Will Allen.

Her store of wisdom was almost exhausted, but she had one precious tidbit: "Think what your mother would say."

Will turned back to the fire. His mother could still have her say, although she lay upstairs in a semicoma, her face pulled into a grimace. Will thought his mother would have her say long after she died and went, as he hoped and expected, to heaven. She would tell him to do his duty and make her proud.

"You can't let yourself be disgraced." Had Nola Lerner said this? Or his mother, calling down from above, or from his own mind?

Will Allen retained sufficient integrity to know it was his own mind.

But his own mind needed reinforcements. And he needed them immediately. He needed a chorus of male voices—damn these women—to tell him that he must not let himself be disgraced. To agree that Lucy was hysterical, dangerous, a thief, a whore and a lunatic. To tell him that although he had done wrong, it was nothing that discretion couldn't erase. And the Sacrament of Confession.

That the asylum was where Lucy belonged.

Asylum. A comforting word. A place of coolness, light and peace.

"I have to change my clothes," he told Mrs. Lerner. "I'm going to drive up to the Cities."

"It'll be dark before you get there," she said.

Yes, he thought. Spring contained her light till after nine. The unseasonably chilly weather made no difference, made the twilight crisp and interesting, dislocating in a pleasant way.

But night was coming on.

"Take your light suit, then. It could be hot tomorrow," she said.

Mrs. Lerner embarked on the reliable topic of midwestern weather. It had snowed all through March, but the hyacinths were budging through. She had seen them in the short-lived thaw. Today there had been a dust of sleet.

•

Was it insane to imagine strangling her with her own knitting wool, Will wondered. The yarn was too light. For whom was she knitting such bridal lace?

58

He'd have to find a rope.

But these were the thoughts of a madman.

Or a moral imbecile.

Jesus had made the point. To think evil made you as culpable as the act. *Whoever commits adultery in his mind is guilty...* This text had always seemed unfair to Will, the freethinker of his theology classes at St. Thomas College, the joker. But perhaps it referred only to sexual acts, not the murder of housekeepers.

Well, he had had his fill of sexual acts as well. Never again. *Lord*, he prayed, *never again.*

Did the Lord care?

Will thrust this thought from him, as he should have thrust so many others. He must not add sins against the first commandment to his catalogue. Or risk the darkness of despair, the unforgivable sin against the Holy Ghost. Which would cast a soul into eternal damnation, *where the worm never dies.*

What worm was that, he wondered irrelevantly, and shrank from any answer.

He thrust a hand into his trouser pocket. Despite the deeds he had done, his rosary offered its worn comfort. "Holy Mary, conceived without sin, intercede for me."

Nola Lerner heard the familiar click of his beads and her lips tightened into a line. Catholics thought they could do whatever they pleased. They just went to confession afterwards. Or bleated to the mother of God like so many children lost in the woods. She wrapped the yarn around her thin pointed steel needles and thrust them into her knitting bag.

She, herself, was a Methodist.

•

How could she resist the temptation to stab somebody with those needles? Will wondered.

Women were lethal creatures. It was exactly as his confessors had taught him. The beautiful female exterior, curvaceous, tempting, the smiling lips. (Well, excluding Mrs. Lerner.)

Female seduction, calculating and canny in its slithering approach. But inwardly a body of death and corruption. The devil's own refined instrument of a man's destruction.

What a slut Lucy had turned out to be. His slaps, his reprimands, had been in order. His father would have beaten her, as he had beaten his own wife. Beaten his son. Knocked sense into them, of which Lucy had little.

His mother had prevailed, or at least outlived her reprimands. She survived upstairs, in her twilight sleep.

"Are you going up, then?" asked Nola Lerner over her shoulder as she turned in the doorway, indicating with a lift of her nose his mother's bedroom.

"Check on her, will you? Ah, no, I haven't got time." There were two stairways leading into the sitting room at opposite sides of the fireplace. One had been, in earlier days, for servants, housemaids. Will took those stairs, two at a time. Up to his unpretentious little room, which had once been the room of a hireling. He would pack his summerweight suit, his spring coat, his carapace, his manhood. He would drive. He loved to drive.

"Listen, Mrs. Lerner"—his demand made her step back into the room. "I'm sure I don't need to remind you. Everything that's happened in this house is between the two of us alone. I expect absolute confidentiality."

The housekeeper turned, her hand on the brass doorknob. "Of course. Try not to think too much about it."

She herself had mastered the art of not thinking. But Will, Will had always been a worrier. What a burden of conscience for a man of his waywardness! Sometimes he seemed to be two people, like that Dr. Jekyll and Mr. Hyde: the man who sinned and the man who repented.

Some of it was the drink, of course.

For her part, she valued her employment too much to jeopardize it with loose lips. What chance would she have in the outer darkness, a widow, and broke?

There was the poor farm, so handily close to the insane asylum. Nola Lerner had no way to support herself, no means of making a living, except by keeping this house.

Or perhaps—it crossed her mind—by blackmail.

CHAPTER EIGHT: LUCY

IT'S THE FIFTH of May, 1921, and the laundry room is getting hotter.

You get worse, I'll get better.

These silly words are scrawled in pencil on the starched detachable cuff of a dress that comes at me through the mangle. I look up over the machine in amazement and incomprehension. Annie, on the opposite side, grins, and then quickly erases her face.

I shrug my shoulders at her. *What do you mean?*

Quickly, I lick my finger and smear the light pencil marks. I slip the dress onto its hanger and button the cuffs in place. It's one of the big muslin smocks that hang from shoulder to feet, like the dresses Christian missionaries make women wear in tropical countries to cover their nakedness.

We mangle girls like to work with these dresses because they are easy to handle without wrinkling.

I know now that the bulky smocks are worn in back wards by women so manic or dangerous that nobody wants to take charge of their buttons and snaps. The sleeves are overlong and, if a patient gets out of hand, a nurse can simply cross them behind her back and hog tie her till reinforcements come with the straight chair and the chemise.

You get worse, I'll get better.

I widen my eyes at Annie again to show I don't understand. She shrugs and feeds dresses.

Matron's bell.

An aide is beside me. I've been observed making faces.

I show her the smudged cuff and speak a word that everyone in the asylum takes seriously: dirty.

The aide says *tchhh* and holds the material close to her face as if to smell it. She will find nothing but a smear.

"Why do they need starched cuffs anyway?" the aide asks of no one in particular.

For show, I think. So that visitors will remark upon our model institution, women tied to chairs, screaming and pissing themselves, their collars and cuffs aglow.

Get worse.

The light dawns! Two floors separate our wards. A little more hysteria might earn me a shift to 3 North. A little less—what? murderous intention?—might get Annie moved down a floor. We could be together.

Ridiculous idea.

I have no desire to change floors, not even for Annie.

I stick out my tongue at her across the whirling dresses.

She smiles. Just a joke, maybe.

Matron's hand on her bell.

•

I don't want to go to 3 North, I want to get out of the Northfield State Hospital. Go home. Find a home. Since my sojourn in the dark room surrounded by dim and sighing women, I am terrified of getting worse. Perhaps that's why they put me in solitary. It was a way of saying *control your imagination.*

They have the power. They could move me to the back of beyond in my starched white cuffs.

Folklore about the upper wards figures heavily in our storytelling on docile Ward 2 North. One of my companions in the dayroom, Liddie, is a survivor, even, of those horrors. Liddie's a tiny, wizened woman with a deformed back and neck that curve in such a way that her chin meets her chest and her eyes cannot, without an enormous effort of painful twisting, meet yours.

I assume her deformity results from some injuries she suffered on the upper wards, being lowered into ice water, wrapped in rubber sheets, tied down till she ruptured herself and endured the attacks of other maniacs.

But that's just my gothic imagination. More likely she was born that way, and abandoned to the institution by parents who couldn't cope with a crippled child.

Maniac. One of our favorite epithets. Lunatic. Another: mongoloid idiot.

My father had raised me never to use such disrespectful language, but we pick up these words from the staff. The doctors and nurses use them with scientific precision. All of us inmates are, for simplicity's sake, *insane* to the outside world. But, within the institution, the specifically insane are those on the back wards. People tied to their beds or to straight chairs who rave constantly, kick, bite, tear at their own bodies or the bodies of anyone who comes close.

"Maniacs," by contrast, go in and out of their spells. With good behavior, they are promoted from shackles and straight chairs even onto the freedom of the grounds.

Liddie has told me about life among the insane; she has a lively tongue in her twisted head.

"Lunatics"—well, perhaps I am one of them—cycle in and out of their tragedies. We have good days, then sink into despair or rage.

"Idiot" refers to one or another feeble-minded patient—palsied, deaf-mute, untrainable, feral. "Mongoloid idiot" is a subspecies of these. Most of them are children.

Yes, I had been stunned to be told there were children in the hospital. I'd seen only a few girls in their teens. I imagined the little ones off by themselves in a ward full of beautiful toys like those I'd seen in Will's old nursery at the farm. Heaven for the feeble-minded.

Though I have my dark moments, I tend to take an optimistic view.

That's how Will charmed me, I realize, playing on my expectation that the world offered mostly good fortune.

Perhaps that was my inheritance from Papa. He raised me to think it a blessing to live in the skin of an artist. A blessing to live in any skin. To live.

I wonder what becomes of the asylum children? Few young people are in evidence on the wards. Perhaps they go home in their parents' pony traps, cured.

I create these positive outcomes in my mind as I feed dresses to the mangle, or push a broom around the wards. I am getting to be "quite the helper," as Nurse Malloy has remarked. Perhaps someday I will graduate to ironing the Sunday frills of the staff families.

Well, a woman must keep busy. That's why I got involved in the work of Will's family farm, while he went to his city business. I don't think he liked to come home on those odd free days of his and find me mucking out the pens. Work Mrs. Lerner would never soil her hands with. He expected to find me where he'd left me, at the dressing table in a pretty gown putting up my hair.

Neither did he like the sketchbooks I filled with precise studies of animal life in all its cycles.

I drew mating, birth. I drew the innards of dead sheep.

Will was squeamish about real life. When I got my monthlies, he slept in the attic.

As for my studies of Arvid, the hired man, whose haunted eyes filled me with compassion—Will threw them in the fire.

I snatched them out. That was the second time he locked me in our bedroom.

Why did I ever think Will was serious about art?

Nellie comes to push my rack of dresses. She is one of the "mongoloid idiots," a fat girl, but short and thin-skinned, with Chinese eyes. Well, Mongol eyes. Nelly smiles at me and huffs a little, with her large tongue between her teeth. There are several of these young women around the place, mostly sweet-tempered and affectionate. Nellie likes to climb in my lap and cuddle as we sit in the day room looking out at the trees and lawns.

But, "Don't get attached to her," Annie whispered last week as we queued for laundry coffee. "They die young."

This a corollary of another of her edicts: "Don't get attached to anything." Not to the chipmunks Nurse Malloy likes to feed on the back stoop. Not to the birds we throw our salvaged bread to. Not to Nurse Mercy, who is becoming a rock of stability in my life, especially now that she takes me every afternoon at two to the art room. Not to Nurse Passmore's dog, Rufus, who lies under the table in the day room, available for petting.

Not to Annie, eternally out of reach across the mangle.

I often long for Norah to kick me again, so I can be taken out and soothed, petted and allowed to sit with my foot in Annie's lap. I long, just now, for the collation bell, so we can steal a few minutes of conversation before Matron sends us to opposite benches. Then I will have to simmer with jealousy, watching Annie feed green tomato jam from her finger to the mongoloid girls.

Across the room. Always across the room.

They are on to us.

We are two wards apart in the great scheme of things. Annie rules—she tells me—over infamous Ward 4 North, which people speak about in whispers. I've been here over a month now, and I'm only beginning to get a bird's eye view of the institution.

Much is revealed on our daily walks—we will take one right after laundry—when Nurse Passmore and Nurse Malloy line us up like schoolgirls and take us outside. Nurse Mercy will bring up the rear. In imagination, I put a switch in her hand, like a goosegirl's. Nurse Passmore takes the lead. She is the Director of Nursing. She likes to stride along, and she likes to head the procession.

Nurse Malloy circulates, encouraging, scolding, commenting on the progress of spring, giving us little quizzes to test our approximation of reality. "What's that building, then, Nellie?"

"Cow barn," the girl will say. Most of the patients grew up on farms and even the feeble-minded can tell a Holstein from a Hereford.

"Good girl. What building is that, Dora?"—Dora is an old woman with braided gray hair who turns her head restlessly from side to side as if checking for the unseen danger that stalks us always. Dora declines to respond. She never speaks, but Nurse Malloy always includes her in the quiz anyway.

I like that about Nurse Malloy. She, too, always hopes for a good result. Looks on the sunny side.

"Admith—admith—" Nellie always tries to answer every question, her tongue stuck up against her lower teeth, which protrude quite a lot.

"Admissions," says Nurse Malloy. "Nelly, can you pull your tongue back just a little, like this…" Malloy opens her mouth grotesquely and waves her pink tongue at the girl, curling it back in her mouth.

We all laugh. Nurse Malloy smiles at her own performance. Nellie experiments with her tongue, making "ah, ah" sounds.

What must we look like to any passerby, as we trot along the circular drive of the Admissions Building?

And there will always be passersby.

There is Sheriff Wally Norton in his black sedan, a frequent visitor. Here is an autobus full of new student nurses who have been trained not to stare. Thus they sit in artificial stillness, looking straight ahead, like gulls at the lakeshore. They seem proud of their new caps, which resemble upside-down pudding pans.

"Anchor Hospital," I say. We all know the taxonomy of nursing caps.

"Excellent, Mrs. Allen," says Nurse Malloy. I wrinkle my nose at her behind her back. What I do *not* like about Nurse Malloy is her teacher voice, and the way she speaks to us all as if we were as mental as Nellie.

Well, "mental" is relative.

Still, Nurse Malloy remembers to call me by my married name, even though they have stolen my ring.

Even though Will has not been to visit, as he promised.

As I gain some perspective on Will and his world, however, I am ceasing to long for the sight of him.

There will be some schoolboys on the hill next to Admissions, playing truant, perhaps, in the sunshine. They'll laugh and point at us. There are always such people around the grounds. No one stops them from their recreational excursions to the Northfield State Hospital for the Criminally Insane, Crippled, Feeble-Minded and Indigent.

I imagine what we must look like through their eyes. It's finally getting warmer, but we all go outside in our odd selection of ratty coats. Our dresses are uniform and presentable, some gray, some flowered, some dotted, all of the same pattern, cut on Ward 3 North, where the ladies have a big sewing room. (No, I do not want to get worse and pump a treadle all day!)

But our coats come from the institutional rag bag—men's coats, nurses' coats. Nellie parades in a maroon drum major's uniform, with gold trim around the collar.

"Nurse, I'm hot." Bella will raise her big sad eyes and start to unbutton.

"Leave it, or we'll go inside. We wear our coats until May 10," Nurse Passmore will say.

"It *is* hot," Nurse Mercy responded yesterday under her breath. "That seems arbitrary."

"It's not for you to say, Nurse," Miss Passmore snapped. She has good hearing, for an old woman.

CHAPTER NINE

Spring, true spring at last.

It brought to southern Minnesota the lightening of earth, of clothing, of manners. It put the Armistice almost three years into the past, a reasonable distance from which to view what had been gained and lost. Nostalgia and romance became the dominant emotions. Romance, especially.

Decoration Day was coming up, the new holiday devoted to picnics in the cemetery.

A fashion spread among the nurses for wearing brooches on their uniform capes, each with a tiny reservoir to hold a sheaf of violets. Nurse Passmore quickly put a stop to it, though.

"It has something to do with the war dead," Dr. Dominic Kennedy explained. He tended to be on the side of Romance.

"That's poppies," she snapped.

Poppies would not bloom for weeks yet. Now there was hepatica, bloodroot. Those who had been too young to fight the war seemed particularly eager, even precipitate, in their embrace of life. The head gardener, over a long weekend, married the least competent cook. Dr. Jessen-Haight began courting a German widow in town. He called her "Alsatian." (He called himself "Viennese.") Gossip had begun to link Dr. Dominic Kennedy and the pretty daughter of the head of physical plant. She was a sophomore at the local college.

By contrast, those whose youth had been wasted on the war seemed to wake to their condition of solitude, now that they had the maturity to name and endure it.

"*Are we down-hearted?*" That was a chorus they'd sung in the ranks.

The brave answer was "No." But Dr. David Grafton, the realist, sighed over his accounts. May meant that he had a legislative report to submit. All the courtship behavior going around had unsettled him. He, himself, needed to get on with marrying somebody. It was expected.

He couldn't bear the idea.

Popular gossip, he knew, coupled him with Nurse Mercy—as everyone had begun to call her behind her back. The younger nurses were on her side.

More mature onlookers (Nurse Passmore, Nurse Malloy) noted his indifference. It seemed more than studied, as her reticence seemed more than maidenly. Dr. Jessen-Haight smirked, as though he knew things a gentleman could never say about sex in general.

Things he himself did not know, certainly, thought David Grafton. He was still behind on his medical journals.

•

Grafton fastidiously addressed the new nurse as "Miss Winstead." He kept up a level of formality with all the nurses, even during the coffee hour.

It had taken him a while, after he was demobilized, to break the British habit of calling them "Sister."

The first time he'd done that in America, what a titter of laughs.

"Yes," Grafton said, to no one, as he shut his ledger. He was down-hearted.

Dr. Kennedy was knocking for his appointment. Grafton reached for his white coat and opened the door.

"Let's take Miss Winstead along," Grafton told the junior physician. "We need a newcomer's perspective on this business." They were going up to 4 North to interview a patient for promotion, as they called the shift to a lower floor.

Kennedy dropped his eyes as though keeping a counsel.

"*Oh, fuck,*" Grafton allowed himself, well under the breath.

It annoyed him to think he and Miss Winstead were the subject of some narrative going around staff quarters. He set a brisk pace down the hall, out the door, and across the grounds toward North. Let the Boy puff along; he was getting fat.

Two nurses' heads were bowed over the charting station on 2 North. "Nurse Winstead," Grafton called out "would you care to accompany Dr. Kennedy and me to the fourth floor? Miss Malloy, can you spare our probationer?"

They had been deep in their work and Miss Winstead scrambled to her feet. Raising her head, Edith Malloy said, "Certainly, sir." A head nurse stood up for no physician. Indeed, that had been Grafton's own order.

Nurse Winstead's very fingers, fiddling with a set of index cards, blushed. That red hair.

She swung into line behind Dominic Kennedy (was he daring to grin?) and they both followed the superintendent like goslings.

Head down, clipboard in hand. Grafton noticed the shine on the floor, white tile, green tile, white tile. So calming, the repetition. Sterile. He admired the polish on the wallboards. He raised his eyes to the curvilinear carving above the doorframes as they passed through. No dust anywhere.

There was little one could control, but one could control the cleanliness of a place. He hated dirt because he hated vermin. Because rats and mice carried germs and germs caused disease. Why did the staff laugh behind his back about his obsession?

Why did he have to defend Louis Pasteur?

Passing a glass door inlaid with chicken wire, he caught the distorted reflections of Dr. Kennedy and Nurse Winstead hurrying behind him. White coat, white apron.

He took the stairs.

He felt, he admitted, a slight frisson in the presence of the new nurse. It flared just at the edge of consciousness and lifted him on a little wave of energy and anxiety.

The keys. He patted his pockets. He had them. He produced

them. They reminded him of who he was. How fortunate he was to be alive and carrying the keys. How precious the status quo. Order. The light rein he kept on himself always.

"Have you been up to 4 North yet, Nurse Winstead?" he asked politely, over his shoulder.

Her eyes were bright behind her glasses.

"Just on my second day, Dr. Grafton," Mercy said. She seemed a bit breathless. "When I got the grand tour."

"And what did you think?" Dr. Dominic Kennedy, beside her now, wanted to know.

They were always asking her what she thought. Mercy groped for a response that would manifest her mastery and intelligence, but in no way undercut the authority of a senior doctor or nurse.

As for her tour of 4 North, frankly, it had been horrifying.

"Exemplary," she said.

"In what way?" Grafton shot back.

Oh. She exhaled.

Mercy was petite. Why did they all rush? Her short legs had to paddle twice as fast as the men's.

Grafton looked through more chicken wire into the ward designated 4 North. He tapped at the glass. Would this mesh really stand up to attack?

Kennedy mentioned it was some new material that didn't shatter.

Grafton fingered his keys. "In what way exemplary?" he repeated.

Mercy tried to calm her breathing. There had been two flights of curving stairway at a male pace. There had been Dr. David Grafton's scent of lime and cherry tobacco, which went, just a bit, to her head. "Why, I'd only just seen the 13th floor at Deaconess, of course."

That had been a ring of hell, in her recollection. "And read about Bedlam." She laughed nervously. She settled on "Clean. They manage to keep it so clean."

Grafton's lips tightened. Disappointing. She was playing to his much-mocked obsession. His *phobia*.

It was not a phobia if the danger was real. *Rats!* Had they any idea?

And why would people not be straight with him? He wanted them to speak up, to be a band of brothers. And sisters.

"I'm sure Deaconess is clean," he said. He relaxed the muscles of his face. He relaxed his judgment. The poor girl was panting, for godsake. Did she lack for exercise or had something upset her? He judged her to be on the flighty side. He remembered Nurse Malloy's report about the patient who lost her skin.

Well, 4 North would frighten anyone. Even psychiatric nurses.

Chivalry was prominent in Grafton's temperament. He subdued his own feelings, still volatile, to the role of teacher. He apologized rhetorically for 4 North. "On a ward like this we recognize the limits of what medicine can achieve today. Someday, I hope—" He shrugged.

What was on the horizon? He mentioned the new fad for association therapy. (But it was useless with mania and dementia, delusionary psychosis. It was useless with Evil.)

(Though it was becoming unfashionable to talk about Evil.)

He wondered aloud how the new abreaction therapies were coming along in Europe. Insulin shock. Coma induction with bromides. Jolting patients with electricity. Infecting them with malaria to raise a fever. Russian doctors had experimented with sticking an ice pick into the prefrontal lobe.

Just as he mentioned Russia, the earth seemed to shudder under Grafton's feet. He reached for the wall to steady himself.

The quake felt something like the minor concussion of gun batteries along the Somme. Grafton tried to breathe consciously and buck himself up. Sometimes images rose unbidden in his mind—well, why ever would he bid them? The engulfing dream could make him lose contact with where he was: *Northfield State Hospital, Minnesota, the USA.*

It helped to say those words, locate himself in space and time. Nine a.m. 4 North.

When these concussions reached for him out of the past, the smells, even, of the forward dressing station would waft back to him: gangrenous wounds, the subtle scent of rodent feces. The cries. In a dressing station, someone was always screaming.

Sometimes, it had been David Grafton.

When the tiles wavered as they wavered now, Grafton would finger the ring of keys, rub his forefinger against a serrated ridge of brass till discomfort nudged him to recollect the present moment.

He paused a moment to observe his mental processes dispassionately.

Something had tripped him into a flashback.

Likely his unguarded thoughts about European experiments and lobotomy.

Very well.

He must remember to observe at all times the most rigorous mental hygiene, especially on the threshold of 4 North.

Must replace the nightmare vision with positive images.

He allowed himself to admire the lift in Mercy Winstead's white bib, where her nurse's watch hung. He tried to feel what the whole institution seemed to want him to feel. His interest in the contours of her small breasts—which religion might consider an occasion of sin—seemed to him, at the moment, an appropriate therapeutic modality.

For him, at least.

Of course, he must not linger with a sexual fantasy. But it served to turn his mind away from trench warfare and the dark arts of his own profession. Thinking about Mercy Winstead's bosom constituted what some of the more positive treatment protocols—those he himself espoused—called "reinforcement."

Anyway, he would have to marry someone, someday, in order to be promoted. People were starting to call him a confirmed bachelor. Among doctors, this could be code for "invert."

Pretty soon, he would have to work through his concerns about marriage. Well, his fears.

Mercy Winstead was peering at him with pursed lips.

(*Why is he staring at my nametag,* she wondered. *Did he not remember who she was?*)

The superintendent shrugged in his white coat. He turned the key. At some point he seemed to have stuck it in the lock.

"That was a major shock," said Dominic Kennedy.

"Hmmm?" said Grafton. Kennedy had felt it as well? Then it was no hallucination.

As they crossed the threshold of 4 North, they met two female aides running toward them.

It appeared that Lady Catherine Stewart, a lost descendant of James II's illegitimate line, had managed to heave her iron bed against the door of her room, which abutted the corridor. That accounted for the earthquake they'd felt.

Thank God, who did not exist, Grafton thought. The shock had not been only in his mind.

Damn, where were the male aides?

As his nurse and junior physician fanned out, Grafton locked the ward door behind them.

Dr. Dominic Kennedy noticed: the superintendent always keeps his hand on the key ring. It must be a point of practice with him. A security measure he, Kennedy, would do well to imitate. A gesture that conveyed authority and reassurance. The younger doctor was always scanning for whatever bits of playacting would get a man ahead.

Nurse Schaeffer was bearing down the hallway from the nurses' station. The oversized flaps of her cap rattled like sails in a freshening breeze: St. Xavier's Hospital, Chicago. Kennedy recognized the nurse's field marks without thinking about it.

Rarely flustered, always in control. Nurse Schaeffer nodded to them at the same moment she rapped sharply on the barred window of the adjoining room. "Stop that, Mrs. Haugen. At once!" There would be no "Lady Catherine." She never gave a moment's quarter to a patient's delusions. "Mrs. Haugen. Do you want to be in the muffs?"

Grafton said mildly. "Don't threaten what you can't perform, Nurse. At least until Max gets here. In fact, do not threaten at all."

Miss Schaeffer took the rebuke with a tightening of skin over her cheekbones.

There was a speaking tube just past the entrance door. She went to it. She called down in a voice neither agitated nor diffident—Nurse Mercy Winstead recorded this as exemplary—"Max! Henry! 4 North!"

Grafton went to the patient's window and tapped lightly. "Madame!" He chose a neutral address fit for maniac or royalty. Playing into a patient's delusions tempted him as an experiment, though it went against common practice. He didn't want to risk failure in front of his subordinates. But later, when they got Mrs. Haugen into restraints, he thought he'd offer her a glass of water, much courtesy, and the title she demanded. He wondered what might result. It was worth a try.

Max, the attendant, was already knocking at the ward door. He had no keys. Kennedy turned the bolt.

"I can take her on my own," Max said, the little muscled man, with his rippling tattoos.

Grafton recalled irrelevantly that the aide had been, on some other planet, a circus performer.

No emergency, they all realized. Mrs. Haugen was calming to the sound of Grafton's voice, its gentle authority.

Mercy Winstead felt a surge of tenderness. How could she have thought the superintendent cold? In the past few days he had seemed, well, warm.

Four or five ambulatory patients were responding to the welcome intrusion. One wore the shapeless smock of the uncontrollable, her sleeves just now dragging on the ground, cuffs filthy. Here was a toothless young girl, who had licked her lips so compulsively that the margin of her mouth had enlarged into a red wound. Here was Hattie, with the mutilated earlobes.

They looked like figures in a sketch by Daumier, Grafton thought. He must ask Nurse Schaeffer to attend to those dirty, trailing cuffs.

Why did everybody want to be royalty, Mercy Winstead wondered. Why not want to be a head nurse?

She did.

Here was Mrs. Anne Leary, leaning against the wall, her arms crossed over her chest, looking on with amusement.

She looked as sensible as any of the staff, Mercy judged. How could that be?

They had keys.

PART TWO: BLUE HEAVEN

CHAPTER TEN

AFTER THE FRACAS on 4 North, Dr. Grafton had seemed to notice the aide Max Bahlke for the first time. He gave him an extra hour for lunch.

Max felt the superintendent's eyes follow him as he left the floor, his swagger a little muscle-bound.

Max liked to be noticed. He had grown up on a big prairie, where he had felt himself to be a very small child. But he had learned to excel at "physical culture," as they called it in school. That was more than tossing hay on the farm; it meant working out methodically in a corner of the barn loft with Indian clubs and weights made from scraps of abandoned machinery. Max didn't know, then, what he was preparing for, but he knew it would be magnificent. He practiced walking on his hands till his fingers were as calloused as his bare toes: *Maximiliano the Magnificent!* When the circus came to town, he retrieved posters and papered the loft with vision: lion tamers, aerialists, even the life of a clown would do, if you could turn back flips and, when night fell, ride the train.

His dream, the dream of every boy he knew, had been to get out of Northfield, Minnesota. They talked about joining the army. Of saddling up with Jesse James.

Of all those farm boys, only Max had broken free. Northfield had gotten him back in the end, but he'd had his run. And now there was Carmie, the garden, the house.

Now. He had two hours free for his own devices. As he walked along Division Street toward the river he whistled a song the nurses played on their gramophone: *"I'm happy in my blue heaven…"*

Past the college, past the bank.

Within living memory, some thirty-five years ago, Jesse James and Cole Younger's gang had failed to rob that bank. The outlaws' defeat robbed the Northfield boys of one active fantasy. Max's imagination, ever adaptable, had taken a moral turn. He idealized the heroic teller who wouldn't turn over his till, who gave the alarm and met his death before the outlaws scattered into wilderness. A posse had rounded up most of them. Jesse himself had escaped on a limping horse back to his wife in Missouri.

Max, as a boy of seven, had hiked twelve miles to the neighboring town of Owatonna, where the Younger brothers sat in a cell awaiting trial. He had climbed a trellis and a drainpipe to peer in the window, not much of a feat for an athletic boy.

That long walk determined the course of Max's life. He would pursue adventure, but not crime. Seeing the outlaws, short, wounded, and disconsolate in their cell, had finished his romance with the James gang.

Yet they had seen the world.

As Max walked back to the farm, a circus train from Wisconsin went chugging by, so slowly that the boy could toss pebbles at the lions in their cages; he could waken them to roar. As the caboose passed, a man in spangled tights, hanging off the back of the train, leapt to the railing and made the young boy a bow.

Maximiliano flipped over in response to stand on his hands. He entered his destiny.

It would be the circus for him.

Passing now on the boardwalk, Max tipped his bowler hat to the bank manager at his desk. The manager waved back. So did the pretty girl who offered tea to the more prosperous clients.

Max himself was one of those.

But only the bankers knew that. Between Carmie's settlement and Max's own frugality, they had enough money to buy any farm in Scott or maybe Goodhue County.

Farming: a sentence to penal servitude. Instead he had an exciting job, which required him to raise his fists several times a week on the side of justice or at least order. Like a lawman. He had a beautiful wife unravaged by sun and toil. He had his memories. He had six-hundred-thousand dollars in a bank Jesse James had failed to rob.

When he nodded to the sidewalk strollers of Northfield, they would nod back with a touch of envy: "There goes a happy man," a lawyer or professor might say to his wife. What could his secret be? A small man in a shabby bowler, clean overalls and long-johns, with a grunt-job at the state hospital.

The pleasure of a simple life, they might imagine, as Max disappeared down the path to his small house by the river.

Max's whistle was famous in Northfield, a birdlike trill that passed for real music. It rose in pitch, like a piccolo, as he passed out of sight of the townsfolk. At the end of the path, he closed the gate. He entered a walled courtyard Moorish in design with elaborate mosaics on the private side. Hidden down the dirt road it looked, from the outside, like a bunker.

But from within!

Max's whistle trilled on.

Hundreds of bulbs were pushing through the soil of his raised beds. Last week he had turned on the fountain. Paths of old brick were laid out, mathematically perfect. By mid-June, it would look like a garden out of the Arabian Nights.

Max chose a square of compacted zoysia grass on which to execute three flips in front of his kitchen window.

His back ached a little from moving furniture on 4 North. But if he did his routine every day at noon—and now he heard the whistle blow from the cereal factory—what was to stop him, ever? He could remain, into old age, *Maximiliano!*

If only to Carmie. She tapped at the window, smiling and clapping as she did every day.

The train, on the other side of the river, hooted as well. It was spring, and one of the trains would be from Baraboo, where the circus wintered. Its passage would exert a gentle tug, as though someone had got hold of his overall straps and urged him away. Often he could hear the lions roar at the crossroad.

But Max was going nowhere.

He flipped once more, because he needed to defy the pain in his back, and landed on one hand. Inverted and breathing a little hard, he could glance through the window up Carmie's low-cut dress—it was a made-over circus costume—as she sat atop the kitchen table kneading bread. He watched her dust off her hands and reach for the trapeze he'd mounted from the ceiling above her head. Her hair, prematurely white, shone in the sun as though footlights had flared.

La Carmencita! Max's lips formed her name.

Using the trapeze, she lifted herself up and over into the child-sized wicker wheel-chair he'd ordered from Chicago. Max knew she rarely used it—only to please him. She much preferred the system of bars and pulleys he'd strung through the house and garden. Her strong acrobat's arms carried her anywhere she needed to go, dragging her legs. Outside the garden gate she was a cripple, inside, *La Carmencita!* Therefore she stayed home. This suited both of them.

Max whistled again about his blue heaven.

CHAPTER ELEVEN

DAVID GRAFTON HAD watched the aide, Max Bahlke, exit the locks of 4 North. An amazing character, he thought, but something weak in the gait. Hip dysplasia? The man shouldn't be bench-pressing heavy iron beds, designed to defeat mania. Nobody should.

Of course he and Kennedy had looked on while Max set the ward to rights. They had no intention of injuring themselves.

He'd given the aide an extra hour of lunchtime.

Two female assistants in white, and one in the green uniform of a kitchen worker, were knocking on the ward doors. Tall, strong, blond women. Nurse Schaeffer let them in and, as a team, they surrounded Mrs. Haugen. She was docile, now, in the embrace of a Mayo Hospital student. They led her off toward the hallway marked "Treatment Rooms." She would be cuffed and muffed and tied to a chair.

Later, the superintendent resolved, he would visit her. But first, Mrs. Leary.

"Mrs. Leary!" Nurse Schaeffer said sharply. The head nurse needed to assert authority. She was embarrassed by the disorder in her ward. She had sent people scurrying in all directions. A tea cart rattled ominously in the distance.

The patient detached herself from the wall.

David Grafton disliked tea drinking and the little ceremonies of civility the nurses loved to improvise. They carried him back to Britain, to places like Wellington Spa, where he'd been sent to heal after the explosion at the forward dressing station. But he resolved manfully to follow Nurse Schaeffer into the nurses' sitting room with Mrs. Leary and his staff in tow.

Unexpectedly, Annie Leary offered him her hand. Reflexively he pressed her fingers though he tried to avoid touching patients. Touching anybody. A sentence from the deportment manual of his youth rose to consciousness: *If a lady offers her hand, a gentleman takes it lightly by the fingertips and returns a gentle pressure.*

The French officers would kiss a lady's hand. The Brits and Canadians snorted at this, but they envied the sweet sensuality of the gesture.

No sensuality for the prairie, Grafton remarked firmly to himself. To some other self.

Annie Leary was looking at him like a gracious hostess, and he returned her gaze with clinical discernment. The woman seemed at ease. If two doctors and a small nurse in a silly cap filled her with either hope or apprehension, she gave no sign.

"It's you we've come to see," he said. Of course she knew that. "You've asked for a review, I understand? You hope to move down a few floors?"

"We talked about it two years ago," she said bluntly, as though her time were valuable.

Indeed they had.

He nodded to his goslings to fall in behind Nurse Schaeffer and the tea cart. He put an armload of file folders between himself and Mrs. Leary, lest their bodies should touch as they followed Nurse Schaeffer's whipping skirts. They went down a different hall from the one marked "Treatment Rooms."

"So you've been thinking about it?" he ventured. He stepped back to let her precede him.

"There were complications, then," she replied. She shrugged lightly, looked over her shoulder.

Two years ago he'd been the new superintendent, fresh from Toronto, eager to right wrongs and initiate reform.

Grafton sighed. It seemed long ago.

He'd discovered Mrs. Leary on 4 North with her shelf of books and journals. Bright and industrious. Apparently sane, though the word *psychopath* had been scrawled on her commitment papers. Careless penmanship.

The woman did no harm; even misanthropic Nurse Schaeffer admitted she did the work of two nurses on the understaffed ward. She cleaned, she tended the other patients and taught a few their letters. She sang; she had a great talent that way. She quieted the unruly.

To be fair, he hadn't simply discovered Annie Leary, he'd been directed to look for her. His workload didn't allow a lot of time for wandering the wards.

He'd been directed in a sharply worded letter from the editor of the *St. Paul Pioneer Press*, a man called Erik Strommer.

A servant of the legislature had to pay attention to crusading journalists.

It seemed that Annie Leary had been writing occasional essays and verse for the paper.

This Erik Strommer had corresponded with her at length, become a sort of pen-pal. He judged her mentally competent. He considered her a friend.

Psychopaths could charm people that way. Some of the psychiatric literature argued they were not insane at all, but morally bent.

With this reservation in mind, Grafton had opened Strommer's sheaf of newspaper clippings.

A stunning surprise. He didn't understand Annie Leary's gnomic verse, but he thought her essays very fine. Up to the standard of an avant-garde ladies' seminary at least. Sketches of hospital life and the passing seasons.

So many passing seasons.

Erik Strommer had called her "an original and authoritative voice." Brilliant, even.

David Grafton had to reserve his opinion on that. What did he know about literature?

Erik Strommer had demanded to know why a woman of such intelligence was incarcerated in the secured unit of a state hospital. How could a woman of sensibility be guilty of the crimes she was accused of? Should they not reopen her case? He was the man to do it.

What, had the journalist fallen in love with her? Hard-bitten reporters were often sentimental at the core. They could be easily duped, especially by a manipulative mental patient.

Still, the editor's letter had sent him to Mrs. Leary's file. Then he had sought her out on 4 North.

We talked about it two years ago.

In this same room, he realized.

Grafton pulled out a chair for Annie Leary at the round table while Kennedy tended to Nurse Winstead. Two years ago, Nurse Schaeffer had bustled off, as she seemed prepared to do today. Burgundy velvet curtains muted the light. Drawing the eye, a series of photographs: severe lines of nurses mounted on the outside steps of North.

Back then, David Grafton had had some hope of moving Mrs. Leary to a more congenial ward. He saw no hope of reopening her commitment case. What a mess that would be. But, perhaps, an accommodation…

Now he queried the patient with her own word: *complications*? She merely averted her glance.

Nurse Schaeffer passed a plate of sweets and made for the door.

"Please remain, Nurse," said Grafton. "I'd like you to take notes."

Lydia Schaeffer nodded and took out the kind of pencil stub they used on the locked wards. Now they could begin.

"Two years ago," David Grafton reminded her, "you had no interest in leaving 4 North."

"But now I do," she said. "I have an interest. Would you like a lemon cake?" She addressed Mercy Winstead. She passed the plate that had reached her. "This is the last one."

"Oh, forgive me," Nurse Schaeffer said. "May I please introduce Miss Mercy Winstead and Dr. Dominic Kennedy."

"I hope you don't mind if we listen in." Mercy spoke up politely.

"Not at all." Annie Leary's voice was low and strong, with a note of ironic detachment. "Sugar?" She turned a silver pitcher toward Dominic Kennedy.

Something, perhaps the tea service, had drawn them all into the atmosphere of a drawing room comedy. The actors seemed to convey to the audience that their pretensions would soon be punctured by pratfalls, hilarious misunderstandings, men caught in ladies' chambers with their suspenders down, and the wrath of elderly husbands.

With difficulty, David Grafton controlled his impatience. He declined his part in the play, but paid attention to the stage business.

Did Mrs. Leary consciously hold herself as far away as possible from any of the caretakers?

Were they, for their part, unconsciously bunching together behind a plate of biscuits?

Mrs. Leary was looking well. Her thick light hair was bobbed; her color, even on the dim ward, was high. She looked healthy. Her family had farmed. She was allowed outside to work in the gardens, he knew, and they would soon be planting. A student nurse on either side, as the state legislature required for a patient with a history of homicidal violence.

He hadn't visited her since his early rebuff. He'd drawn back and cut his losses. Unlike most patients, who clamored for a physician's time, she seemed to prefer reading. He was busy. There were always twice as many patients running amok than the doctors could attend to.

There had been the ridiculous recurring business of her smoking. Really, that had to stop.

Aside from carrying matches, as far as he knew, she behaved and read Jane Austen.

The patient met his gaze with eyes that were forthright and brightly blue.

Grafton smiled. "You're very well, I see." He felt his smile was stiff.

Nurse Schaeffer handed him a brown folder and a sheaf of notes. "Yes, thank you, sir."

What if she were that rare bird, a true psychopath? They were difficult to diagnose, but sometimes you could catch an element of playacting...

Amateur theatricals were a staple of the hospital community, mounted by the recreational therapists. With a great expenditure of foresight and leadership, which waxed and waned, patients and staff would sometimes produce a play together, like last year's abbreviated version of *The Tempest*.

David Grafton disliked such co-productions, though others thought they were good for morale. They blurred the distinctions between appearance and reality. That line was important not to cross in a properly functioning psychiatric asylum. He hadn't liked to see Dominic Kennedy groveling across an improvised stage playing Caliban, while a delusional patient from 3 North put on her overweight Miranda. That patient, when last he'd checked, was still inhabiting the role.

But perhaps that indicated progress for Miranda, he thought.

Grafton let Nurse Schaeffer warm his tea.

He was on the side of education and culture, certainly. He had values beyond cleanliness! Theater, though he might personally dislike it, could at least offer patients a higher quality of delusion. He smiled to himself and pretended to drink from the porcelain cup.

Mrs. Annie Leary now, would have made a fine Miranda, but she had not been able or willing to appear.

Perhaps she'd been tied to a bed somewhere.

But no—he opened the file Nurse Schaeffer offered—Mrs. Leary had not been in restraints for four years at least, and the last tie-down had been for "fits." He traced the head nurse's fine copperplate hand, so much more delicate than the woman herself.

He must ask Nurse Schaeffer how the fits manifested.

Patients often had a canny genius. They could play at being well, play at being ill.

Grafton drew a hand across his eyes. It was too confusing. He was a little tired today.

"When last we met, Mrs. Leary," he began, "I offered you a—shall we say—promotion to an open ward."

The doctors and nurses smiled encouragingly. Mrs. Leary looked from one to another of them with a face full of limpid charm.

Grafton went on. "But you refused. You indicated your wish to remain on 4 North. You said"—he pretended to consult his notes, though he knew well what she had said—"you had friends here and 'people who depend on you.'"

·

Dominic Kennedy cleared his throat, but the junior doctor was afraid to speak up. He wanted to inquire about the legal implications. Annie Leary had been indicted for a capital crime—a particularly heinous one. She'd been remanded to the institution when she proved mentally incapable of standing trial.

Kennedy wondered: *did Annie Leary know that if she got better she might become vulnerable to the law?* Her trial could be reopened. Minnesota had revoked the death penalty, but who wanted to live out their life in the state penitentiary? Even a lunatic asylum might be preferable. He wondered if his superintendent, a foreigner, fully understood that.

Annie Leary had a private cubicle in which to read and write, happy as a nun in her cell.

Kennedy munched on cake, playing out the options in his mind. This was not a good moment to raise the problem.

Grafton nodded to his associate. The American legal system confounded him, but he had pondered the problem. If a deranged person committed a crime, he was not morally responsible. But if he got well, he became responsible, retroactively.

Pursuing such a case involved a muddy set of distinctions.

Grafton imagined a roomful of prairie lawyers and grocers and farmers up at the legislature. He imagined them laboring at their slanted desks, pencils in hand, tongues between their teeth, attempting to define "mental illness."

Which he, himself, admitted to a poor grasp of most of the time.

Usually the asylum didn't have to worry about the legal consequences of recovered sanity because the insane rarely got well. For practical purposes, the law distinguished hardly at all between criminals, drunks, cripples, the insane, and the incorrigible poor. It was pretty much a matter of luck whether you wound up in the state hospital, the poor farm or the penitentiary. In any of those locations, seldom did anyone improve.

There were exceptions. Most likely, they'd been misdiagnosed in the first place. But, after years in the asylum, how could the survivors live outside? Where were their people? Who cared?

He thought of the aide, Jane Robinson, with her club foot.

Mrs. Leary's chart indicated an unusual story. She had been admitted in something like a catatonic state. She had emerged from it, regressed now and then, and finally begun acting like a model school girl.

He turned to the patient again. In the drawing room scene they were playing out, it seemed rude to bring this up, but he ventured, "No more of the falling sickness?"

·

Quaint term, Annie thought. She liked it. It conveyed the sensation of dropping off the world, into an illness that felt familiar and friendly, into a space where there was no responsibility, no god. That described her experience quite well.

"No, sir," she answered.

Well, there had been the occasional aura, some blank spots like smudges on the glass of the day. But no, she had not, for a long time, *fallen*.

·

Nurse Mercy Winstead was rapidly scanning the file Grafton

handed her. Nurses were not privy to patient records, but they read them, when they got the chance, like forbidden novels.

She found no backstory in Annie's file. Perhaps it had been expunged. (Why?)

There were just the daily notes on how the patient spent her day: reading, mostly, and writing in a set of copybooks she'd been given. There were some fifty of these lined up in her cubby on the ward, Nurse Schaeffer had noted.

•

"I'd love to get my hands on those diaries," the superintendent thought, as he watched Mercy Winstead's finger pause on a line of script.

He weighed the invasion of privacy against therapeutic intent. He came up short.

"What do you do all day?" he asked Annie Leary.

The patient repeated what he already knew. "I help out. I read a lot. I write."

Nurse Schaeffer had reported that Mrs. Leary considered herself "college educated" by now. An autodidact.

"What are you reading these days?"

"Everything I can find. I like literature. I just finished *Middlemarch*. I like poetry. I've read a lot of botany and all of *Hoskins' Studies in Abnormal Psychiatry* that's in the library. We're missing volume seven." She looked at Grafton expectantly, like a scholar confronting a stingy librarian.

•

Volume seven, *sexual aberration*, thought Dr. Dominic Kennedy.

Nurse Winstead blushed so easily.

Someone always had volume seven out.

•

"And I'm reading about cures for deafness," the woman went on. "Because of Sylvie…"

Yes, Sylvie. *There are people who depend on me.*

Grafton called to mind the patient's comment from his last

interview. This had been—it occurred to him now—the major complication. Sylvie Sztamburski was a feral deaf-mute, age about twelve, confined to 4 North because she bit and kicked and had never been toilet-trained.

Full of rage. She should have played Caliban.

Grafton wondered why Annie Leary was interested in Sylvie.

"I can make sense of her," the patient said, responding to his cocked eyebrow. "She knows about a hundred signs now. I can ask her to use the bathroom and comb her own hair."

"Well, what about Miss Sztamburski then?" said Mercy, inserting her two cents' worth as the superintendent seemed to expect. "Are you ready to leave her now? What will become of her if you go to another ward?"

Annie Leary returned a confident smile. "Oh, I want to take her with me. She doesn't belong here. She's not insane. She's deaf."

The doctors and nurses exchanged a look of controlled surprise.

Dr. Kennedy cleared his throat. "Oh, then we are considering *two* transfers today? Mrs. Leary, you must understand that's a lot to work through." He determined to push hard, challenge the serenity of her affect. "You're not making a pet of Miss Sztamburski, I hope."

•

Annie Leary dropped her eyes.

They're trying to trap me, she thought. Trying to make me rise to the bait. Sylvie, the bait. No, Sylvie is not my pet. Nurse Passmore's dog, Rufus, is not my pet. *Attach to nothing.* That was the message of one of the pious books Nurse Schaeffer had offered her: *The Imitation of Christ.*

Annie thought it was a sissy book. But she honored one piece of advice: attach to nothing. It had served her well.

Lately, though, the counsel had outlived its usefulness. She had become attached to getting off this ward. That seemed like progress, not backsliding. She had become attached to Lucy, and surely this light in her heart was holy.

"You get worse, I'll get better," she had written to that beautiful, dim girl, so stunned and innocent.

Then they could meet somewhere in the middle, say, 3 North.

That plot had seemed to her brilliant in the flash of its conception.

Only moments later, too late to pull it out of the mangle, it horrified her. She saw the peril for Lucy: regression backward through a carnival hall of mirrors, the cuffs, the chemise, hydrotherapy. Once regressed, Lucy might not know how to find her way back.

That happened around here. Insanity was catching. You put an innocent, vulnerable girl among raving, twitching, shitting, maniacs who thought they had a claim to the British throne and—the girl might catch it. Annie had seen such things happen to others. The curriculum of sanity was more than most of them could master.

Had she, Annie, mastered it?

Really she wasn't sure. But far better for her to make her own journey back toward sanity—and quickly!—than for Lucy to get more sick.

The poets were her counselors. Miss Emily Dickinson, her kindred spirit. Annie knew many of the dark and accurate poems by heart. Knew by skin and bone. Poems that told her own story:

And then a plank in reason broke,
And I fell down and down,
And passed a world at every shift
And finished knowing, then—

That was it, in a nutshell. Surely Miss Emily had some experience of *falling.*

Either that or Miss Emily was insane.

Or we are both sane, thought Annie Leary.

Or we both have grand mal seizures (*Hoskins' Studies in Abnormal Psychology*, Volume 3).

How had Miss Emily avoided the asylum, Annie wondered. Wealthy family, no doubt. That came in handy.

The intensity of her desire to be with Lucy rose and ached in Annie's chest.

She had forgotten to breathe.

She breathed. She sat quietly. Detached.

•

To everyone's surprise, Nurse Winstead spoke up. "If I can be spared the time, I'd be happy to work with Miss Sztamburski. If that would help to move things along." Eyes swiveled to her own. She looked down. "I—my little brother is deaf. I have some experience." Her blush now was a malarial burn.

Oh Lord, thought Mercy Winstead, *I've confessed to an hereditary congenital taint. No one will marry me.*

•

Annie Leary put on a smile that she hoped was unreadable. God. What had she set in motion? Would Sylvie be able to bear a transition? And what if her own healing put her back under the power of the trial attorneys? Perhaps instead of reading poetry she should have been reading law.

Annie felt a clutch of terror. She soothed herself by totting up in her mind the risks and benefits. No one else was talking. They were all sitting there like dropped puppets.

She had trained herself to be calm and strong. She had observed rigid discipline. Think about this, do not think about that. Two hours a day of physical exercise. Four of "helping out." An orderly course of study, memorization.

All undone in the laundry building…Her insouciance, how she had taken the pins from the girl's hair, her flirtatious jokes and playacting boldness. Showing off. Now the fear returned. Fear she had repressed for years, of what she might be capable of.

She could not, could not, remember what she was capable of.

It was easier to stay on 4 North, it was easier to let yourself be tied to a bed.

Anxiety. Suffering. *Life.*

Because she'd folded laundry with Janina Lucy Valenta.

You and your partner took opposite ends of the hot-smelling sheet as it came off the mangle. In the same motion, each of you folded your end in half and in half again, snapping the material taut between you. Then you moved toward each other like dancers, lifting the folded fabric off the floor. You met in the middle and touched your half to hers, arms reaching overhead.

That was the moment she'd whispered to Lucy, "I'll be with you forever."

One woman—it didn't matter which—would hold the top of the sheet while the other brought up the bottom. Touch again. Clasp again. Bring up the bottom again. Lady on the right takes the folded square to the cupboard while lady on the left moves to receive another from the mangle.

Lucy had looked over her shoulder. She had smiled, but there was a shimmering sadness in her look, as if something in the light or the heat was claiming her against her will and lifting her away.

CHAPTER TWELVE

As HE DROVE past the St. Paul Cathedral, Will Allen's tires skidded on wet leaves that had lain under the snow since October. The cathedral, as ever, seemed to rebuke him, to rebuke the whole city with sheer mass. The great church spoke only to the massive state capitol building, on an opposing knoll. Rival architects had designed the buildings, set them to dialogue forever about the relative powers of the archdiocese and the political order.

The church commanded a higher hill.

Freed from the entrapments of women, Will thought of heading for the Commodore Hotel. But it was too public, even in the after-hours room where there would be a few rich men and good cigars. Yet he needed male company, male understanding. He needed, he thought, someone with insomnia and a bottle of Jameson's.

He thought of Father Joseph Haggerty.

He drove up behind the Chancery, which housed the archbishop and his aristocracy of priests and minions. He set his brake. For a moment he sat watching the pulsations of the gaslight in the second-floor room he knew was Haggerty's. There was no electricity in the Chancery yet.

Will revisited his decision to confess. The gaslight promised too much intimacy.

But he could depend on Haggerty to get them both good and drunk first. The priest was a New Yorker without illusions or midwestern prejudices. A critic of the establishment. A lover of opera. He had a stock portfolio. He was as good as a Jesuit. And he was *there*, the light in his apartment burning at eleven-thirty.

Will let himself in the back door, never locked, and ascended the stairs. He rapped quietly.

"Billy!" Haggerty stood in his apartment doorway in black pants, undershirt and wool vest. The blessed glass was half full in his hand.

Will knew that Haggerty called him by the old nickname to puncture any self-importance he might be carrying in from the night. The man had assumed that hectoring role long ago, and Will had let him. Just now, he needed the puncturing and worse.

"I thought you were with your mother tonight. How's she doing? No emergencies, I hope." Haggerty set aside his whisky. He pulled a gold watch out of his vest pocket and peered at it through his horn-rims. "Goddamn. I have the six-thirty tomorrow morning." It was a way of saying *this had better be important.*

Will caught the flash of impatience. There would be worse to come, he knew.

"Joe, I'm sorry. No, my mother's as good as she can be. She's breathing. This won't take long." (It would.)

Haggerty rubbed a hand through his carroty hair, set it on end, and gestured inside. It was a man's room, with a single easy chair covered in ratty plush. Haggerty sat down. In front of the chair was an ottoman, on which the priest placed his stockinged feet. A small fire burned in the grate.

There was a straight-backed chair next to the fireplace. Will picked it up and moved it to face his friend. They had played out this scene many times before.

Next to Haggerty's chair was a table and on the table was the holy bottle of Jameson's. Catholics had little reverence for the Volstead Act. "Get yourself a glass," Haggerty said.

Will knew where his friend kept the dishes, in the little alcove with its sink and two-burner. Around them, in other Chancery apartments, Will sensed the innocent sleep of other men who lived without luxury. This was the residence of priests who served the diocesan bureaucracy. Most of them would be monsignori before long. Somewhere in the turrets above them, dwelt an arch-bishop, even, of spartan taste.

Worse, a saint.

Worse, his uncle.

In his own innocent days, now beyond recall, Will had found comfort in the manly atmosphere of the Chancery. It sheltered a cloud of witness, as the epistle put it. He couldn't remember the text, precisely.

Mrs. Lerner, that Methodist, could be relied upon for chapter and verse. She had certainly loosed them on Will in the last months. He shuddered at the thought of his housekeeper's contempt. He had given scandal.

And probably she would betray him.

Or blackmail him.

"Billie, you look like hell." Joe Haggerty said companionably. "Have you found yourself yet? Have you had something to eat?"

Will shook his head to both questions. "Look, if you have a six-thirty…"

"I can stay up all night, Bill. It's just we can't drink past midnight. We have half an hour."

"Joe, I'm not going to say mass tomorrow morning. I already asked Van Cleve to take my eight o'clock."

Haggerty steepled his fingers; they were thin and white. "I have all night," he said again.

•

But Haggerty, anticipating the fast, had taken too big a glass of whisky. And Will could not get to the point. The storytelling began, and, if they hadn't heard two bells chime on some other priest's clock in some other apartment, it might have progressed to ballad singing. From Haggerty anyway. He had a fine baritone.

Will thought about Haggerty's voice and how he could carol out the *Ite, missa est*. A silence fell.

Haggerty let it stretch. It was one of his tricks.

"Look, man, you're not the only fool." His gesture took in the apartment, the building, and its warren of blameless sleepers.

Blameless: that was Will's thought.

Haggerty went on, in a dreamy voice, nothing much at stake. "Every priest thinks every other one is a saint. But I can tell you, Billie, everyone falls down. Ashes, ashes, we all fall down." He interrupted his hand's stretch for the whisky. He remembered the fast. Resolutely, he turned his glass over.

Then he refilled Will's.

"So, you're not saying mass tomorrow morning," he said, letting the words trail off.

Will could not respond.

"Even women," Haggerty said helpfully. "God, if a man never falls with a woman, you're looking at a mental case."

Mental cases was a rich topic.

Will failed again to reply, so Haggerty took off on that reliable tangent. "Oh, Jesus, do you remember Corrigan, that mother's boy? With his nocturnal emissions? It's our mothers make us crazy, let me tell you, especially the Irish ones," Haggerty motored on.

Will thought of Corrigan, with his sheets. He'd tied himself up like a mummy at night—that was in the seminary—to keep his hands off himself—until one morning they found him damp and shivering with pneumonia.

"He could have died of it. Imagine the obituary: *Dead of Nocturnal Emissions!*" Joe Haggerty said.

Will's lip creased. "Whatever happened to Corrigan?" he asked, though he knew. The boy had left before ordination. Scrupulosity did more damage than women to a priestly vocation. More damage than *men*, even.

Well, no one could accuse him, Will, of scrupulosity.

"I dunno. I dunno." Haggerty subsided and gave him another long look.

They heard the clock chime again from the other apartment.

"Goddamn Wilson. The man sleeps like the dead," he said. "I'm jealous."

Then Haggerty reached into the drawer of the table at his elbow and pulled out his clerical stole. His long white fingers shook it out. He drew it to his lips and kissed the cross embroidered into the neckpiece. He yoked it over his shoulders, the businesslike gesture of a priest prepared to administer a sacrament. "Whatever it is, Billie, you know goddamn well I've heard it before."

"No," Will said, "No, you haven't."

•

When the two men drew apart and Haggerty had taken off his stole, he began to curse vividly.

Will said, "You can't give me absolution, can you, Joe?" Lapping around his feet, he sensed the waters of the abyss. And despair was the unforgiveable sin against the Holy Ghost.

Haggerty rubbed his eyes and glanced up. To heaven. To the archbishop. "No I cannot, Billie. As you well know." He grabbed a fireplace poker and Will instinctively recoiled, as though his friend intended to brand him.

Haggerty stirred the fire. He got up and added a log from the brass can on the hearth.

Haggerty was known to have the temper of a demon. Will thought he was going to say the thing a priest must never say: *this is the vilest story I've ever heard.* But Haggerty's flush replaced itself with a look of sadness. That disturbed Will even more.

"I can't give you absolution till you make it right, Will." He gestured towards the floor above, where the archbishop slept, they both assumed, like the saint he was.

"You have to make it right."

Will couldn't imagine a way to fix things, and he had a good imagination. He danced again with the flickering figure of despair that seemed to have crept into the room behind him. "Will you give me your blessing, anyway, Joe?"

Haggerty stood and Will knelt, feeling his friend's hand on

the place where his hair was thinning. "May the blessings of Almighty God, the father, Son and Holy Ghost, descend upon you and remain with you forever," was how the Latin went. Will swayed on his knees.

"There's the couch if you need it—"

"Thanks, no." Will imagined himself at breakfast in the common dining room, the hangover, the shame, the lies, the archbishop's heavy silver plate.

"Listen, what's your schedule like tomorrow?" Haggerty asked.

"Van Cleve's going to cover for me all day. I pleaded my mother. I'm driving back to the farm."

"Remember Father Murano."

Catholicism refined the art of memory. Remember Father Murano. Remember Corrigan. Remember, O Most Holy Virgin Mary. Remember man that thou art dust.

Father Murano, who drove hell-for-leather and drank too much. He had struck and killed a child. And then gone down into the darkness, himself.

Will felt a flare of rebellion.

Did it not warp a man? The burden of perfection? He was able to remember all too easily that he was dust.

•

Just before first light, Will pulled into a circle of stones that marked the new war memorial at the river end of Summit Avenue. He'd only gotten a mile or so from the Chancery. He passed out.

There came a sharp rattle of isenglass at the car window as dawn broke.

Will rolled the window aside.

A voice in his face "What in the hell do you think…?" Then the cop drew back, touched the bill of his cap. "Sorry, Father."

The cop knew him. But the cop would say nothing.

CHAPTER THIRTEEN: LUCY

ON MY WEDDING night, I had no idea.

I laughed about it with Nurse Mercy one day when I was feeling well enough to joke. I told her people think art students are loose women.

Nurse Mercy shook those keys of hers. Sometimes the keys seem to be all that separate us from them.

From me, anyway, because I Am Not Insane.

Nurse Mercy said, "They think that about nurses, too."

I might have gone on. If I had been talking to Annie I'd have told more of the story, but Nurse Mercy was pretty naïve—as I had been—and she wasn't going to get any information from me. She had her textbooks to consult.

I did tell her how I'd run away from Will, down the central hall of the farmhouse, thinking, *O God I'll wake his mother. I'll wake Mrs. Lerner.* Thinking, *I don't care.*

Yes, Nurse, I'd grown up around animals. In my small town of New Prague, Minnesota, I'd seen men put the ram to the ewes. I knew what animals did. But I didn't know we humans did that. I thought we'd have refined the operation. We'd invented, after all, calico, stockings, garters, corsets, and shimmies. Surely, in the course of history, we'd have made some advances over barnyard squalor.

And I was a good girl, pretty fresh from the nuns. I had not let my mind compose any of the private business of marriage before Will came on the scene.

After we drove back to the farmhouse from the judge in

Decorah—me with my gold ring—I began to have immediate and terrible doubts about Will. His roving hands cut right through the haze of romance that had veiled our brief courtship so far.

I was expecting—I don't know—some sweet surprise. Something to equal and maybe transcend the delicate and utterly-unlike-anything-else-feelings that spread down my camisole when we'd kissed and petted in Will's car.

A man, I believed, would know how to deliver this sweet surprise, and would unveil it with quiet chivalry.

But Will's intrusive hands terrified me. I pushed him away and headed for the door—we'd reached the bedroom by then—snatching up the pretty lace dressing gown he'd hung over the bedpost. It was my bridal gift. Well, I flung it over myself and ran down the stairs and out the kitchen. That was in early winter and the crisp snow in the yard cut my bare feet. I broke through a little iced puddle into mud and straw. I fell and he caught me.

He was angry, but he didn't hit me that night. He slammed the door on the marriage chamber and left me there in my damp lace. I managed to wash my feet and get into bed. First I turned the lock on the door but I stayed awake all night crying and praying to Papa and God about what I'd gotten myself into.

Eloping to Iowa with a handsome man from drawing class had seemed, in the unfamiliar haze of gin, an act of romantic heroism.

Now I thought of *Bluebeard*.

Will had the key, of course.

This is a new theme in my life: *Who has the keys?*

He hit me the next night, a little playfully. He'd decided—as I now understand—that I was playing a game with him, art student whore that he thought I was. Experienced Madame. Lucy Unlaced. That was one of his pet names for me, because I'd opened the top button of my shirtwaist one day in class and let the other students draw the bones of my clavicle.

I'd grown up with naked women wandering around Papa's studio and didn't think much about baring my neck.

That didn't mean I knew anything about the Marriage Act, as Will pretentiously called it.

So I struggled.

Will called me those names Norah had tossed out at the mangle.

Then he tried pretending to be the coy suitor of a virgin, which—apparently unknown to him—I was.

Then he showed me a book by a German doctor, which was the dirtiest thing I'd ever laid hands on.

Finally he forced me. He apologized all the while and reminded me that husbands had the right. I bled so heavily we both thought I was dying. He started to laugh and cry at once.

I felt contempt for the performance and then a flare of hatred for him and for myself.

Because I knew in my heart that a judge in Decorah wasn't Marriage. I'd been raised a decent Catholic girl and I'd dreamed— who doesn't?—about the long walk up the aisle to where the priest would be standing with a welcoming smile. The catechism says that a man and woman bestow the sacrament upon each other— Will had explained this theological point to me—but ideally not in front of an Iowa judge who's nearly failed the job of pulling on his pants and smells of bootleg alcohol. As did we.

I'd let Will do the thinking. He had all that education. He had his rosary and his grace before meals. I let him tell me what was right.

My upbringing had been, let's face it, unconventional. I'd come to America at the age of five, steerage. My father was a painter. My mother was buried back in a country that, since we left, had changed its name.

There in Will's bedroom, I started thinking for myself. I felt the first twinge of guilt—no, a stab. Thinking for yourself seems to have that consequence, till you get good at it. Things had gone so badly that I supposed I was being punished. When I thought about it at breakfast, over Mrs. Lerner's strong coffee with the egg in it, I discovered plenty to punish myself for.

There I was on the prairie, sixty miles from home, tripping the wires of madness.

"Anyone would have suffered after all that," Nurse Mercy said helpfully as we were walking down the corridor together. She unlocked the door of the art room.

I had given her the sanitized version of my story, trying to make her laugh instead of scream. She was innocent, for a nurse. I didn't tell her about the cuts I had soon begun making down the tender inside flesh of my left arm, nicely spaced, like cross-hatching. The scars had faded by then.

In retrospect, that was crazy, cutting myself.

"You had no mother to guide you..." she soothed.

My mother had died young, as mothers will. I had Papa, and, in the new country, he'd rather quickly become a successful artist. Verging on famous. Of course he'd drawn the female figure over and over. But I think that—as I myself would do—he shrouded certain implications of the exercise from his mental gaze.

People do that, you know. Artists, nurses, farmers.

Or not.

Sometimes, after Will, I wondered about Papa. He was a man, and now I understood more about what men looked at and dreamed of and wanted.

Still, I couldn't imagine Papa wanting the things Will wanted. And Papa, of course, had given me no warning about how a man's desire might affect my life. These things were unspeakable between a father and daughter.

Papa hadn't even warned me about my monthlies.

Why do women bleed this way, as though their wounds fester and break open in secret? Is it the taint of Eve?

Will would say so.

He did say so.

Alone at the farm, I read the Bible attentively—it was one of the few books Mrs. Lerner kept around—seeking escape from my nauseating fear of punishment. Instead I found plenty to scandalize me. There was the story of a woman thrust outdoors to be defiled, in order to save her brothers.

Where was God?

Why had no one told us these stories—by us I mean *girls*? I didn't even know about rape till Will came at me.

Though that wasn't rape, of course. Husbands have the right. If he *was* my husband.

In the Gospel of Matthew there was a story about a woman who bled constantly. I feared something like this this would happen to me; it was only a matter of time.

Everybody left the woman alone. She was an outcast, because the touch of her hand, her clothing, her very glance would send a man right to hell.

But she was a bold one. She grabbed Jesus's robe as he passed by. She had courage; there were a lot of people around and they might have taken up stones, as was the custom in those times. And Jesus was a rabbi, an important man in a small town.

But Jesus didn't hit her or run away. He looked at her with love and healed her. The bleeding stopped on the spot.

What a crude story, I thought, though Jesus came off well. I'd never heard this part of scripture. Catholics don't read the Bible. We take in what the priest reads on Sunday, which gives us an odd, disjointed sense of how it all goes together. And they skip the coarse parts.

My mother died young—to go on—so it was just Papa and me. And art. My father's reputation spread, not only in our small town of New Prague but beyond: the Cities, Chicago, even.

"Have you heard of him, Nurse Winstead?" I asked her.

I looked around the little studio to which we had come. I took in the supplies, the light, the easel, the clay. "Anton Valenta, who did the murals in the St. Paul Cathedral?" I told her shyly that I been the model for the young Virgin Mary, standing at the knee of St. Ann, who was played by one of the cleaning ladies. St.

Ann and I both got sick from sitting there in the cold sanctuary. Though we had a thermos of coffee—it was the first time Papa had let me drink coffee.

"Weren't you clothed?" Nurse Mercy asked, her voice a little tremulous. She often questioned me about how I posed for Papa. Later I discovered they thought I had been *interfered with*, which was far from the truth. I had been coddled. People in the Midwest—Will included—have a lot of prejudice about artists.

"I had on a thin dress," I told her with some exasperation. "It was supposed to be Palestine."

I thought back to when Papa had gotten his chill. Certainly those winter sessions in the cathedral hadn't helped him any. He'd coughed a lot as he worked in the chapel of the Blessed Virgin.

Just then I wasn't paying much attention in parochial school and Papa didn't care. What he thought was important—English grammar, color theory—he taught me himself. In school, I doodled and woke up for soap carving or something artistic. My first toys had been brushes and colors. Our conversations at the dinner table were about perspective and Michelangelo Buonarroti and what artists were doing in England. Papa loved the pre-Raphaelite Brotherhood. He dreamed about forming a community like that in America. After supper we'd sit in his studio copying the sketches of Michelangelo by lamplight, and I seldom did my arithmetic homework.

Papa's renderings were, of course, better than mine.

Often he repeated to me what Michelangelo, as he lay dying, had said to his apprentice: *Draw, Antonio, draw! Draw and don't waste time.*

It seemed an odd thing to say on one's deathbed. But I know Papa would have whispered the same thing to me—*Draw, Lucy!*—if I had been with him when he passed away. That commandment breathed itself through the very air of our house.

I was not with Papa because he had had to go to the TB sanitarium in Bayfield, Wisconsin. I was fifteen. I'm sure I was sketching when he died. In fact those sketches exist some-where, maybe at the Cannon Valley farm. Papa on his pillow, Papa with his sunken eyes, his mouth falling open a little with the final breath.

From imagination, because I was not there.

Yes, I know I had those drawings at the farm, because Will admired them. He has a good eye. He admired them a little, anyway, and found them morbid, perhaps. He laid them in the back of the folder, as though they might escape and haunt his imagination.

As they haunt mine. But in a good way. What we draw with love becomes part of our spirit. Annie believes what we love survives the body and goes on to life after life.

"What about heaven?" I asked her, anxious for Papa.

"Heaven seems a little static," she answered. After 4 North, she craves variety. "Boring to me. Boring to Jesus, I can imagine."

How can I get those drawings back?

I'd like to show them to Annie. She loves to hear about my life. She missed so much of her own.

"Perhaps you can draw them again," Nurse Mercy says, when I tell her I hope to retrieve my work.

No.

Everything must be new.

From this moment on—I select charcoal, pencils and paper from the shelves of the art room—I'm not practicing any more. I'm not correcting my old work or even copying the masters as a useful exercise. *Draw, Lucy, draw! Draw, Lucy and don't waste time.* Without a doubt Papa whispered those words as he lay in the sanitarium. I hear them in the rhythm of my daily heart.

I will never again be without the stub of a pencil.

Blunt. I will not eat it. I will not harm myself with it.

I will draw.

CHAPTER FOURTEEN

DR. DAVID GRAFTON wanted no one, least of all Mercy Winstead, to know he was courting Mercy Winstead. It was a cautious experiment on his part.

The hospital was a self-contained village and a man couldn't, with impunity, "walk out"—as the locals put it—with a woman. There could be no quiet chats on the porch swing, no visits to the bandshell. Jealousies might erupt or concerns about promotion and preference.

Cooing might erupt, and the premature tatting of lace.

Besides, both he and his nurse had reason to avoid entanglements.

But mutual interests brought the reluctant couple together in the course of a day. Mercy was monitoring Lucy Valenta in the art studio and David Grafton was writing a paper on the Therapeutic Applications of Art. Therefore they needed to meet and discuss the progress of the case.

"For it interests me from the psychiatric aspect," Grafton told the young nurse, "that so many of our patients are talented in one way or another, dramatically talented even."

They were sitting, at a respectable distance from each other, in wicker chairs on the verandah that ran the length of staff quarters, where the nurses and female aides lived, above the parlors and refectory. The junior physicians had a lean-to apartment off Men's Detached, while the superintendent, as befitted his rank, lived in a house built for the family he didn't yet have, and needed to have if he hoped to rise any farther in the ranks.

Dinner was over and now the nurses and physicians had an hour or so of freedom while a skeleton staff maintained order on the wards and fed the patients who were crippled or tied to chairs.

Typically the doctors and nurses spent this time in the parlors, or walking the grounds or enjoying the verandah as weather dictated. Sometimes they had musical evenings or played charades. It was a time for catching up on conversations relevant to patient care. Freud would be invoked among smokers playing canasta in one corner. The nurses played with fancywork and chatted mostly with each other.

On this particular evening in late spring, most of the staff were walking outside. The superintendent and Nurse Winstead had the verandah much to themselves. They sat at a corner table, she with her coffee cup, notebook and pen at the ready.

"There is Orenstein from Men's Detached, who can calculate numbers up to thirty-five places in his head," Grafton continued.

Nurse Mercy nodded and sipped her coffee.

She must sleep well, Grafton thought. It was her second cup. He himself had not slept a full night since Second Ypres.

"And Goldie Reynolds on 4 North can play on the piano any tune you hum, with both hands, even though she can't tie her own shoelaces or dress herself," he said.

Someone had told her—Mercy Winstead commented—that Miss Reynolds had never even seen a piano till last Christmas pageant, when she was allowed to gather with the others around the parlor grand. "And here's me with my eight years of lessons. I can barely play 'Country Gardens.'"

Mercy tittered.

Grafton wondered if the coffee was making her nervous. Her laugh was a bit annoying, he thought. Or was he upsetting her again? Why did he have that effect on people? "Well, I guess it's not a gift I'd trade my sanity for," he said.

"You do play, though? I've heard you," said Mercy with some boldness. As if she'd been skulking in the parlors listening to the superintendent riffle through Schubert.

She had been skulking.

Such passion, she thought, for a man otherwise reserved.

"Yes." Grafton fed his pipe the cherry-scented blend. "I played pretty seriously at one time. Thought about conservatory. Before medical school."

"So many physicians are musical," Mercy said noncommittally.

"A talent we apparently share with the insane," said Grafton.

"I've heard Annie Leary and that dwarf-child on 4 North sing harmony," Mercy said.

"No!" Annie Leary's music interested him, now he'd begun to listen for it: strange, pentatonic, modal tunes she'd brought from her people in the southern states. He intended to discuss her singing in his monograph. "But no, it can't be Sylvie Sztamburski," he said. "She's a deaf mute."

Nurse Mercy said it could well be a different dwarf. She knew a lot about deafness and muteness but she hesitated to disagree with a physician, especially the superintendent. Though, lately, she did not hesitate long or often.

"But I believe I've heard some toning from her." Mercy pressed on.

"There's the screaming," Grafton conceded.

•

Mercy could distinguish between toning and screaming, but she let it go and tugged the conversation back to their mutual interest. She turned over her coffee cup, because the waiters were circulating. She opened her notebook. "And then there's Lucy Valenta, who draws like Michelangelo." Nurse Winstead's face grew thoughtful in the gathering twilight.

"In somewhat the same style," said Grafton fastidiously.

"Lucy's not a savant, of course. She's had a lot of schooling."

Grafton gave his nurse points for knowing what a savant was.

A faint breeze wafted through the screen porch. The asylum had been located high on a sunny hill, so it might catch such breezes. Now a warm lift from the south, with its fecund smell.

Now a chilly cat's paw from the north, where, in early May, snow still lay rotting in the shade.

Grafton was aware of some similar current between himself and the young nurse: now warm, now chilly. Approach, retreat. Grafton was not innocent of the sexual act, but he had never before courted a woman. There had been no courtship in France or Belgium, just desperate coupling and sometimes barter or making change.

As he looked at Mercy Winstead, a virgin, of course, he flushed. How did he dare imagine her in such a role?

No, he must not dare.

Anyway, there remained the problem of her brother and the hereditary taint.

Though deafness could be a manageable affliction. Such children did well in attentive families. Nurse Winstead's seemed to be one of those. Grafton thought he would like to know more about her people, but to ask would seem an intrusion; indeed it could be taken as evidence of courting behavior.

Between them, the current rose and fell, as though their very breathing attracted and then repelled an act of imagination. Did Mercy feel it?

Women, women like Mercy, were innocent. Even nurses. He must remember to call her, even in his thoughts, "Nurse Winstead."

•

Mercy felt the passage of energy between them and had no idea what to make of it.

She had worked hard to become a nurse, and felt conflicted about her place in any world beyond the wards: the world of husbands and children or even of maiden aunts. To become domestic, she would have to give up nursing.

Some days she found herself longing for the things other women seemed to want and she'd catch herself studying the men on the place. What was on offer.

Most days, however, she immersed herself in the work and

meditated on the life of Florence Nightingale. Though David Grafton attracted her: his reticence with its promise of secret passion.

But in professional life, a woman could do good. Florence Nightingale had had no time for passion. She had made do with the company of a parrot, or was it an owl?

In any case, it was illogical to believe that a cold exterior hid a warm heart; more likely it indicated a chill to the bone.

•

Resolutely, Mercy Winstead turned the conversation back to psychiatry. "If I may be bold," she began. She'd copied this formula from a ferocious head nurse at Deaconess (unmarried of course). "If I may be bold, it seems to me that many of our patients are not all that different from people one meets on the wards of a regular hospital—or on the streets of Minneapolis. Who defines them as mentally ill?"

Grafton thought this brave, indeed, and rather intimidating.

It touched on the question of his own professional competence. A truthful answer would be, *I* do. He bore the ultimate responsibility, signed the papers that committed or released an inmate.

Though, with the current backlog, he found himself slipping into the habit of relying more and more on the sheriff, on Olivia Passmore, even on the aides, to assess a patient's status. "Well, I can't imagine Goldie Reynolds playing the piano in a—what do you call them?—speakeasy bar. Finding her way home at night to a little flat."

Grafton knew he sounded defensive.

"Of course not," Mercy responded. A breeze seemed to drift in from the north and shift the space between them. "But I wonder about some of the others. Many of the others."

"You haven't seen enough yet," he said. What an upstart she could be, after a few weeks on the wards. Questioning their decisions.

Grafton enumerated in his mind the reasons one might be confined to Northfield State Hospital, excluding psychosis: poverty, stupidity, congenital alcoholism, palsy, sexual deviance, petty crime. Women got locked up in Northfield because their husbands tired of them. Men, because they wouldn't keep themselves clean. Because the sheriff had no room in the jail.

"Where else are they going to go?" he wondered aloud. He thought about the crippled, he thought about the family of albinos divided between the men's and women's wards. Such people couldn't farm. They were prepared for no future but the circus.

Grafton smiled grimly. Think of Max, the indispensable aide, who had run away from the farm to the circus, from the circus to the hospital.

Mercy squirmed a bit. Grafton's criticism stung her. All her life people had said, "You don't know enough. When you're older. Don't question the physician's orders, Nurse." But newcomers, she thought stubbornly, brought a fresh perspective. The staff ought to listen to her, instead of ignoring her point of view.

Grafton, for example, often asked the nurses' opinions. Then he discounted them. Was it just a game to him?

Perhaps she should return to the game every woman knew how to play. Draw out the male. Play to his ego. Be the humble student.

She was, in truth, a student of Lucy Valenta's case. She knew the girl had come to see her as a friend.

Dr. Grafton had invited her onto the verandah, playing on her interest in Lucy. His choice of a secluded spot had warned off other circling nurses and doctors who assumed, perhaps, that they were courting.

What might be his intentions, anyway?

In some distress, Mercy reconsidered the superintendent's earlier invitation. "Let's chat after dinner about your work with Mrs. Allen," he had said. And now, for twenty minutes they'd twiddled their coffee spoons, feeling the gathering breeze alternately warm and cool them.

Mercy drew a light shawl around her shoulders.

She knew how to fend off men, even doctors, who thought that nurses were loose women.

Did she *want* to fend off Grafton? She shivered slightly with fantasy.

"Chilly?" he asked.

"I think I'll go in soon. I'm off duty tonight." She yawned discreetly into her small hand. Here she'd sat wasting time, offering up her career on the altar of matrimony, if only in imagination.

She told herself, lying, that she had little interest in Grafton as a man. She just wanted his learning, his astute grasp, the authority of his intellect.

"Let's quickly chat about Lucy Allen then. Sorry, I've let that go," said the superintendent.

"Indeed," said Mercy. She gathered her shawl. "I confess to being rather confused about Dr. Kennedy's theory of seduction."

Mercy was not confused. However, she thought that a virtuous woman, from Deaconess School of Nursing, ought to be confused

Grafton felt his color rise. He encouraged himself: of course he could speak about this, teacher to student. Of course he could.

He couldn't.

He bunted. "What do you think, Nurse? The girl will never share her past with me. It's you who'll be able to get her story."

Mercy could not repress a sniff. *I'll get the story and you'll write the paper,* she thought.

No one on the medical staff had even done an intake interview with Lucy Valenta. They were all too busy to see actual patients. But let that go.

"I've read some Freud, of course," Nurse Winstead admitted. "I'm not sure I find it persuasive." She left "it" vague: galloping libido, infant sexuality, obsession with the private parts. "Anyway,

Miss Valenta seems to have had a perfectly normal upbringing. If you count it normal to be raised by an artist, with no mother on the scene."

Mercy now referred to Lucy by her maiden name whenever she pulled the patient into consciousness. After insisting for a month on her married status, Lucy had dropped the whole matter as soon as she got access to the art studio. That was an interesting shift. She must update Dr. Grafton on the change.

Grafton confided, "My mother was a concert pianist," he said. "And my father died when I was seven." As Mercy seemed to withdraw from him, Grafton instinctively approached. He offered the bait of personal history.

Mercy felt he was making a bid for sympathy. She was not in the mood for revelations. Rather, she felt a flush of longing and jealousy for a world in which women could be concert pianists, or maybe study medicine.

She returned to the agenda. "The girl is often depressed," she reported. "She feels herself to have been abandoned by her husband—though she rarely mentions him now."

"Has the fellow visited?"

"Never once. I assume he signed the commitment orders?"

"Seems to have been some other relative. Nurse Passmore's misplaced the record."

"That's not like her." Mercy quickly amended: "From the little I know."

Grafton bit his lip.

His imagination abandoned Nurse Mercy and shaped in the waning light the blooming form of Lucy with her curly, abundant hair and pale skin. Her case was shaping up to be one of those tragedies where they locked someone up and forgot why. Forty years from now, an old woman would come blinking into the sunlight, her life utterly wasted.

Really, he must not let that happen to Lucy Whatever–Her–Name.

"We need to know more about her background. The life of a painter is often unconventional," he said. He sounded, to himself prudish, Canadian, though he was thinking about studios, voluptuous drapery and naked majas. Again he censored his imagination and tamed it to the therapeutic. "Can you get her to confide in you?"

He didn't want it to sound like a physician's order. He liked the idea of a collegial relationship with Mercy. He settled on that for the moment.

"I'll certainly try," she answered.

A flock of cedar waxwings dropped to chatter in the bushes below, discovering red berries. Their voracious appetite made David Grafton feel hungry, though his own dinner had been adequate. Fresh salads were coming out of the greenhouses. But he felt an uncharacteristic longing for—something more substantial.

Promotion? The superintendent of Men's Detached was retiring. Working with male patients was considered more prestigious.

No. He longed for his own life to be unconventional.

He was restless. He would practice the new Rachmaninoff this evening, now he'd got hold of the score. He would submit himself in the same motion to discipline, beauty, and the sanity of art.

Two years ago, after the war in Europe, Northfield, Minnesota, had felt like paradise to him. A beautiful site. He would have authority. Scope to do good.

But so few patients got well.

And there were not many charming women.

He looked at Mercy Winstead critically. She had fine, kinky red hair and freckles. She could be called intellectually aggressive. She was short-sighted and her brother was deaf.

She didn't seem all that attracted to him.

Grafton stretched and prepared to excuse himself from the experiment in courtship. "I would like to take a look at Mrs. Allen's drawings," he said. "We'll ask her permission, of course."

Mercy Winstead nodded and took out her tatting. She was making a baptismal bonnet for her sister's child.

She hoped it wouldn't give any of the doctors a fantasy life.

Grafton excused himself and headed inside to the grand piano.

CHAPTER FIFTEEN: ANNIE

AT DAWN, I station myself on the screen porch that runs the length of 4 North. The asylum architect wanted us to have light and air, a model designed for tubercular patients. Really, it was progressive at the time, 1878.

My perspective befits a country estate. "Pemberley," I sometimes say to myself at first light, and smile at my own joke. Below me, hill cedes to hill and then to valley as far as the horizon stretches. In the foreground lies a small pond with ducks. The farm buildings behind it seem to pulse gently in the dawn light with their stir of animal life.

In the western sky today, a yellow moon sets low, flanked by Venus and Mercury.

My jaw drops all on its own and I can't keep from singing out.

Bright morning stars are rising.
Daylight is breaking in my soul.

"Shut up, Leary," comes Nurse Schaeffer's call.

If Dr. Grafton could hear her. If Grafton knew how they talk to the ladies when his back is turned. And punish.

I am powerless to stop singing.

Oh where are our dear mothers?
O where are our dear mothers?
Daylight is breaking in my soul.

"I said shut up, Leary. Not everybody wakes up at 6:00 a.m."

If you can't sing in an insane asylum, where can you sing?

My throat just opens to it. The song starts in my belly and swells upward as though I am somebody's instrument and I have been touched.

Daylight is a-breaking in my soul, sings Belle Tyler, tied to her bed just off the porch. Belle and I know the same songs. She's from Mississippi. Few people know our songs anymore. After us, who will know these songs?

I think I sang them to my children, but my children, I'm told, are dead.

I'm trying to teach them to Sylvie. She has enough residual hearing to drone on key when I give her the cue. It pleases both of us.

"Everybody s'pose to wake up at 6:00 a.m." I hear Belle call out. She likes everything in order, all the rules to be kept.

Though she herself murdered somebody somewhere, a husband or a pimp or an overseer. She was born into slavery, she's told me: a woman so big they keep her tied to the bed in case she decides to roll on somebody in a homicidal moment.

Below me on the farm, I see two men in overalls from Men's Detached push the feed carts up the path toward the barn. I sense, though I cannot quite hear, the caterwauling of the animals who know they are going to get alfalfa hay.

I used to love that sound, going out at dawn to my own animals on my own farm. My farm and Samuel's.

To be fair, sometimes I hated it. You can paint the past with a rosy glow.

They have gone to heaven shouting, I sing.

They have gone to heaven shouting, Belle takes it up in her Mississippi voice.

A rattle of carts comes on to the ward behind the dormitory. I hear one crash into the wall. The wall out there is scarred and peeling its green paint after many such accidents. I picture the coffee sloshing out of its urns. For breakfast it will be real coffee, though cold by the time they line us up and get us out there.

To say something good about Nurse Schaeffer, she manages to keep the oatmeal warm. She throws a couple of blankets over each cart. Why don't they bring them up an hour later, when most of the women are untied and ambulatory? Those at least who won't be tied down all day. They should put Belle Tyler in charge of the place, with her sense of logic.

At least about certain things.

"Leary, you could give me a hand," Nurse Schaeffer calls out to me.

I have to finish my song. It's a way I have of checking my progress. How that high fa flips across the break between my chest and my throat and then into my head. The warble among the syllables that tells me my breath has a clear channel.

That I won't be falling any time soon. I won't need to ask for the cuffs or the chemise or any other madhouse underwear to keep myself from bashing my head against the wall like a wayward breakfast cart. Likely that green paint has some of my hair in it.

I've heard them say at Report, me sitting there mute with my eyes down, that I didn't sing for years after they brought me to Ward 4 North. Dr. Dominic Kennedy, with his damp cow eyes, considers my vocalizations to be a sign of something therapeutic he has personally accomplished. Probably he is writing a paper on it.

Well, I am writing a paper on *you*.

To say something else good about Nurse Schaeffer, she doesn't touch my notebooks, which are locked in the glass case in the nurses' station beside the sterilization kit. I have laid traps. I've placed a yellow hair between the pages of my current notebook—just so—that will fall out of place if they meddle.

They promised they would not. And mostly the nurses keep their promises. It's all right, I tell Nurse Schaeffer, if she reads my books: Emily Dickinson's poems, which I personally own, and my novels from the library.

The patients, on the other hand, do not keep their promises. That's why I have the *privilege*—a word much emphasized on 4 North—of locking my words away in the nurses' cupboard. It's not easy to keep anything to yourself around here. We each have our cigar box with our daily stuff in it. We have no place to put these boxes though—which we guard jealously—so we have to carry them with us all day.

Some people around here are always waiting for a chance to get into somebody else's things. Just for the fun of it. Just to cause a little chaos. Even though I have my private space—it used to be a janitor's nook, off the porch—the door is always open.

Nor can the other women return to the dormitory once they've gotten out of bed, dressed or been dressed and shunted into the halls and dayroom. You can't ever lie down, or take a nap. Napping is not, as the nurses say, good mental hygiene.

The patients get so bored. They sit on the benches lining the hall and nod off. Sometimes they fall on the floor.

But I, with my *privileges*, can ask the aide for my current notebook and a blunt pencil. Or my Emily Dickinson.

I'll lay down the song for now. I'll help Nurse Schaeffer get the ward ready for breakfast. Privilege or punishment? It depends on your point of view.

Belle has wet the bed. I know where the linens and rubber sheets, the smocks, are kept. I can make myself useful.

Only I am allowed to waken Sylvie, who in her deafness doesn't hear the rising gong. I know how to place a gentle finger over her lips to call her out of sleep, so that I get a head start on her terrified animal thrashing. I can make signs into her hands to remind her where she is and what we are having for breakfast. I can trace a little smile on her lips with my finger and make her follow its outline.

They should pay me whatever they pay the aides.

Nurse Schaeffer nods at me because I've stopped singing. "Reinforce sanity" is their motto. Not a bad idea. But my singing is not insane. For me, silence would be insane. I was silent for three years, I heard them say at Report.

I don't remember.

I help Mrs. Czerny to the lavatory. I get Mrs. Doran a bed pan and check her restraints.

What will they do without my help?

For this is my last day on the job.

Tonight I am graduating. They always move patients at night. Even the dead. I'm taking my cigar box. Someone will pack a cart with my books and notebooks and I will graduate to 2 North. A promotion two floors down.

I need to sing. To check my barometer. Because I am more excited than I can bear to be, though I try to move slowly and not spill myself. Not *fall*. I have a lot to lose with this move.

A lot to gain: Lucy.

As I look out across the hills of Pemberley over Mrs. Doran's bedpan, I see, just where the sun came up, a girl on a white horse riding into view. To be free like that.

Snap! Pop! I think of the crackle of celluloid in the film projectors of the movies they play for us once or twice a year, which make us hoot with laughter at the fraught images and dramatic gesture. I smile.

Still.

CHAPTER SIXTEEN: LUCY

Downward through the evening shadows
In the unremembered ages
In the days that are forgotten
From the full moon fell Nokomis,
Daughter of the moon, Nokomis.

ANNIE WOULD BE amazed to hear that I know much of that
poem by heart. Papa used to read it to me at bedtime, trying
to pour America into my brain. It's a soothing poem, the
edges of the words rubbed with the soft consonants of Papa's
Czech accent. That's the way my mind offers it up.

It's a poem about the Indians around here. A romantic version, as I now understand.

I don't know what brought a famous poet upriver to our
little city, why he picked up his pen and made an epic out of the
local story, but he did. So now we have streets and lakes and car
lines—Hiawatha, Nokomis—all over Minneapolis named for
poor Indians. These days, they keep out of sight up north.

Papa said it was the kind of transformation that went on all
the time where he grew up, in Bohemia. Let a poet get hold of
your story and he'll make you look good.

Or let an artist.

No, that's not our job. Maybe it's not the poet's job either. I'll
ask Annie about that.

But we'll make something out of you you won't even recognize. It will have all the power we can give it.

I think that happened to Jesus.

I think about Jesus because I'm praying at the moment: *Jesus forgive me.*

Suicide is a mortal sin. As if a suicide didn't have enough problems.

I lean out of the castle window: that's the top floor of the bell tower. We call it the castle. I look dizzily at the brickwork below.

> *Downward through the evening shadows.*
> *From the full moon fell Nokomis…*

You could go to sleep to the rhythm of that, or kill yourself.

•

I didn't want to die. What I wanted was for Will to visit me. I needed Will to refute the terrible story Mrs. Lerner had just told me in the visiting parlor.

I imagined him visiting my grave. Girls are silly. I had taken the pins out of my hair and let it roll into the wind, that's how foolish I was. Illustrating my own story, an excellent composition signed by me.

Will might be down there, I thought, his Daimler coupe in a pool of moonlight, the moon conveniently full. Watching me fall with my hair in a picturesque torrent.

That's why they call it lunacy.

I swung out, my hair a flux of light.

It was Nurse Mercy who grabbed that hair and then my apron and dragged me back into the room.

•

I'm on the gurney now, speeding down the halls toward 4 North. They've inserted a tube up my nose and inverted a bag of something that swings on a pole over my head. That's protocol, Nurse Mercy tells me, *I'm sorry, Sweetie, I know this hurts*—when I can't or won't answer her questions—*Did you take something? What did you take?*

I'm crying too hard to tell her what I want: my cigar box, which I've left behind on the window sill of the visiting parlor. It contains my wooden comb, my monthly supplies, a poem of Annie's, and the fat wad of hundred dollar bills Mrs. Lerner just gave me in the parlor. I'd thanked Mrs. Lerner politely, said good-bye, and slipped behind the curtain to figure out how I was going to kill myself.

Darkness fell, and nobody missed me. Then I'd left my box and slipped up the service stairs to the bell tower at moonrise.

The scenery was stunning from up there.

What I want—now that I find myself alive—is my box and Mrs. Lerner's money. My money. And Annie's.

•

Annie is coming down the hall between her two nurses, or am I hallucinating? The nurse pushing my gurney and the nurses leading Annie stop to chat.

"Severely regressed." I hear my nurse say these words.

Annie is coming down the hall from 4 North. The moonlight from the clerestory windows plays on her bright hair. They always move people at night, when the maniacs are settling in their restraints and everyone is heading downward through the evening shadows. Of Veronal.

My gurney bumps away over the red Spanish tiles that add charm to this particular corridor between worlds. I writhe and twist my neck to catch her eye. She gives me a look of horror and her lips form an endearing word. I see her pull at the arms of her nurses and crane her neck back toward where I am disappearing.

Too late, I fully understand the note she'd passed me through the mangle: *You get worse, I'll get better.* We'd meet, she wanted to tell me, on Ward 3 North, a transitional ring of the inferno, where the ladies were bound to strictly supervised craft projects.

Maybe she'd planted the idea in my mind. But I got worse all on my own. Or Nola Lerner made me worse.

Whatever Annie's plan was, it has gone severely wrong.

I am speeding, *severely regressed,* on to 4 North just as Annie is being taken off. No crafts in our future.

•

"Baths tomorrow," says Nurse Winstead to Nurse Schaeffer as they finish working over me. That will be welcome. For twenty minutes after they took the tube from my throat they held my head over a basin where I've thrown up every bit of food I've eaten since coming to Northfield State Hospital for the Criminally Insane, Crippled, Feeble-Minded and Indigent.

Nurse Malloy says reproachfully, "Oh, Miss Valenta, just when you were doing so well."

The nurses, working as an efficient team, right to left, pull me out of my soiled gray dress and into one of the Hawaiian smocks, a white cotton one for sleeping. They tie the sleeves to the bed. Then, for additional security, they cuff my wrists to the frame.

My bed's wheeled to a position in front of the night nurse's station, where, at the moment, Max, the aide, is sitting in lamplight. He leers at me as if through the distortions of a crystal. I mistake him for the devil, vividly tattooed.

Who tempted me to throw myself off the parapet.

The devil will do this.

I can't hold back from screaming, and now there are groans and complaints around the ward. Two student nurses in identical teacup caps bend over me. I hear Sylvie's low drone.

Has anybody noticed that Annie has taught that deaf girl to sing? If you touch Sylvie on the belly, she will hum "fa," and on the chest, "la" and on the forehead "sol." It's an amazing game, which we play at collation in the laundry. She seems to have perfect pitch, and finds her way by vibrations. It makes her happy.

But she is not happy now, she is blubbering. Probably she is blubbering for Annie. Alternately she drones her scales.

I blubber for Annie as well. How have I managed to arrive here just when they've taken my friend away? I wish I'd listened harder in high school when the English teacher explained "irony." I believe I'm having a dish of it.

Max and the two student nurses station themselves at the head and foot of my white iron bed and I am flying again on castors down the hall to another of those rooms without windows. One of the women stays with me. She gently wipes my eyes from time to time. She holds a handkerchief to my nose and says "blow" every now and then, like a mother.

I am lonely for the moon.

•

When I wake it's full daylight, but what? another day, another week, another corridor? There are opaque, full-length windows down one side of the room and lights overhead as well. My limbs feel paralyzed, dead.

Disoriented, I imagine I have accomplished the suicide. I have become a mind, horribly alert, in a body on the undertaker's slab.

I see, I feel, I smell, I am tied in—a rubber sheet. Distorted pictures of the tube winding above me, the moonlight on Will's auto, the seductive call to flight from the belltower rise in my mind.

I have no idea what's real. I have no idea how to control my imagination.

They lay the dead on rubber sheets and wash them.

I have seen it.

Dr. Grafton would bite hard on his pipestem if I told him this story. How Papa would take me to the mortuary, Zelleny and Peters. Pavel Zelleny was Papa's friend from Bohemia. He would take us down to the crypt under the funeral home, where he prepared the dead for burial. Me with my sketch book under my arm. I used to quake at first, but later I became accustomed to the journey.

It was, of course, cold. Papa and I would keep our wool coats on. Pavel didn't seem to mind the cold. No doubt he was used to it.

This may seem like a strange story, but I was sixteen years old and already a serious artist. Papa's prize student.

How else could I learn the terrain of the body?

Michelangelo had to pay a grave digger to steal corpses and dissect them before his eyes while he sketched.

This was nothing so crude.

There'd be the human form, sheet-covered on a black marble table. We'd stand there on the stone floor. Pavel Zelleny would start a prayer and we would join in the familiar responses: "May the souls of the faithful departed rest in peace, amen."

Sometimes I felt the souls of the faithful departed pressing around me as I worked. They were a friendly presence. I imagined they'd enjoy having their portraits drawn.

It was respectful. Papa and Pavel Zelleny had worked out a gentler curriculum than the art academies of old. I repeat: how else was I to learn?

There were life drawing classes at the School of Art and Design, but girls weren't allowed in. We had to go to Still Life, where we drew bowls of daisies, perhaps a crock of butter and, if they had one handy, a dead rabbit.

•

Thankfully, I discover I am not at the moment on a mortuary slab.

A new student nurse is holding a spoon full of food in front of my face.

The dead do not require pureed carrots.

My hands are bound to rings on the side of—my God—it's a shallow bathtub. I stretch out my feet; they are free. I am not paralyzed. I slosh. I'm in warm water. The rubber sheet stretches out over my tub, my head sticks out like the head of a turtle knocked onto its back.

The nurse presses food, I turn away, a reluctant baby. "Where am I?"

The persistent question.

"You're in hydrotherapy. You had a manic episode."

"How long—?"

"A week."

"I've been in this tub for a week?"

She laughs, that giddy student nurse giggle. It tells me she's thinking how to tell this story back in the nurses' home.

That makes me angry.

I turn my chin resolutely away.

Around me, I become aware of a chorus of crazy women singing and shouting like a bunch of Holy Rollers. Mine's not the only tub in the room. There's a line of them. And nurses and aides in raincoats and boots, scolding and feeding and making sure none of us boils or freezes or slips under the water.

"And now, aren't you comfortable?" The young nurse plumps some kind of rubber pillow under my head. "Just lay back and enjoy the warm."

"*Lie* back," I snap. Papa was careful about my English grammar. He hated the way native speakers looked down on immigrants.

In the hallway, which I can see from my tub, naked women are being paraded and draped and herded toward the next turn of fate. More screaming around that bend.

My eyes search the women's bodies. I compare the curves in their spines, one of nature's loveliest lines.

I paddle my feet again, experimentally. Perhaps this is all intended to give us the feel of babies in the womb.

We are about to be born again.

PART THREE:
Finishing School

CHAPTER SEVENTEEN: LUCY

IN REAL LIFE, life beyond the asylum, there are people we turn our heads away from if we meet them on the street. This passes for politeness.

Papa had taught me from my earliest days, "don't stare." Paradoxically, he also taught me to look closely and to study the contours of everything that came within our ken: the way a dog's hair flattens on its muzzle, the angle of ridges on a pine cone.

Still, a polite person does not stare at crippled people, demented beggars and the general riff raff of humanity loose on our city streets. Drunks. Elderly ladies in unbecoming hats, bosoms too tightly laced.

From them we avert our eyes.

But on 4 North, I started to look in earnest. There was nothing else to do and there seemed to be no social sanctions, so I began to sketch people as soon as I got hold of my materials. They wouldn't let me off the ward. I'd lost access to the art studio. But they gave me charcoal after deciding it wouldn't harm me if I ate it. The stub of a pencil, at last. Nurse Mercy brought me thick books of the best quality drawing paper. I think she must have bought them with her own salary.

Drawing increased my license to stare, and my work passed the time for all of us, nurses, as well as patients tied down or cuffed to chairs. Everyone liked to watch me sketch, and I had no fear of audience reaction. I'd grown up in studio conditions: Papa's gentle admonishments and, later, every level of critique from my fellow students and professors at the art school.

"Oooh, Miss, you've got her. That's exactly what she looks like!" an aide would say to me. I enjoyed the little bit of celebrity that came from my skill.

I spent a month on 4 North.

It was my finishing school. It's where I grew up.

I drew and drew, I did not waste time. I took it all in with my sketching hand. I thought about my friend Wanda, from St. Paul—another talented girl from an immigrant family—who had gone away to art school in New York. Her postcards and letters had detailed an exotic, enviable life.

Getting mixed up with Will and his shenanigans, I'd lost touch with Wanda. But now I pondered the difference between the chances she'd had and my own portion.

I felt a red swell of jealousy, and then I laid it down. What could be more exotic than my exile on 4 North—if the purpose of life is to gain experience and love a few people against the prevailing odds?

That's one of the things I mean when I say the locked ward was my school. I accepted that Wanda was living her chances and I was living mine.

First I enlarged upon Papa's curriculum: *Draw, Antonio.*

For a graduate exercise, I followed Annie's.

The day I woke up in the hydrotherapy room I realized what Annie had gone through, and what she'd made of it. I tried—because I loved her—to follow the trail of insight she'd left, her scent on the air.

Perhaps I'll never get out of here. She had faced down that thought.

And then, *how shall I live my life? What choices do I have? What does it mean to be sane?* Without Annie's spirit to guide me, to the extent I could summon her, I might have stumbled over some of those questions.

•

After hours in the tub—sometimes women are in there half a day, gibbering with mania—the nurses rub down your naked body, a prune by then, and take you round the corner. At this station of the cross you are cuffed to the wall in a bath smock and soaked again, now with freezing cold water from a hose. Nurses in their rubber aprons accomplish this job while you scream and thrash.

Then they rub you down again and wrap you in a damp sheet frosted with rime from the ice chest.

It sounds horrible. It is horrible, if you have sufficient consciousness to experience it fully. It was one of the treatments the doctors were experimenting with that year. It sounds like torture to the outside world, but it often encompassed a transformation.

After being bundled into the icy sheet, you're tied into a few layers of flannel and wool deliciously heated on the radiators. Then you'd be bound to a bed in a dark room. Immediately, the most maniacal patient would fall into an exhausted sleep. Sometimes we'd sleep for days and awaken in an altered state, namely, better. Most patients loved hydrotherapy and learned to beg for it when they felt their episodes coming on, or even when they just wanted some peace.

It put the brakes on mania, and often turned around the crushing sadness that oppressed some of the women on 4 North. Not everybody got the treatment. Women who were hearing voices or tied down in catatonic fits didn't seem to benefit from hydrotherapy.

Then there was Sylvie, who didn't hear *any* voices.

Or so they thought. I noticed she raised her head to the clatter of the meal cart.

In art school, mostly I liked to draw beautiful people. Sylvie was the first ugly person I drew from life. She looked like a child—though she might have been in her teens. She had a pale monkey face and red-rimmed eyes; her blond hair stuck out from her head, very curly and stiff and burned-looking. Her tiny body was contorted and deformed.

I once heard a woman on the Grand Avenue car whisper to

another (for it's whispers young girls tune in to) that someone had "given birth to a little monster."

This secret obsessed me for a time. I paged through my father's anatomy book, which had a chapter on "monstrous births." Anencephalics and hunchbacks found their way into my sketchbooks for a time until my father scolded me mildly for my perverse interest. He assigned me medical illustration till I got bored and went back to drawing bowls of fruit and the gradations of color on a dead rabbit.

Sylvie must have been one such monstrous birth; she was crippled, she couldn't hear, she had no language but random animal cries until Annie somehow taught her to sing.

Like me, Sylvie was mourning for Annie. Her behavior on the ward became more and more incorrigible. Besides looking a bit like a monkey, she could climb like one, despite her twisted body. The nurses would be constantly chasing her up the bars and screens laced over our long, salubrious windows. They didn't like to lock her down too often. It was unhealthy, and her feral screaming disturbed us all. She didn't just cry and moan, she cultivated a weird inhuman shriek that set everyone off. So the strategy was to keep Sylvie tame.

"An ounce of prevention," as Nurse Schaeffer frequently observed.

This is how the breakthrough came about.

"Sylvana Maria Sztamburski!" Nurse Schaeffer yelled one day, as though to a mischievous toddler. Sylvie was hanging by one—paw—as it seemed—from the scaffold of a containment bed.

I'd never heard Sylvie's surname. On other wards, patients were called Miss and Mrs., but this polite custom broke down on 4 North. Here, women were as likely to answer to a call for Nurse Passmore's dog as to the name of some dimly remembered husband. Those like Sylvie, who had entered the asylum as toddlers, were often sorted out by nickname—not that Sylvie knew who she was, in the verbal sense.

But, for me, the name "Sztamburski," stuck a probe into memory.

That was my aunt's married name, a common one in Bohemia. My mind went back to nursery days and the language Papa had suppressed in me when we moved from New Prague to the sophisticated city of St. Paul.

A synapse fired.

"*Přestaň, miláčku!*" I said reflexively to Sylvie in Czech. "Stop that, sweetheart."

Though, if you'd asked me ten minutes before, I'd have told you I don't speak Czech. Papa had forbidden it.

Sylvie's head spun around and she dropped from her bars to the mattress. "*Dívka!*" Two distinct syllables of my father's language emerged from her gabble.

Nurse Schaeffer had been pushing a cart down the dayroom, handing out tin cups of this and that. I'd been hoping for cocoa. Nurse Schaeffer's eyes whipped from Sylvie to me. Say this for the woman, she was alert.

"*Přestan, dívko!*" I said loudly to the crippled girl. Stop it, baby.

Sylvie grinned, her face a monkey's ecstasy.

Papa had taken away what Czech of mine he could control. He'd sent me to elocution teachers to erode any trace of accent and then to the Irish nuns for polishing. Rarely did he call me by my birth name—*Ya-ni-na*—with its yawning foreign vowels, because he rarely got that impatient.

Nurse Schaeffer rolled her cart over to where I was sketching Sylvie's grin. Nurses never left their carts unattended. "Sylvie said something in what-was-that-language," Nurse Schaeffer observed.

"Czech."

"Can you say anything else to her?"

"I don't speak Czech," I replied.

Nurse Schaeffer rolled off to the speaking tube at the end of the corridor. "Attending!" she called into it.

Later there was a kind of party on the ward, far different from the usual diversions of screaming and praying and throwing collation dishes. Dr. Jessen-Haight came up, his white coat tails flapping, and, finally, Dr. Grafton himself.

I was made to repeat *přestăn! dívko!* and Sylvie to grin. When I ran out of Czech, a gardener from Men's Detached was led in to manifest his languages. There were experiments with whispers and ranges of tone.

Sylvie loved the attention.

I drew and drew, the beautiful along with the ugly. Here is Dr. Jessen-Haight with pince-nez and haughty air, Dr. Grafton looking sad as ever. Ethereal, wandering Eileen Hoolihan, plaiting a torn sheet into mystery knots.

It soon became clear to us all that Sylvie was, according to the common understanding, deaf, but not profoundly so. She had some latent hearing and she had the apparatus for making words beside her screams and musical drones and glottal stops. What she didn't have was the English language. Perhaps she was feeble-minded also: how could we tell?

There was a lot of fuss for several days and Sylvie blossomed under the scrutiny. Then it all died down. Staff had other work to do.

•

I began by telling how 4 North was my finishing school, and how I followed Annie's curriculum. I was on the ward for thirty-two days. Annie had been there for seven years. I was speeding through the lessons she'd tried to teach me, what she'd taught herself on 4 North. *Control your imagination. Exercise your power to choose. This is your life; it might never get better.*

I caught on to the set of subtle choices Annie had made: stay in your right mind, take care of people when you can.

I took care of Sylvie. Annie had taken the first steps into the girl's silence with her *fa-sol-la*. I couldn't do anything with music, but I could hold Sylvie's chin and force her to meet my eyes. I could say, exaggerating my lip movements *dívko!* and then repeat by the hour *baby* till she learned to spit out the English word. And a spit it was, across her overbite and her disinclination. *Baby*. She mimicked with her arms the rocking of an infant. She climbed into my lap.

Finally, they sent me down to 2 North, where Annie was. And they let Sylvie come with me.

CHAPTER EIGHTEEN: ANNIE

THE BLOODROOT IS coming up now, mid-June, late as ever it's been, in the glen by Men's Detached. They let me walk there now that I've graduated to the docile ward.

I love these secretive blooms. First they pole up through the silt and compost left over from last year, looking like little green mushrooms. Then the sun strikes them and they open to large white stars, low to the ground. Their roots are thick and crimson—*if you prick them, will they not bleed?*

Which is from Shakespeare.

I read also that the juice of bloodroot has some medicinal use to the Indians who used to roam these parts.

Indian medicine is likely as good as ours, or as useless. I wonder what the Indians did with their insane, crippled, feeble-minded and indigent people. Leave them out in the snow? Make them into gods?

If the sun shines too brightly, bloodroot wilts within days. I like a good show of spring ephemerals. It takes cool weather, though, and who wants that in June? After such a long winter.

Just take what comes.

Here's the little scattering of light in the underbrush called "springbeauty," one of the purslanes.

Here comes Lucy, in a procession of madwomen.

Oh, please make them take off her ugly smock. They are short of dresses on our ward, so she still wears the long shapeless costume of 4 North. It horrifies me, forced to think of her time up there.

Sylvie has gotten into some kind of child's pinny, and

she's full of energy. She runs as far from the queue as the nurses will let her, arms outstretched. She makes gobbling bird noises.

My family, my new family, is close enough to touch. Lucy and Sylvie are "in transition," held on the outskirts of the resident population. Tonight or tomorrow they'll be bedded down in our dormitory. I've lost my private space and gained—oh, my! I take a slow, conscious breath. I whisper *thank you thank you thank you* and try to calm my blood pressure. All my pressures.

Three male patients with their aide are launching a boat down at the lake. The men are allowed to go fishing, and even spend time in a little cabin in the woods.

We women have no such freedom, but, after 4 North, who's complaining?

Gardening will be my therapy, as soon as the beds warm up. They think I love it, but I'm really not interested this year. In the past, I just wanted to get outside, away from the ward. I felt I needed the exercise. They made me wear smoked spectacles and this, I learned, kept the auras at bay.

But now Lucy will be here. I want to walk with her, look at her, listen to her talk, with her tiny imperfect hesitation on the sound "th." She thinks she has no accent, but she teases me about my slow southern speech.

She tells me the south comes roaring back when I sing. I don't hear it.

I guess we're all fooling ourselves. Everybody knows who we are. Only *we* don't know who we are.

The minute I saw that beautiful girl across the laundry room I wanted to get well. Really, completely well, I mean. She called out to the wholeness in me. A river of it.

By then, I'd made my peace with 4 North. I felt safe there. For years, the staff had been encouraging me to progress. As soon as I came out of my twilight, it had become clear that I didn't belong on the high-security ward.

But the Legislature wanted me there. I had committed murder, so they said.

Every little while some wet psychiatric resident or student nurse would discover me with my books and papers and try to rehabilitate me. For what?

I resisted being saved. On 4 North, I had my jobs, an element of privacy, poetry, novels. I had sufficient objects of study: Nurse Schaeffer, Nurse Passmore's dog, each patient's unique crazy spoor. To the calm observer, 4 North is much more interesting than the lower wards.

I know as much about insanity as Dr. Grafton. Which is almost nothing. But you should see my case notes.

Now everything's changed.

These days I am studying how to be whole, which is different from sane. I watch Lucy and study that robust body—she has gotten chubby on 4 North. I want to lie next to her at night and hold her in my arms. I want my sanity to leak into her and hers to leak into me. That's how it works. People can make each other crazy or make each other whole.

Sweet rivers of redeeming love lie just beyond mine eye.

Had I the pinions of a dove...I sing as I walk in the glen.

The figures of Samuel and our children have begun to rise in my mind. My first family. Images come if you don't try to grab for them. Not quite memory: shadow play. I think Sam and I did well together. We drew some kind of arc on the world. I recall the landscape of Indiana, the pursuit of spring across Iowa; I remember southern Minnesota (bloodroot by the pump). There are stories in my body about building the house, planting the first crops. I wish I could read them.

Or, no.

Too many babies, too fast, but that's how it is. How can you stop it?

Were those my words or something I overheard in town?

It's not true what the lawyer said in court, that I turned on my family because I was worn out from childbirth, had no mother or sister to help me.

This passed for *defense*.

I didn't believe it and neither did anybody else. I just sat there in court, without language, like Sylvie, till the long white windows began to sparkle and splinter. I tried to warn the bailiff that the sky was falling and the Terror of That Day was upon us. The judge descended with fire in his hair, pretty much on schedule.

I woke up on 4 North. Three years or so had passed.

My babies were nowhere to be found.

Nor Samuel.

I don't think about Sam all that much. I'm able to repeat what they told me, though I don't understand the story. It never became real to me. He is "poor Sam" in the shadow he left in my mind. I don't believe he was all that intelligent. I think I confounded him.

They said I killed him.

"Did you think he was better off dead, Mrs. Leary?" the opposing lawyer had demanded, closing in on me with his sickly breath, his old-fashioned whiskers.

"Nobody's better off dead," I told him.

Though sometimes, on 4 North, I lost that thought.

·

I am thirty-two years old. Not young. But today I feel like my life is starting over.

In Indiana, in the Holy Ghost church, I got myself born again whenever I couldn't withstand the pressure. Of the Falling Sickness, as I now know to call it. I thought it was Jesus. Maybe it was. I'm told he works in mysterious ways. Sets fire to the world now and then.

CHAPTER NINETEEN

CARMIE WOULD NEED her wheelchair to get out of the house, through the woods, and into Buell Fricke's pasture. She was lucky to have it. Thanks to Max, who, she thought, her a little ungrateful. She seldom used it in the house, his gift. He knew nothing of her secret journeys.

He adored her and wanted to control her. That was his way of loving.

At this moment he would be on the wards. He would have a cup of bad coffee in hand. He would be jingling the limited number of keys in his britches' pocket. He would be saying his prayers of gratitude, by now unconscious, for every key that separated him from the patients he tended: for his freedom, her freedom. For a world he could master.

She sent him grateful thoughts.

For they weren't the most normal people on earth, Carmie thought. Their fate could have been as dark as anyone's in the asylum.

She swung herself from her counter top and then down to the wheelchair's velvet cushion ("World's Fair" garishly embroidered, that day in St Louis still shining in her mind). It was Max who kept them *normal enough*, by making an income and managing so competently her bit of settlement from Barnum and Bailey.

It could just as well have been the poor farm for Carmie.

She gripped the brake to keep the chair from sliding out from under her.

Without Max, she'd be a powerless cripple.

Instead, she was the Queen of Blue Heaven.

But the wind carried its smell of new grass, and Carmie felt keenly the strictures of her confinement, like a queen in a tower. Max never took her out. At first she thought he was ashamed of her, and she had been too weak to care. Later she realized how fearful he was, how protective of his secret treasure.

She'd gained strength. He'd noted the wistful look in her eye. He'd planted the garden for her and engineered the wheelchair. Once he had caught her past the front gate, tooling toward the post box. The terror in his face made her lie to him: "I don't really like it beyond the gates. The road is too bumpy. I'd rather stay home."

Not quite a lie: she'd learned to roll out the back way into the woods.

And now Carmie had a goal in mind. She loved her husband, but the excitement of her mission was impossible to resist.

The brick paths were easy to navigate, paths she and Max had laid together. Max had fixed the pavers, while Carmie, pulling herself handily along, had knocked them into place with her rubber mallet. She could manage the back gate. The path through the woods, though—it might be challenging.

Carmie took from her pocket the sharp little clippers she used to prune roses. She'd let blackberry vines thrive on the edge of the forest; now she clipped them when they got in the way of her passage. Max disliked the woods and thought of the hedge, if he thought about it at all, as a sturdy barrier. He preferred nature in its domestic disguise, as he preferred his wife.

Carmie smiled.

Summer had greened its way in. Not a trace of dampness. Deer hooves had hardened a path. Her grip on the wheels was strong. She burst out of the bushes into the sunlight of the neighbor's meadowland.

The stile and the wire fence would pose no problem to La Carmencita. (Her name had appeared in lights. The circus posters used to follow it with an exclamation point. But these days Carmie cherished anonymity. Best to keep a low profile. Keep things to yourself, what you knew, what you could do.)

She could not stand alone, but all winter she had carefully exercised the power of her knees and thighs to grip. She had not been—as Max might boast—the greatest bareback rider in the world, but she'd been good, an aristocrat. It wasn't only that she could stand *en pointe* on a galloping pony, but that she understood, with preternatural attention, the mind of the animal. Together, she and a horse could do things that looked miraculous: the famous stunt in which her mount appeared to balk, skid to a stop, and toss the rider over his head. How La Carmencita would flip in the air and come to rest on one foot, horse and ballerina bowing together.

(It wasn't the Appaloosa who had hurt her at that matinee performance, Tulsa, 1919. It was the clown, careless with his props.)

Pulling herself to the top of the stile, Carmie spread her arms and whistled. The horse galloped her way, a flawless white Lipizzaner. How had the mare, rare animal that she was, come to find herself in Southern Minnesota, on the Buell Fricke farm?

How had Carmie?

She grabbed for the horse's mane, launched herself, clung, and cantered.

•

Max whistled under his breath as he came through the swinging doors of 2 North—no locks here in the daytime. Yet he fingered his keys. It pleased him to see pretty Lucy back down among the living. He would make a story of it for Carmie over lunch. The girl, still in her mended smock, was pacing restlessly back and forth in front of the cabinets that lined the front of the ward. He patted her shoulder, as he turned to greet Nurse Malloy, who swept up to the nurses' station just then.

"Run up to 3, would you Max? Their gaslight is sputtering."

Lucy stopped pacing and looked up as though the sound of the nurse's rustle delighted her.

"You've missed me, haven't you?" Nurse Malloy's brogue was affectionate. "I hear you've been naughty. None of that now. Right?"

The nurse gave the pretty girl a stern look, which Max knew was all pretense. She raised the patient's chin and made her meet the assessing eyes. "Run along, then," she said to Max. Try to finish before lunch."

All of her attention went back to Lucy.

Peeked, but strong, Nurse Malloy thought. *Stronger than before. A dose of 4 North often had a therapeutic effect, if the patient ever managed to get off. Thank God Lucy had.*

Lucy seemed to be stalled in front of the cubbies where the nurses stored the patients' valuables.

"What are you doing up here, my girl?" Nurse Malloy didn't try out "Miss" or "Mrs." Why couldn't the doctors make up their mind about that?

Lucy said, "I was wondering if I could have my things."

"Your box, do you mean? Did you leave it up on 4 North?"

Lucy looked puzzled. "I-I don't think I had it with me."

"We'll ask Nurse Winstead, then. She'll know. Meanwhile, what do you need?"

"My hairpins. My—my…" She dropped her eyes.

"Your sanitary towels?" Nurse Malloy intuited. "Oh, my darling girl. We'll take care of that. Come along here."

Edith Malloy led Lucy up to the pen that surrounded the nurse's station. Susie Atkinson was on duty, one of the cupcake-hatted students from St. Joseph's. "Mrs.—ah -Allen needs her monthly supplies, Nurse, and some hairpins."

Miss Atkinson was mastering, all too quickly, Nurse Malloy thought, the bright artificial smile of someone who was keeping her heart out of the work. She handed over a paper bag and checked her pockets hopelessly for pins.

"Let's just braid that hair for now, shall we?" said Nurse Malloy. How had the girl gotten away from Lydia Schaeffer without a bob? "Do you know where her cigar box is, Nurse Atkinson?"

"In her cubby maybe. Nurse Winstead would know."

"Well, ask her, will you? And do we have any decent dresses? I'm sure we're tired of this smock."

"Yes, we are," Lucy said, with a hint of her old spunk.

"They're hanging in the hall by the lavs," Susie Atkinson said.

"I think we always feel better with something decent to wear," Nurse Malloy said. She bustled Lucy along the tile. "It's a small, isn't it?" She looked the girl up and down. Who could tell in that smock? She grabbed a cream-colored dress with tiny blue flowers out of the press. This month's issue.

Lucy's spirits lifted at the sight of it. She hadn't gotten close to Annie yet. She wanted to look nice for her. She wanted her comb.

"Do you need some help?"

"I can do it, Nurse."

"Well, let's have a bit of a wash."

Lucy shrank back.

Of course, there had been the hydrotherapy.

"No, just under the arms a little," said Nurse Malloy. "Before we put the new dress on."

Lucy let herself be trotted into the lavatory and ministered to. She liked the feel of Nurse Malloy's hands in her hair. She tried to see herself in the heavy mirrors over the sinks; they were unbreakable slabs of polished metal. She raised her arms obediently and let the ugly costume of 4 North drop down around her feet.

She caught Nurse Malloy's look of surprise, distorted as it was by the unreliable mirror.

"Mrs. Allen!" (Let's settle on that) "Didn't you tell me you wanted your sannies?"

"No. I just want my box," said Lucy (my comb, my *money*).

She hoped she didn't sound like a petulant child. She thought she did.

Abruptly, Nurse Malloy grabbed Lucy's slip and pulled it back so the material stretched over her belly. "You're putting on flesh, aren't you?" said Nurse Malloy. She quickly moderated the remark. It seemed unkind. "Well, you need some meat on your bones in here."

Then Lucy felt a wash of bubbles tickling her armpits and a gentle sponge and dry, while Nurse Malloy kept up a line of conversation. "When did you have your last monthlies, my girl?"

The intrusiveness! Lucy blushed. The question, besides, took her back to the farm and the shame of Will's bedroom. "I don't remember."

"Well, you've been through a lot, haven't you? Are you pretty regular?"

"I-ah-no."

Brisk pats.

The flowered dress didn't fit. "I'll get a bigger," said Nurse Malloy.

Lucy leaned into the mirror as the nurse charged out, charged back.

"This is just as nice, don't you think?" Nurse Malloy held it up.

Lucy tried not to pout. It was one of the grays.

"Never mind. I'm going to find you a pretty apron," Nurse Malloy said.

•

The call from Sheriff Norton had gone to Nurse Passmore's office.

"You have a man there named Maximiliano—ah—Bahlke?" the sheriff said in his barky way.

"Max. Yes." Olivia Passmore pushed her glasses up into her hair and reached for a scrap of paper. "Yes. I'll send someone over to find him. Is there an emergency? Oh, my. I see."

"Well. Well." Nurse Passmore was huffing as she wrote,

and huffed again as she handed the note to her assistant, Miss Merriwell.

"Max is on Three. Run up, will you, and tell him to dial Sheriff Norton right away at this number. He can use the phone in the nurses' station."

"Max, the aide?" said Miss Merriwell.

In response, Olivia Passmore made the impatient shooing gesture with her fingers that she habitually used with underlings. "I'll be along in a minute."

Miss Merriwell took off, glad to get out of the office and smell grassy air wafting through the open skylights.

Up the stairs of North, she found Max on a ladder, attending to the hallway lights. When she called him down and led him to the telephone, he didn't seem to know what the device was for. She roused Central and asked for the sheriff. She left the station when Max gave her a savage look. Then she had to go back when she heard him shouting, "Yeah? Yeah? I can't hear you."

Was he talking into the wrong end of the phone?

Miss Merriwell heard him say. "Is she hurt? I'll be right there."

Max threw the phone. The stick clattered to the floor, the mouthpiece hit the blotter. "I have to go to town," he told Miss Merriwell. "Tell them I have to go."

She had never seen the impassive man distressed. His hands were shaking in the air.

"What's wrong? Let me drive you." Northfield was six miles away. She would borrow Nurse Passmore's car.

"No, no." He sprinted away, almost upsetting the Director of Nursing as she panted up the stairs.

At that moment, Nurse Malloy emerged from the double doors of 2 North. She carried a sheaf of aprons over her arm. She, too, dodged the aide. She clamped her aprons, and clutched for Nurse Passmore's hand. Then, "May I speak to you please, Nurse?" both women said at once.

152

They ducked into a niche in the hall. It had been designed for classical statuary which had luckily never appeared. Miss Merriwell, toiling after Max, heard them cutting off each other's sentences. She caught the word *wife*. Like many whose hearing was poor, the Director of Nursing spoke loudly.

"I'd no idea he had a wife," said Nurse Malloy clearly, as one speaking to the hearing-impaired.

And then Nurse Passmore said urgently, "Wally Norton has her at the jail."

"What in heaven's name…?" said Edith Malloy.

There was a sentence that had the word *horse* in it and then the head nurse claimed Olivia Passmore with her own story. It was about dresses and aprons and "where the husband might be."

Miss Merriwell had no excuse not to keep running downstairs, and anyway, the women on the floor above lowered their voices.

CHAPTER TWENTY

DAVID GRAFTON WAS raging. He blamed himself.

Nurse Olivia Passmore listened to him because listening was her job. She valued her job above all else, except perhaps her immortal soul, which she also cared a great deal about.

Grafton let himself rant at Nurse Passmore because she was the old-fashioned kind of nurse, the sort he might have been dealing with in Toronto, a nurse who did her work impeccably and understood that part of her job was listening to her superiors let off steam. At the same time, she sat upright in her formidable dignity and let it wash off her. Grafton imagined the Director of Nursing in a good waxed field jacket, letting his words roll off her.

"Here's Kennedy ranging on about some German seduction theory while you all nod wisely—"

Nurse Passmore nodded wisely.

"…and nobody takes the trouble to pull up the girls' chemise and look at her. I *asked* about her physical condition, did I not? I *asked* if there had been a gynecological examination?"

Another nod.

"And here we are, tying her to the wall and spraying her with hoses while she's, for Godsake, excuse me Nurse Passmore, *in the family way.*"

The Director of Nursing nodded with an intimation of finality. "To be fair," she responded, "Mrs. Allen is tall and perhaps natu-rally"—she seemed to grope for a clinical term—"*curvaceous.* There were the smocks. Her condition is only now becoming apparent."

Grafton did not seem to hear. "And you, Nurse," he continued, "have misplaced her people…Is she married or is she not married? Who is responsible here? We need to establish paternity and make sure somebody claims this baby." Grafton riffled through a set of files that was lying on Nurse Passmore's desk.

The invasion made her cringe. She hated her things being tossed around. "It is not there, sir."

"Well, where is it then?"

She didn't know.

"Six months, give or take." Grafton went on. He counted off on his fingers, waving them under Nurse Passmore's nose. " At least they can't blame it on an aide, or accuse us of poorly supervising the male and female patients. But how could we not have noticed?"

Olivia Passmore thought that we were overly concerned with matters above the neck and rarely troubled by anything below. She thought perhaps that's why we'd gone into the psychiatric profession in the first place, but it wasn't her place to say.

It was, though, her place to produce a file, and he could not.

"I think, sir, we'll have to ask the sheriff. He'll have a copy of the commitment order."

Perhaps the only copy, Nurse Passmore thought. She did remember what a big mess of paper had come along with Lucy Valenta, how she'd thought it might require two brown folders instead of one and how, when she'd come back to neaten the file, Janina Lucy Valenta's paperwork seemed to be missing. *Seemed to be*, she had put it to herself, because there'd been that fire in the wastebasket on 3 North—one of the doctors' pipes—and then Jessen-Haight pawing through her cabinet looking for some monograph in German.

"It'll turn up," she'd said to herself, "any minute." And then Nurse Malloy had stormed in about the fire and the rules on smoking materials—Nurse Malloy did tend to obsess, having survived that fire in the Dublin Women's Infirmary—not that her concern wasn't justified.

But the missing file hadn't turned up in the normal course of things and within an hour Nurse Passmore had forgotten even her intention to search.

Now she wondered was she perhaps growing too old for so much responsibility? "I'll get the sheriff on the phone," she said.

"Never mind. I'll get him," said Grafton. "Jesus God—forgive me, Nurse Passmore—is the poor woman married or isn't she?"

"I don't know, sir," said Olivia Passmore. "She had a gold ring." Nurse Passmore stuck to that point. The ring seemed to be lost as well.

CHAPTER TWENTY-ONE: ANNIE

WE'RE GOING TO have a baby.

I should have known. I'm not stupid about things like that.

Our baby was conceived in that first glance between us across the laundry room. My eyes found hers and love sprang into bloom.

This is the story I tell Lucy.

We both know it isn't strictly true. We are not crazy. I know I repeat that sentence too often. But it's a sentence necessary to our survival. I've never needed to prove sanity before—it wasn't even expedient to do so. I had come to terms with my fate and the label didn't matter. *Insane* worked for me.

But then, you meet someone and your fate shifts. The future had looked like this: day after day on 4 North. I'd sing out the back windows, I'd teach Sylvie a little sign language (yes, I could tell them, she is feeble minded), I'd pat Sarah's hair till she stopped hitting herself, I'd admire Eileen's intricate pattern of cuts, the tattoos of a warrior queen. I'd help Nurse Schaeffer feed those who were in restraints that day or forever.

Singing out the back window was the highlight. And reading, and writing in my copy books.

I'd started to write letters to the *St. Paul Pioneer Press*.

A man named Erik Strommer, the editor, wrote back. He encouraged my essays. Published some. Turned down most of my poems. It wasn't a bad life. Think of Miss Emily Dickinson—as I often did—scribbling away in her bedroom. Any life is what you make of it, and I've seen some chilly fates.

Then you meet someone and the spirit calls you, the way God used to call my dad.

With that kind of terror and brightness.

Daddy was a Holy Ghost preacher from Sand Mountain, Georgia, a lonely part of this earth. Never mind, we didn't stay there long. I guess I was born on Sand Mountain, or maybe somewhere on the way to Tennessee. My father had his nose to the trail.

When the power of the Lord was off him, my dad was a responsible, prudent man, who kept good accounts. He planted his crops and often harvested them.

Other times he'd be under the burden of the Word and we'd be giving away all we had, not much, and taking off to wherever he felt called to preach.

My mother believed in his mission and followed along in her lamblike way, keeping the six or eight of us fed and clothed, trying to send us to school. My brothers and sisters didn't take to it. I did, because I was smart and because my Gifts made me unfit for helping in the fields.

My Gifts were also useful in keeping us out of the poor farm.

I was possessed by demons—this was my father's initial diagnosis.

He made an honorable profit from that idea. A preacher who can drive demons out of his own flesh and blood is a hot commodity. It gave my father an advantage in the ministry, though he was modest about it.

I only know what others have told me. Back then, I would be out cold or out somewhere when the Powers came upon me. My brothers and sisters, however, would describe how the devil made me writhe on the ground and wet myself, my eyes rolling back in my head.

"Unclean Spirit, depart from her, HEP, I abjure you by the Living God, by the power of the Holy Ghost. Amen. HEP!" My brother, Tom, the eldest, expected to become a preacher in his turn. He loved to imitate my father's rites of exorcism.

After Daddy shouted and pranced around for half an hour,

I'd fall back like a dead cat and sleep on the damp church boards till the women picked me up and carried me into the back room. My father would go on crying and preaching and calling people to the Lord. I'd wake to ecstatic singing and come out when I was able—these events used to go on for three or four days.

They'd dress me in white lace and prop me up in the tenor section where I'd sing even louder than I'd cried out in the grip of the demon.

All of us kids sang well and that helped the collection basket.

> *O when shall I see Jesus and reign with him above?*
> *And from the flowing fountain drink everlasting love?*
> *O had I wings, I would fly away and be at rest…*

Love, love, it was always about love. I could feel it pouring over me in a river of light. *O had I wings…*

My father was sincere, and as incorruptible as any of us are in this world. Overly sincere. My mother managed to hold him back from snake-handling. If my demons were an advantage to the ministry, well, that was the Lord's providence. He could make a silk purse out of a sow's ear. And it wasn't a long-term advantage, because after a lapse of several months, my demons would return.

A preacher who can't *keep* the demons out of his own daughter has a lot to answer for. Besides the show got stale after a number of repetitions.

That's why we moved a lot, Garden City, Centralia, West Fork. In every state there are towns with those names.

At a certain point, my dad went into himself and gave it all some thought.

We'd just gotten a little place in Canaan, a one-street town in northern Indiana, where my father had been called to preach at a Free Evangelical Independent Church of God in Christ. There was a wave of religious fervor sweeping the country just then. Dad rode those waves and rode them well.

Maybe he started them. Whatever starts a wave.

People came from all over to hear Daddy preach. It was a change from the liturgy and the tamped-down worship of those parts. There was a lot of music and anyone who wanted to showed up with instruments. They let the little kids play tambourines.

Daddy would preach love, there'd be singing from the *Harmony* and dinner on the grounds. People would go home happy and make babies. I'm telling you.

During his period of prayer and retreat, the power of the Lord came down on my father and overshadowed him: because how were my fits going to play out here in Canaan, where we had settled in so nicely?

Well. The Lord revealed to my father that I was not possessed by demons but by the spirit of prophecy!

I think, now that I've had more than enough time to ponder, that Daddy had a bad conscience about the way my life was turning out. Puberty was on me. My spells got worse and worse. I suffered as well from my reputation as a girl possessed by demons—or, alternatively, angels—which was hard to outrun no matter how many times we moved. Try out that story at your new school.

Daddy wanted to retire me from his ministry. I think he was afraid I was going to die. The Lord revealed to him that I needed a reclusive life, like some of the prophets of old. The power could come upon me, somewhere in the back of the house, and Daddy would carry it forth and preach the Word. That was his plan.

I had a plan of my own, however. It did not include Canaan, Indiana and throwing up in the back bedroom.

It involved Samuel Leary, who sang bass in the Canaan Sunday night shape-note meet.

As I said, all of us children had grown up to be strong singers. My brothers and sisters and I knew the whole of the *Harmony* and we could sing the shapes and the words without ever opening the book.

Samuel Leary was a strong bass singer. His voice had already changed; he was five or six years older than I. The basses sit next to the tenors, and so I spent a few years blaring at Samuel and he at me. I hadn't the brains to know I was being courted until they were ready to call the banns; word got around and people started to hold us to account.

I decided that was just fine.

From there my plan developed. Girls are romantic fools. The way we look for men to save us, it's pitiful.

•

I was fifteen by then, and dubious about my powers of prophecy. What if I came out of the back room with nothing much to say?

Left to my own devices, I'd started to read voraciously. The Episcopalian minister's wife in Canaan had noticed me. She volunteered at the little library in the back of the drug store. She loaned me her own books. She got to know me. She took me to Richmond in a closed car, in fact, to a doctor. At her own expense. The doctor came up with a theory about my "seizures"—I loved this word, which seemed to validate my ecstatic trances. He attached several French words to them, which was also pleasing. But he could offer little in the way of treatment.

Keep calm. Don't look at flickering light. Stay out of the glare of the Holy Ghost.

Damn, I would marry Samuel, I decided.

He would be a strong shoulder and a good provider. He longed to get out of Canaan as much as I did. We wanted to go farther north, Samuel because there was a lot of open land to be homesteaded, and me because I thought I could leave the demons down south. Foolish me.

We set out on the train for the northern U.S. just ahead of the dust storms. Everybody in the Free Evangelical Church showed up to cry and eat and say good-by, my sisters and brothers and my Dad praying and prophesying.

I never saw them again. Did any of them know how to write,

even Dad? He took his orders in the old-fashioned way, from God.

•

I'm telling Lucy this story as we spoon in her bed after lights out. I lie at her back and wrap my legs around her legs and my arms around the growing presence of our baby—which, yes, I know isn't really our baby—and we exchange histories, in defiance of the rules.

Spooning in bed isn't against the rules.

One thing about the asylum, they let us find what joy we can in human contact, so long as it isn't male to female. Some people don't keep the male/female rule either, but I can't tell you anything about those secret romances. It's not my story, Lucy's and mine.

*You meet someone and the Spirit calls you....*Before us, as we bundled on Ward 2 North, the future stretched out like a field of summer wheat. The only obstacle was that we were under commitment orders in a state asylum.

And I—if I got well—would likely go to prison. A conundrum.

•

"Baby, we have to get a lawyer," Lucy is saying as we fall asleep. "Or we have to run away. Or both." She has a good head on her shoulders, my little wife. She is full of plans.

"I have a lot of money," she tells me, as she drifts off.

Lucy is still a bit delusional.

I see her as Seduced and Abandoned. I read a lot of lurid novels on the way to refining my tastes. Lucy is a novel I long to read over and over, to separate out the truth from the fiction. Crazy people lie habitually, and I believe it is her residual madness that tells these tales of *stealing, whoring* and, now, *riches*.

Will Allen confused her mind. He told her lie after lie until she didn't know who she was any more. I've watched her come back to herself, day by day, in the art room. She's one of those rare people—like me—who can use the asylum to get well. Such people were probably not insane to start with—though I've seen people come in here pretty normal and become, as the diagnosis runs, *severely regressed.*

Who told the sheriff those stories about stealing and whoring? Will Allen.

Why?

Who told the stories about me, that have put me here for life without parole?

I don't know.

The State of Minnesota, maybe. The State of Georgia would have hung me by the neck until dead. But these pale-faced Norwegians and Germans can't get their minds around a woman who'd do what they say I did. They had to declare me insane in order to sleep at night with their philosophy intact.

Not that I'm not grateful.

Is an insane asylum worse than prison? I don't think so.

We play out the cards we have. Though I grew up in a family that didn't hold with card playing.

Lucy wants my story, and I would give it to her, but, frankly, I can't remember much.

Mostly the forgetfulness feels like mercy, grace abounding. Every detail I can call to mind stings like a nettle in a bed of nettles: Samuel's kindness, Samuel coming in on the bass line. Samuel leading me out of my father's house with its love and limitations. Our farm, wildflowers where the pump dripped.

My memories of marriage cannot struggle past the first minute of the first hour I knew I was pregnant with Julia. All coherence gone. From Julia, my mind skips to that falling-fit in the courtroom: *O will the judge descend? And must the dead arise? And earth and sky must pass away at those discerning eyes?*

The song goes.

So what could I say to a lawyer? What can I say to Lucy?

Our histories are all we have, but it's a struggle to control them. We can't remember, or we lied in the first place, or somebody saw something that never happened, or we didn't know how to write the words. Other people write down nothing like we would say.

I feel for the kick of the baby in Lucy's belly, little bloodroot, but it is too early. And anyway, they sleep. Babies.

CHAPTER TWENTY-TWO: LUCY

THE SUPERINTENDENT HAS summoned me to his office to explore my sanity, as I am in the habit of examining his. He opens my file. I sit still, watch his face, and ponder the notes I'm keeping on him.

Dr. David Grafton is crazy.

I love to throw that diagnosis around.

He's not neurotic—my delicious new word. If you're neurotic you do not hear voices, harbor delusions about your royal blood, think the radio is sending you messages from God and so forth—the usual run of fantasies. You are just a little abnormally sad and selfish.

Neurotic is what I aspire to.

You might have a *complex*. You think, like Nurse Schaeffer, that you are superior to everyone else, or, like Dr. Kennedy, so beaten up by religion, that you are inferior. We can all live with our complexes.

But David Grafton is one of those unexploded bombs I hear they left behind in France that blows up a farmer now and then, trying to plant crops.

I think he knows it, too. I watch him at his work, so controlled. Icy. So carefully polite and kind. But slam a door behind him and he starts to twitch. He'll have something like one of Annie's *petites*, as she calls them. Her eyes go glassy and she isn't with you for a minute.

Grafton will do that.

Why does he have the keys and we don't?

To be fair, he hasn't killed anybody or "threatened the public peace," that phrase the sheriff blessed me with. He can wash and brush himself.

No doubt his family has money.

"I think it was the war," I told Annie once. We love to put our heads together and psychoanalyze the doctors and nurses and aides. Our experience in the hospital has given us a way of looking at the world, and in it all we find little sanity.

"What war?" Annie said.

No doubt she thinks the War Between the States has broken out again.

"There was a war in France since you came in here. Grafton was a soldier, a medic." Every patient in the hospital carries a notebook of a mind that covets every detail of staff history we glean in our wandering and eavesdropping. We are generous, we share.

"That would rattle a person," Annie said. "But he's kind. He tries to keep a hold on things."

This was Annie's own survival strategy: *be kind, keep a hold on things.*

"But you can see how the others stand back from him. He just isn't easy," I answered.

Watching staff interact with each other is theater for us, Saturday melodrama down at the Shubert. They are almost as incarcerated as we are, off on the prairie, shut up together with their own dining room and laundry. They have their little dramas: Nurse Schaeffer and Dr. Jessen-Haight despise each other. Dr. Kennedy is in love with some college girl and Nurse Mercy as well.

Well, everybody is in love with Nurse Mercy, except Dr. Grafton, who has a chance there, if he'd push it.

He's afraid. Afraid his craziness will leak out and harm her.

Poor Dr. Grafton. I study his face as he leafs through my folder. But he has the keys.

Today, in his office, we have gone through the preliminaries. "What date is it today, Mrs. Allen? How are you feeling?"

"July 18, 1921. I'm feeling extremely well, thank you."

So far, so good. I rehearsed those two sentences.

Don't start to blurt out paragraphs, Annie has warned me. Don't say, *I'm well and I'd like to be released with my friend Annie Leary so we can live together in Minneapolis or maybe Paris with our baby.*

Being sane involves a lot of play-acting.

"I understand you're enjoying the art studio," says Dr. Grafton.

This blindsides me. I had expected questions about Will, questions about my interesting condition. I'm quite intelligent enough, thank you, to know what a problem my pregnancy creates for Staff.

What a problem it creates for me, that's a cliff from which I draw back my toe. *I am having a baby. I live in an insane asylum. They'll take my baby away. Put it in an orphanage. Give it to Will.*

Focus, Lucy, I hear Annie's voice in my mind.

To my surprise, Grafton puts another folder on his desk. I recognize my portfolio from the art room.

Private, keep out! It took me a while to feel a sense of safety about the work I was doing down there. *Draw, Lucy, draw and don't waste time!*

"Do you mind if we look at these together?"

If I say "Yes, I do mind" will that be marked down against me? I have no power in the matter. He has the keys. He can do as he likes.

But Grafton leans forward, carefully putting on an empathetic expression, as an actor might don a mask. I have to give him credit for trying.

"Mrs. Allen, I removed this folder from your shelf in the studio, but I haven't looked at it and I won't do so without your permission. We are all entitled to privacy."

I almost believe him.

Annie would not. She would not believe him, but she would forgive him.

That's the difference between us.

Dr. Grafton goes on. "I'm writing a paper for a medical

convention. It's on the use of art in treating emotional distress." He stops, apparently for applause. "I would love to look at your work with you and hear you tell me about what you're doing."

Emotional distress, what a polite phrase. I have been promoted to the Northfield State Hospital for Emotional Distress.

But I have endured many a studio critique both from Papa and the art school faculty. I explain that to Grafton in a saucy attempt to establish my professional credentials.

"But I will not play the critic, Mrs. Allen." His smile relaxes. "And I understand that professionally you use your maiden name, Lucy Valenta?"

Well!

I will promote this dual identity back on the ward and solve that recurring problem of what they are to call me.

And now he will get around to Will, I think.

But, at my nod, he opens my portfolio. I watch him lose himself. I can read faces the way Annie understands a line of music. I can read the tiny crinkles around a young man's eyes and recapitulate his baby face. I can anticipate his old man's grizzle. I'd know what grade my professors were formulating the minute they leaned over my easel. I knew on April 10, 1921 that Annie Leary and I would be together as long as we lived and potentially beyond because I saw it in her face, though I could not imagine what my own eyes played back to her.

"I promised I'd not critique, Mrs. Allen, but, really, I'm surprised by the quality of your work," Grafton says.

I nod. This is what I do, who I am, what I've practiced since I first held a pencil and heard the imperative *draw*. I don't bother with a pretense of humility.

"You've done more? I just picked up the top file."

"Yes." It's who I am.

He smiles, softly now, over a study of Nurse Mercy sipping a cup of cocoa. He looks up at me as he comes to the sketches of 4 North. "Have you seen the work of an artist called Daumier?"

I do not say "of course" in the uppity way I used to have, but just "yes."

"Your work is exceptional. It should be published. Hung in a gallery."

Of course.

He comes to my drawings of Annie's face. This is how I memorize her. This is how I read her, how I will hold her in mind for eternity.

"Ah, Mrs. Leary." A tiny muscle at his lip registers caution.

Now he closes the portfolio and gets down to business. "You two seem to be very fond of each other."

I say boldly, my love on the line. "You should talk to her, sir. You should write a paper. I don't think she did what they say she did…" I stop myself with a little snap of teeth on the tongue in my head.

Lucy, focus. Don't blurt out paragraphs.

Grafton looks at me and allows the moment to lengthen. I know this trick. He thinks I'll get nervous and make some terrible mistake. But I meet his gaze and smile a little. Like a docile, rational girl.

"There is no one here in the hospital whose good I do not have in my care," says Grafton in his convoluted way. *My eye is on the sparrow.*

He taps a little drumroll with his long fingers on the papers in front of him. "But it is you I must concern myself with now. Your welfare and that of your child."

At last. I nod humbly.

"We would like to be in contact with your husband."

I hear an electric buzz, which is either from the new institutional wiring or mine. But they have only to ask. I repeat my address in Northfield. Isn't it in the file?

"Thank you. That information never made it into your record."

"I thought he would be visiting, Will," I venture.

"Is he on the phone?"

"Ah, no. And mostly he lives in the City." *He kept me at the farm,* I want to say. *Rather like you keep me here.*

Would Grafton be sympathetic? I doubt it.

"What does he do there?"

"Business," I venture. Will's secrets, now that Mrs. Lerner has handed them over to me with her wads of cash, are safe. To divulge them would start a conversation that might end with me screaming. I could lose focus.

"Do you know a way he can be contacted?"

I shrug. I give up Mrs. Lerner's name. Let her take it on.

"Oh, yes, the housekeeper. She did visit." Grafton looks up from his obviously inadequate records.

"She did," I say. Offered me her blood money. Propelled me off the cliff, *downward through the evening shadows...*

Grafton's eyes have gone the steel color of the star sapphire in his tie pin. He tries the silence trick again.

But I sharpen myself.

"If you really want to find Will, maybe Nurse Passmore can help you," I say.

I try on an ingenuous face.

Where have I picked up a secret about the Director of Nursing I did not even know till this moment that I knew? I blink myself back to some druggy moments in Admitting. The sheriff had held me upright while signing papers Nurse Passmore thrust at him... I heard the word *discretion* fly back and forth.

Annie schools me daily in the grasp of reality, though she admits to only a light hold on it herself. All of us here—and I include the staff—lose our ability to distinguish between the dream world and the waking world. We hear so many secrets, so many lies; there's a taxonomy of lies: lies you know are lies, lies you think are true, lies you have to tell to survive, lies you simply think are amusing.

What kind has Nurse Passmore told? Lie # 3, I believe. She has to keep her head up in Northfield, where she means to retire to a little cottage on Front Street. She's buddies with the sheriff. They sing in the same choir or something.

We get lost. Dr. Grafton is lost in his paperwork and maybe in his war. Nurse Schaeffer gets lost in things from the medicine cupboard. Annie gets lost in her books and her writing, I in my drawing. Sylvie can stare for hours at a caterpillar climbing a twig.

With reality so much in flux, Annie says, you have to pay attention when you can. You can't afford to lose your grip.

I look at Grafton and see that he knows this, and that it isn't easy for him, either: keeping a hold.

CHAPTER TWENTY-THREE

Nurse Winstead went to Nurse Passmore with her story.

Junior nurses report to senior nurses, that's what the chain of command required, though her first impulse had been to presume on her friendship with Dr. Grafton.

Instead, she stopped Edith Malloy. Nurse Malloy's rustle halted in mid-corridor, like a rest in music that lets you get your bearings.

"Whuh?" she said. And then, "You go straight to Miss Passmore."

The Director of Nursing had a corner office overlooking a small garden where sometimes in the evening Nurse Passmore herself could be found at work. This afternoon, drowsy as it was, she sat at her desk and looked out at the oncoming color. She almost, not quite, nodded off.

Nurse Winstead knocked.

Nurse Passmore dipped her pen in the inkwell and prepared to resume business, uncertain of what had alerted her.

Nurse Winstead knocked again.

"Come in." Nurse Passmore swiveled in her chair.

"I'm sorry to disturb you, ma'am."

Miss Passmore sat upright. She had never been, as a girl, allowed a chair with a back. She didn't need one now, even to nap. She didn't ask the younger woman to sit down. Junior nurses shouldn't expect to sit down.

"How are things going, Nurse?"

"Very well, ma'am, thank you." Mercy took in the windows, the sunny lift of the day and the garden beyond.

When you went into nursing, it was all "service, service, service." Mercy's feet hurt.

But here were pansies, cornflower, butterfly weed.

If you were very good at your work you would get to sit down and have a window in your office.

"Miss Passmore, Nurse Malloy suggested I speak to you about an issue that's come up about a patient."

"And which patient would that be, Nurse?" Olivia Passmore thought it would be Lucy Valenta. A bit of a narcissist. Such people created drama wherever they set foot. It made life amusing, really.

"Lucy Valenta," Mercy said. "Mrs. Allen."

Nurse Passmore herself preferred the more respectable mode of address at present. Her brow creased. The *poor, foolish child.* Seduced and abandoned. The punishment seemed out of proportion to a bit of fun. Why did the men always go unpunished?

Power, she knew. Especially in this case.

Mercy Winstead watched these ideas flit over her supervisor's face. It was a white, papery face with many small lines and pouches. Perhaps Nurse Passmore looked older than she really was, Mercy thought. Or perhaps she was very old.

The Director had seen a lot. She had served in the war. She had led a hospital team. Mercy bowed her head a little in recognition of this history. "Miss Valenta has recently come down from 4 North, as you know."

Miss Passmore smiled faintly. She liked to see progress, and saw so little of it.

"…and asked for her things, of course. Her box."

Miss Passmore's lips squared themselves. These boxes were a recurring problem. The patients owned little, and what little they had they protected fiercely. As they had no secure storage space they carried their pitiful cigar boxes around all day. Of course, there was loss and pilferage, which took up a lot of staff time.

"No, no, I don't think so. It's this: when we took Miss Valenta up to 4 North after that incident at the window, I left her box in the tower room. The Castle, as they call it. I was distracted, you see."

"Of course."

"But I did come back for it before lights out."

"Very good."

"And I opened it to see that all was intact, her hairpins and handkerchiefs and so forth. Because I wanted to make certain she'd have nothing dangerous in her possession, even the pins, say."

"Yes, Nurse." The pen tapped and a drop of ink flew.

"And Miss Passmore, there was *money* peeking out. Cash. With a hanky on top. I locked it up, of course, in her cubby on 2. And frankly I forgot about it. I didn't take time to look. Just thought, *O, Lucy.* Because there was that *kleptomania* in her admission. But I forgot, I went to bed. It was so late by then."

Miss Passmore nodded. She carefully blotted the ink spot.

"I mean, I thought, just a few bills." *I shouldn't have gone to bed*, Mercy rebuked herself.

"Continue."

"Mrs. Allen has been asking for it, her box, now that she's back on 2 North, and finally somebody thought to come to me. The penny dropped, you know, and I went to the cubby and looked. I opened it. Maybe I shouldn't have. Miss Passmore, there are hundreds and hundreds of dollars, rolled up and tied in rubber bands."

Miss Passmore drew a breath. "In her *box*? In the *cubby*?"

"Yes ma'am."

Nurse Passmore scowled. "And it hadn't been there before? You're sure?"

"Oh, no, ma'am. Of course not. I've looked into her things, Lucy's, plenty of times, fixing her hair and so on. She had nothing before but the usual."

And her ring, Nurse Passmore suddenly remembered that item. Her wedding ring. What had become of it?

The Director of Nursing stared into the left corner of the room. Mercy's eyes followed hers. Both of them watched a small spider spinning a web in the cornice.

"Now of course, she's asking for her things, and she has a right to them," Mercy went on. "We don't want to instill a paranoid reaction or cause her to regress, especially not with things as they are…"

Her pregnancy. Her progress.

"Patients have a right to their privacy." Nurse Passmore repeated one of the institutional mantras.

"Exactly. But we can't have all that money lying around on the wards. Nor do I want to tell Mrs. Allen that I rifled through her things, so as not to…"

"…precipitate regression."

"Yes. And here's the important thing…"

Olivia Passmore had already grasped the important thing, or at least the dangerous element of the case. She carefully arranged her face.

"…Lucy must have gotten that money from her visitor, the night of the…um, the incident. The suicide attempt. I can't think of any other time it could have gotten into her box. On visiting day, I helped her do up her hair. Gave her her comb. The box was half empty as always. I put it into her hands, I gave her a pat, I sent her off to the parlor."

That hair, Nurse Passmore thought. Her mind tried to avoid a tide of panic. It grasped at the irrelevant. *That hair really must be cut.* She let some silence gather, then, for the sake of her own poise. "This Mrs. Lerner," she said.

Nurse Winstead said, "I think the visitor must have given her the cash. Mrs. Lerner. Who else? And I think that had something to do with why Lucy crept off and tried to throw herself out the window."

Nurse Passmore felt a chill. Experience had taught her that in a moment she might begin to shiver. She had been a fool, worse, a coward, to collude with the sheriff. You could work hard all your life. You could try to be perfect as your heavenly father was perfect. And then, in an unguarded moment, the animal instinct betrayed you. You just tried to save yourself. Or guard your nest, even if it's no more than a little cottage on Front Street. Power had that effect on a person.

She gathered her courage. "You've thought this through carefully and I believe you are correct," she told the young nurse in her measured way.

"Lucy was in tears today about 'her things.' That's why the students came looking for me. But I couldn't just give her the box, once I saw."

"Dear, no."

"What do you think I should do?"

The Director of Nursing seemed to flinch slightly. "What do you think you should do, Nurse?"

This was the common feint of a teaching hospital, and lately Mercy had been prepared for it. "I think I should sit her down very calmly and say, 'Mrs. Allen, when I brought you upstairs to 4 North I put your box in the cubby because I saw there was a little bit of money in it. And now that I think about it I don't feel it's safe to leave those bills on the ward. So why don't we get you another box and put this one in the Admissions safe?"

"In other words, treat it normally."

"Exactly."

Mercy's clinical eye took in the pen Miss Passmore had laid down, the bloodless look of her fingers. But as she watched, the older woman gathered her forces.

"We'll confer with Dr. Grafton. Of course," she said briskly. "He's working intensively with Miss Valenta. As you know. Everything else aside, we have to sort out the paternity issue. And if this money has a bearing on her suicide attempt, we'll figure that out."

Mercy Winstead nodded at the reassurance. "I wonder if we could bring Lucy over here to Admissions and have her put the money in the safe herself and sign for it," Mercy said.

"Treat it all normally," said Miss Passmore again. And then

her look became a little sly. "Why don't you confer with Dr. Grafton yourself? You two are collaborators on Lucy Allen's case. He's probably writing a monograph."

Nurse Winstead's color rose.

But Miss Passmore seldom calculated Romance into her equations. Instead, "Make sure you get your name on it," she said.

Oh, my, thought Mercy Winstead.

The old woman wore a predatory frown. "Have confidence in your own power, Nurse."

CHAPTER TWENTY-FOUR

DAVID GRAFTON FLUSHED to the extent he was able. Pallor retreated from his cheekbones and he felt for a moment the pressure of blood in his veins: *dear life*. Mercy Winstead had called him "David."

Mercy did not change color. She had not noticed her own slip. She sat across from him at the tea service, chattering, pale, freckled. She had carried the crockery in on a silver tray, here to his own office. The ribbons on her cap had streamed with the current of her excitement, and she had called him "David!"

The superintendent recognized that she had not heard her own words. What would Sigmund Freud have to say about that, he wondered. He pursued this thought conscientiously. He missed Mercy's next sentence. Experience had taught him, however, that women re`peat themselves, if a man simply holds his peace.

Mercy repeated: "Lucy refused to put her money in the safe! She told me she wanted it in the First National Bank where it would draw interest. She wants it in the name of Janina Lucy Valenta and she wants the deposit book to carry in her pocket!"

Grafton carefully lit his pipe. This was another action a man could perform in order to play for time while the flush of life receded. "Excellent," he said at last. "Amazing, if you think about it." *Wanting* was an assertion of life, of healthy ego. A patient who had come to them drooping between two officers, no sense of self to her at all, was now asserting a right to manage her finances.

He considered it a personal triumph, a vindication of his reforms. "Let's get the deposit book locked in her cubby, at least. But give it to her any time she wants."

·

People tend to enter the profession of psychiatry because of a yearning to save a loved one irrevocably lost. Usually a mother. Coupled with Presbyterian rigor, a man's compulsion to do good becomes the driving force of his career. Personal suffering matters little on the Presbyterian high road: he must do good.

And when, as now, he feels his efforts bearing fruit, such a man feels an almost religious exaltation. David Grafton smiled.

His own nightmares had withdrawn a little. His favorite patient, Lucy Valenta, was progressing. His favorite conundrum, Mrs. Annie Leary, seemed to be opening herself to his new experiments with the "talking therapy."

Human affairs often swirl toward these satisfying climaxes, like the first movement of a concerto. There had been the transformation of Sylvie, the supposed deaf-mute. Dr. Jessen-Haight, a perpetual subversive annoyance, had calmed down under the influence of his Alsatian widow. He thrived under the flattery of Dr. Grafton's humble questions about psychoanalysis. Dr. Dominic Kennedy had lost weight. Nurse Mercy Winstead had managed to train most of her hair under a cap. She had stopped giggling. She had called him "David."

He relaxed his face and allowed himself the pleasure of the moment, though he knew the music could soon change key and demons awake, demons in, say, A-minor.

Nurse Winstead poured more tea, "playing mother," as she put it.

Grafton drew back his cup with a startled motion that rattled the silver.

"I'm sorry, sir."

"No matter." He confided that he really didn't care for tea.

Mercy smiled. The superintendent feared the smile might not

be for him, but for joy in her intellectual quest. "I think," she went on, "we still need to figure out how she came by all this money."

"Did you simply ask her?"

"I did, of course. She told me her husband's housekeeper gave it to her. *Payment for services*, the woman said. This Mrs. Lerner."

It was charming, Grafton thought, how Mercy Winstead could raise one of her brows, darker than her hair, and suggest worlds of irony.

Mercy watched the lines on the superintendent's forehead deepen, tiny fans wrinkle around his eyes. She interpreted: *concern*. Was he worried? Shocked?

She lowered her own gaze. What kind of services had Lucy been compelled to perform in the course of her so-called marriage? This was not an appropriate conversation for Mercy to initiate. She cut her eyes toward the open door of Grafton's office. Nurse Passmore was right next door, her own door ajar. They had asked her, for the sake of propriety, to join them, but she had declined.

"We have to get hold of this housekeeper. She'll lead us to the husband," the superintendent said, quite loudly. Perhaps for the benefit of Olivia Passmore.

•

Upright at her desk, not drowsy at all, the Director of Nursing took up the challenge. Sunlight crept across her desk. It seemed to have absorbed energy from the flowering outside.

She had heard the young nurse carol out "David!" and she had rolled her eyes. No, she didn't want to join them. In her austere and nostalgic way, she supported whatever courtship was in progress.

But, more importantly, she needed to pull herself up to the demands of professional responsibility.

She had to ring Wally Norton.

She was ashamed of her collusion, as she now thought it to be, with the sheriff. He'd told her they had to keep the thing—whatever the thing was, exactly—quiet, but look where that led?

CHAPTER TWENTY-FOUR

Missing paperwork. Perhaps an unjust commitment.

She brooded over the possibility that Wally Norton, with the droopy eyes and droopy moustache that made a woman want to help him out, had lied to her. And implicated her in his lie. And stolen the papers on Lucy Valenta's case?

The sheriff had sealed Lucy's fate, and Nurse Passmore had given him her full support.

Not all narcissistic girls deserved to be incarcerated.

Olivia Passmore felt she had to make it right.

CHAPTER TWENTY-FIVE

THE RECTORY PHONE rang a little after midnight. Three doors opened along the assistant pastors' hallway. Pete Van Cleve still wore his white shirt, clerical bib and black trousers. Pat Riordan's hair was standing up in a crest and his eyes blinked nervously in the electric light Monsignor had recently installed. Will Allen had thrown a bathrobe over his nakedness. He'd been preparing to leave the world; he'd been scribbling a note about the disposition of his worldly goods and had thought it fitting to do that in a state of nature.

Van Cleve started down the hall. His ink-stained fingers reached toward the phone. Van Cleve needed little sleep and sat up half the night studying Greek. Everyone knew he planned to extricate himself from parish work by getting an appointment at the seminary. But for some reason he liked night call, and took more than his share. They called him the Vampire.

This time, Will Allen's hand motioned him back. He got to the phone first. Allen hated running sick calls in the empty, lonely, dark city. He was an extrovert. But lately he'd been doing all sorts of things his nature rebelled against. It was a form of penance.

Suicide? Certainly not! That was the unforgiveable sin against the Holy Ghost. He intended to enter a monastery. An austere seclusion more radical than priesthood. This was the archbishop's solution and Will had snapped at it gratefully.

"Hello, Central, I can't understand you," the other priests heard him say. Then Allen turned his back on the watchers and leaned against the wall, cupping the phone to his ear.

So it was personal then. The other men retired to their rooms.

It was a poor connection and Will barked into the mouth-piece as if to clear the wires. "Mrs. Lerner, I can't make out what you're saying."

Her voice came through to him clearly then, the righteous whine all too audible, "I said, Father, I have bad news about your mother."

When had there ever been good news?

"Has she taken a turn? Did you send for Quinn?" The farm wasn't on the phone, yet, and to bring out the doctor meant waking the hired man, that Arvid, and hitching up the team.

Where was she calling from?

"Where are you, Mrs. Lerner?"

"The hospital in Cannon Falls. I had them come and get her in the ambulance"—a shabby wreck of a vehicle, war surplus. "Then I came along with the Bjornsons next door. They have the car, now, and Hal had to be to Northfield for the auctions. Arvid was drunk. I got there before she did. Even after walking that mile. To the Bjornson's."

"Oh, Mrs. Lerner." His mother had begged to stay in her own house, her shell of memory. But Mrs. Lerner was given to petty cruelties and larger ones if she could manage them. It seemed an impulse she could scarcely control. All the while complaining of her martyrdom. "And what's happening now?" Will asked.

"She passed, I said."

In that burst of static from the telephone.

Will Allen felt something like an exhalation leave his own lungs and the world around him, the dim hallway, the priests' residence, the parish, the city of St. Paul. This was what it felt like to lose someone big as a mother.

He would have to remain in this world now for a few more weeks, long enough to honorably bury her.

"Why didn't you keep her at home?" He couldn't restrain the accusation his words implied. Nola Lerner had promised.

The second motion of his spirit was self-recrimination: why should Nola Lerner, why should anybody, honor any request of his?

I am a worm and no man. The words of the psalm came to his mind.

Still, she had ignored his mother's last wish.

"I couldn't cope with"—the static, the interventions of Central: a black-haired monster of a woman, he imagined, listening in. He knew what Mrs. Lerner couldn't cope with. *She'd had it*, as she so often said. She hadn't signed on for this: intrigue, hysteria and death.

Well.

Will Allen sighed and rested his head against the wall. On the other side of it, he could feel Riordan's sorry bumping.

"I'll be down on the milk train," he said. He'd have liked to drive, but the train was faster. "Did she have the last rites?" he asked. But the connection had broken up again.

•

In the lantern light of small stations, the train's window glass reflected more of Will Allen than he wanted to see.

He considered his options.

There was castration.

He had heard about priests seeking surgical intervention, or doing the job themselves—farm boys who'd done the simple procedure on hundreds of ram lambs or calves. There would be a snip, a little blood. Nothing an experienced man couldn't accomplish in the privacy of his bathroom.

Or were those just seminary legends? He'd scoffed. But he'd been a boy, only fourteen, when he entered the minor seminary. Asleep to the wiles of women and the grinding imperative of men.

He longed to be free of that need.

"We all fall down," Joe Haggerty had said. Will didn't believe it. He couldn't imagine Haggerty, for example. Or Pete Van Cleve.

Will knew he was different from other men: more athletic, more charming, more daring, face it, more attractive. Things easily fell into his hands. Moreover he believed his temptations to sexual sin pressed harder than other men's. Likely his vocation to the priesthood had been hopeless from the start. His mother's dream, not God's.

Too late to back out now. Five years ago he'd lain on the stone floor of the Cathedral and felt the archbishop's anointing hand: *Tu es sacerdos in aeternum.*" You are a priest forever." The sacrament of Ordination, like Baptism, made an eternal mark on the soul. And the archbishop, his uncle, had pressed hard.

Will Allen imagined something like a branding iron, searing a holy seal.

The thought of the pain attracted him, stirred him sexually even.

What a monster of perversity he was! Will savored the dramatic phrase.

He was a sinner who should not be allowed to breathe the air of normal people. In sinning, also, he excelled. He needed a well to throw himself down, a dungeon, a cell.

The archbishop was arranging that exit for him: a cloistered monastery where men whipped themselves with small chains in the watches of the night.

The train clicked through rural stations. It devoured the awakening countryside. Light winked in the windows of barn after barn. At each village crossroad, humble men were arriving in one-horse carts with their rattling cans of milk. Then home to their wives. This, anyway, was the script Father Will Allen wrote for the humble men.

He suffered a wealthy, talented, sinful man's envy of dairy farmers.

He needed Lucy. The knowledge renewed his horror at his own capacity for destruction. How many priests, like him, needed one Lucy or another?

Surely, not many. He honored the priesthood in his mind at the same time as he degraded it with his body.

He wondered again about surgical castration.

How could he possibly put things right? He was a wealthy

man, wealthier now that his mother was dead. Archdiocesan priests didn't take a vow of poverty and his father had owned the Bank of Northfield.

He'd already paid off Nola Lerner in spades. What could he, must he, do for Lucy?

A private sanitarium, perhaps.

For the girl was vividly insane. He had no doubt.

But now that Lucy had ceased being a whore to his imagination, she rose in the rags of a ruined madonna. And he had ruined her. Treated her without mercy.

But how else did a man claim his own? His father had licked the two of them, Will and his mother. "Licked" was a mild word. "Took the belt to us," he'd bragged in the seminary dining room once or twice, when the subject of a man's rights and prerogatives came up.

And Lucy was hopelessly insane.

(Or had he made that up?)

He'd tried to knock sense into her. That was another phrase of his father's.

He saw his father's face in the train window, leaning toward him. He despised the image. He thought of his mother, the sound of her body hitting the walls of the bedroom down the hall from his. Her cries. At the age of eleven, he'd conflated this commotion with "the act of marriage." The next day, her bruised face. He would look away. She, on other occasions, would ignore her son's blackened eyes, once, the broken fingers.

He hated his mother. He hated their covenant of weakness.

But, as for Lucy, he must make amends. Though she had brought it on herself, with her manipulative grace, her flirting. Daughters of Eve.

His own conduct? Blame it on the drink. His mother would, with those words, excuse his father. He loved his mother, the long-suffering woman.

CHAPTER TWENTY-FIVE

He forgave himself and deferred castration.
But at least he should visit her, Lucy.
The poor woman. He had promised to visit her.

CHAPTER TWENTY-SIX

WANT. SYLVIE WANT. Finger sign laboriously rendered. *Zadat Sylvie.* Everyone on the docile ward knew that much of her finger-babble now.

Marjorie Salton looks up from her knitting. Her needles are big, blunt, size 12. She's a good knitter and the lack of decent equipment outrages her. All she could knit with these monster pins would be mittens for the giant Santa the workers constructed every year on the roof of Men's Detached.

The yarn they give her is hideous as well. And better suited for the smaller needles she craves. If she ran the skeins together, maybe, it would give her the right gauge. If she mingled black with this lurid shade of rose, perhaps the effect would be more subtle.

She needs to make a case, at the ward meeting, that she will not stab anybody with small needles, nor hang herself with heavier yarn.

Marjorie sighs. Pleading exhausts her. She is sick, not crazy. She used to tell them so. And she's tired of dragging her wheezing body around.1 Crippled, constricted in her breathing. Sad and prone to the vapors, as Nurse Malloy puts it.

The polio epidemic of ought-nine ended her chances. The unfairness overwhelms her sometimes. Her chances for a husband, children, better needles, better yarn.

The feral child, Sylvie, crawls to Marjorie across the floor of the dayroom, muttering nonsense. "Aaahn…" she squeaks. A general complaint, or the name of her beloved? Annie Leary. Marjorie has no interest in what the child's trying to say.

She takes a handkerchief from her box and helps Sylvie to wipe her snuffles. The girl has a cold, and that's why she has to stay in while all the others are picnicking by the pond.

Marjorie doesn't want the company. She couldn't go on the picnic herself because her crutches catch in the mole-holes. If they would do something about the moles, Marjorie could get outside more often. But, no.

Her needs are not high on the ward's priorities. Her needs have never been on anybody's list. There have always been favorites ahead of her. Just now, Miss Valenta and Mrs. Leary. They get taken out on a daily rotation to meet with the doctors. It's assumed they can make significant progress.

Marjorie knows she will not make progress, and no one rotates her any place interesting.

Sylvie screeches like a monkey from the Como Park Zoo. Why doesn't Nurse Cupcake take the child away? To bed, or somewhere.

Marjorie looks hopefully toward the dais, where a student nurse is immersed in a report, her lip caught in her crooked little teeth.

Sylvie grabs hold of the yarn and pulls it out of Marjorie's hands. "Aahn…" she pleads again.

Marjorie takes up her crutch and strikes.

Now the girl is a ball of snot and screaming. Nurse Cupcake has to come down from heaven and intervene. "What the hell?" she says.

Very unprofessional.

The feral child springs and runs down the ward.

Who let her in here? That animal.

This is a ward for docile women, who can cope. Who should be allowed proper knitting needles.

CHAPTER TWENTY-SEVEN: ANNIE

I KNOW WHAT psychoanalysis is. I've read. You talk your heart out to a sympathetic listener until you feel better (Hoskins, vol. 4). It seems a soothing practice in theory, though it requires courage, and truthfulness. Dr. Grafton and I are learning to trust each other.

But who among us can trust ourselves? You who have followed my story so far, do you think I'm telling the truth? Here's a concept I ran into in my studies: *the unreliable narrator.* Huck Finn is the best example. I'm sure we'd all agree on that.

But Huck lies mostly for fun, and there's no harm in it.

Hamlet. There's a player for you. We're putting on *Hamlet* for the fall co-production. Dr. Kennedy is dieting, so he looks good in the tights for his college girl.

Hamlet doesn't know what's real. Which of us does? Or we can't stand to face it. Or we can't remember.

Whatever. I agree to Grafton's experiment. He's polite enough to ask my permission to sit down and listen to me an hour or so a day. He admits he hasn't perfected his technique; he's learning from Dr. Jessen-Haight.

It sounds to me like a good diversion. Much as I like 2 North, I miss my private space. All the to-ing and fro-ing interrupts my thought process. Some of these ladies could do with time in the muffs.

A diversion, but fraught with danger. I don't know what I might remember. What I fear above all is that they were right, whatever it was they said. *They*: faces with moving mouths. But silent.

I'm taking the chance because of Lucy and our child.

David Grafton is asking: "What do you want, above all?"

What we all want is a place to be strong, I think.

But how much to say?

Behind his desk, an alcove of windows opens onto skyscape. With the soft light behind him—he's adjusted the blinds just right so as not to give me that precipitous headache—I can't quite make out his features. It's as though he's erased himself to give me space, made himself into a neutral attention, like a dog's, to whom I can tell my story. Thinking about Nurse Passmore's Rufus, I smile.

Since Dr. Grafton's eyes are not quite available to meet mine, I examine the objects on his desk. I've never seen such toys, little figures in terra cotta, a bronze cat. Lucy would be playing with them by now. There's an ink well and a set of pens. An hour glass, through which the white sand runs. Nothing else.

"You're smiling," he says.

Well, I don't want to mention the dog.

His question about what I want above all hangs in the air. My answer remains stuck behind my teeth: I want a place where I can be strong. Real.

For some, it's easy. They just puff themselves up and fill their clothes.

I used to look out the windows of 4 North that overhang the circular drive to Admitting, where people from town come to picnic. Each of them their own person, leading a horse, catching a child by the dress.

Looking out, I would think about the train ride with Samuel up from Richmond, Indiana to the Union Depot in St. Paul. The porters would smile at us, each porter self-contained, knowledgeable. Couples rather like us and couples very different from us sitting side by side, each person in charge of his own business. Single men with chewing tobacco. Boys running up and down the aisles. Women, young women even, in wool suits going somewhere alone.

On 4 North, going somewhere alone was the height of my aspirations.

Now I want to go somewhere with Lucy. Both of us Real.

I must not say this to Dr. Grafton, however drowsily pleasant it may be to sit here in the sunlight of his office and think about my life.

After that long-ago trip from Indiana, I didn't see much of the streets of St. Paul, Minnesota. But I sit here now, peopling the city in my mind's eye with men and women in charge of themselves, going about daily life.

I picture Lucy and me and our child walking among them. In my vision the child is indistinct, maybe a girl, maybe a boy.

When I remember my father's house, I remember being strong, though of course this power was mostly illusion. Even with my terrible, comical, unpredictable fits, I was protected. Being protected, I was able to be quite a lot of my own person. Contained within a frame that made sense. I couldn't be caught off-base, like a runner in our backyard baseball games. I had a role to play, and people around me who would close the circle if I fell. At home, in church, at the singing meets, I was no shadow.

When I married Sam, I thought he'd protect me and I would thrive. You know, I always thought I'd get over the fits, because that's what people said who loved me, "Oh, I've seen it before. It's a phase they go through, like holding their breath and turning blue. As soon as she grows a little, it'll get better." Even the doctor in Richmond held out hope.

But I didn't get better, and Sam wasn't the protector I'd imagined.

To look at it from his point of view, I suppose he thought that love would conquer all. He thought I'd grow up—for, really, I hadn't even reached my full height by the time Julia was born—I'd be well. He would be a tree for me that I could shelter against till that day I'd be well. His confidence carried me—I was sixteen, with Julia.

•

"You seem far away," David Grafton says.

Oh! I must give him something back! Like Scheherazade in the *Arabian Nights*. I must offer a tantalizing bit of story. It's quite the privilege, my nurses remind me, to be taken off the ward for these sessions. It means Dr. Grafton thinks I can get better.

The thought of getting better fills me with shimmers of warmth, succeeded by cold. But, on the whole, I want to enchant him like any foreign princess. I will my body to flood itself with just the right temperature. I raise my eyes to meet the place where his eyes must be.

•

David Grafton watches Annie's gaze slide from the windows and focus easily on him. Her calmness surprises the superintendent. He's used to the evasive glances of mad people, listening for voices in the radiator or cast down in depression.

The psychiatric literature coming out of Europe tells him that insanity—or that evolving concept, neurosis—originates in childhood trauma, but he can find little of this in Annie Leary's story—nor in Lucy Valenta's, either. (He thinks of them, now, as a unit, a two-part problem to solve.) Both of their upbringings had been, to say the least, unconventional, but he's found no evidence of abuse or mistreatment. Just the poverty.

"I'm not used to conversation." Annie Leary finally responds to his observation.

This is obvious. Sometimes she talks in the cadences of the King James Bible—well, that's the southern thing. Sometimes she talks like a character out of Jane Austen. She's spent the last four years—what Grafton's beginning to call her healthy years—reading in the corner. And watching her cohort with the attention of a medical student.

Now her tranquil face seems ready to respond to further questions. Grafton struggles for the right ones, the ones that will deliver them both to understanding.

What the superintendent loves above all in psychiatric practice is the pivotal moment when he grasps a patient's inner condition. Views it from inside, so to speak. To go there, several elements must be in place: he, himself, must be at rest and *not wanting*. The patient must open to him, not-fearing.

And he must be strong, and brave as a surgeon trepanning a skull.

Because, when he gets into the mind of a patient, deep in, he has to hold on for them both. And get himself out intact.

Psychiatric practice resembled in so many ways the work of the forward dressing station at Second Ypres.

Where must he go to find her? To bring her back? Where is she? The hourglass runs.

He surrenders himself. He lets her condition engulf his own. He allows himself to feel the loneliness of her life, the horror of her memories, the depth of her grief—or shame: which is it? Her hope.

No, he *wants* too much.

Or her inner world is too dark.

He pulls back, reinforces his boundaries.

He will travel that path with her, but slowly, carefully. Careless probing might send her into a regression from which she'd never recover. She might spend the rest of her life tied to a bed on 4 North.

Psychiatry was such a balancing act. You could heal, or you could send a patient into the depths. Maybe along with yourself.

Grafton bows his head, like a penitent. *Deliver us from evil,* he thinks; it's not quite a prayer, but a generalization. He must be ready to back up a little.

"Tell me about your time with us. Do you remember how you came to be here?" he asks.

•

Lord revive us, I think.

He looks so sad.

I want to blurt out, "What happened to you in that war Lucy told me about?"

194

But, no blurting. What would Miss Austen write? She would beat around the bush for five or six pages.

I have to follow the advice I gave Lucy. Keep your focus. Think about what you want and the way to get it. I want to live with Lucy and Sylvie on a little farm in the Cannon Valley, with a couple of goats and a swing for Baby.

I don't want to go to jail or be returned to the back of beyond, 4 North.

Achieving this dream will call for one of Daddy's own miracles.

It looks impossible. But, for the first time in years, I have a goal in mind. Something besides *get through the day, read*. The goal gives me a rush of psychic energy. I fasten it all on Dr. Grafton, whose lips are moving again.

•

"If you take yourself back to the last thing you remember living outside, what might that be?"

Blood on the floor.

It must be mine. If nobody gets to me fast enough in my falling fits, one of my brothers or sisters or Sam—and Sam is dead—I remember now—that fact fills me like a sow caught in the doorway of my mind—if nobody gets to me fast enough, there's always a river of blood. I hit my head, or I bloody my nose. Maybe some fool has stuck something in my mouth and I've bitten him. I'm feeling so mean, as I often do in the fits, that this idea gives me pleasure.

Blood, screaming, shattered glass.

And then a plank in reason broke/And I fell down and down.

When I woke up, three years had passed.

This is not much to report. Oh, Annie, find your tongue!

Grafton bends over his notebook, skidding along with his handsome silver filigreed pen. Apparently I have told him something.

I would like a pretty pen. They give me only pencils.

"Mrs. Leary, do you know you have a seizure disorder?" He looks up to ask me this.

"Yes, sir, I do. The doctor in Richmond told me so."

"Right. Well, since you were admitted in"—he consults his notes—"in '13, medical science has made strides in understanding temporal lobe epilepsy, which is the precise name for your condition."

Congratulations, I want to say. Let Medical Science take a bow. How does that help me? Can we treat it? No.

We. I've promoted myself to staff. Well, I've read every monograph that comes into the library. Probably I know more about the falling sickness than anybody here.

What I know is I could fall forever and nobody would catch me.

A little lick of despair tickles my consciousness. There is always the temptation to give up, slip back into the moving water. Let them drag me out and tie me down and fill my mouth with cotton till I choke.

But, Lucy.

•

Grafton plays with his pen. In a way, he thinks of this as an intake interview. Nobody seems ever to have offered Annie one. He ought to ask her more about her background, her husband and children. But those simple questions, in her case, may lead to the abyss. Perhaps to regression. At best, loss of trust.

"Do I correctly understand that you remember nothing of your married life?" Even this is a risky question. Grafton finds himself praying the prayer of the trenches, addressed to no god in particular.

But she rises to it with her clear and honest look. "I remember my wedding, the life we had on the farm. I remember being pregnant."

•

I come to a wall, there. I push against it. The wall becomes a door. "I'm told she was born. I remember *you have a little girl.*" I offer these details to Grafton's pen.

My body memories end, though, with that turn of a fishtail in my belly. Later, I tied together what people told me, sentences cleft away from any physical reality. "You're going to have another child, Mrs. Leary…You're *that way* again, Annie (accusation in the voice)…You have a boy, Annie…Where is your husband, Mrs. Leary?"

Are these memories? No.

They are sentences on a blackboard, written by a teacher I can't see. Somebody else's words. *Copy these sentences on your slates, children.*

•

Grafton watches disorientation grow in her eyes, and he sees, too, that she is trying hard to tell him something. She is walking a corridor where no medals are given out, though she is as brave as anyone he's seen under fire. "That's enough, Mrs. Leary. That's just fine. Thank you for telling me that. You don't have to remember. Just rest, now."

•

He turns the hourglass over and I watch time run backward. I feel drowsy in the sunlight, warm.

But a snake detaches itself from a pile of snakes that den in my mind. It starts to slither forward. The snake opens its jaws and prepares to speak. I know what it has to say, and I don't want to hear it. "You killed your children, Annie Leary. You killed your husband, who loved you. You murdered in cold blood three little babies."

I know how to handle this snake. *This is old news*, I tell it. Go away with your hissing.

This is the way to send him back to his den. "Come back to me when you have something new to tell."

Because I have no body-story to accommodate the facts the snake puts forth.

There is a wax recording in my brain that spins out other people's words, other people's accusations.

•

Grafton watches her struggle not to get lost. He himself feels rising panic. He forces it back. He should not have pushed her so hard. He feels sweat blooming in the armpits of his carefully ironed shirt.

"Mrs. Leary, can you please just try to breathe with me," he tells her.

He inhales.

•

I don't want to breathe with him.

I want to go inside myself and track a song.

Bright morning stars are rising.
Bright morning starts are rising.
Bright morning starts are rising.

•

I do trust him, I think.

I find myself humming softly despite my best intentions to put on the semblance of a normal woman. He's doing his best.

I smile as the song warms up my mind, repels the cold-blooded reptile.

Grafton doesn't know the music but I sense he's with me. Maybe he can get me where I have to go, for Lucy's sake. Not because he's so smart, but because he's so wounded. Because of what he himself has seen. Blood on the floor.

Daylight is breaking in my soul.

It's not true about the daylight, but it *could* come to be true.

The sands have stalled in the glass. Dr. Grafton has tapped that little button I know he has under the desk, next to his knee. At the glass of his office door, veiled as it is with a lace curtain, I see the shadow of the nurses who will take me back to 2 North.

•

Grafton is alone. His fluent pen glides across his notebook. He feels relief, gratitude and a tiny flare of professional pride: *that was a rather close call.*

But she'd faced it. She did not slide backward. She let him stand with her. He gives himself credit.

He's exhausted. He sits in the middle of a circle of energy, worn out. Annie, Lucy, Mercy. He adds: the Legislature, his peers, the crusading newspaperman who keeps trying to get an interview.

Annie might be innocent of her crime, the voices say, and perhaps that could be proven.

It would take a good lawyer.

Who would pay for that?

Or, other voices cut in, he could be deceived. He must not allow himself to be charmed by her. He might be working hard to release a psychopath on the community, demolish his reputation forever. And endanger the innocent.

Conflicted, Grafton tries to separate the threads. He ponders Mrs. Leary's fixation on Lucy's pregnancy.

Suppose Annie is what the law found her to be: a homicidal maniac?

Psychopath, in more clinical terms.

He thinks it over. Psychopaths are not mentally ill, in the true sense. They are not even all dangerous. Some of them seem to be the products of a purely evil, incomprehensible (to him) gestation and generation. Demonic, the old religions would have said. Such specimens cannot be cured and must never be trusted. But they are not insane…"according to the present state of our knowledge," Grafton concludes, as though he were composing a scientific paper.

He keeps the pen moving.

Probably such people belong in a maximum security prison. That's where Annie had been headed, when the State of Minnesota intervened.

It had taken an act of faith for Grafton to move Annie to 2 North; this signaled a decision, if only within himself, that she was not seriously disordered. That she could be rehabilitated. He had already, at an instinctual level, cast his vote.

She'd been under restraint for seven years. There was something biblical about the number. After coming out of the initial catatonia, she'd had a couple of petit mal seizures and one grand mal but nothing had happened recently. Some patients outgrew epilepsy.

At no time had she behaved destructively toward another patient. On the contrary, she'd befriended the more vulnerable inmates and helped out when she could. She'd written two shelves of journals. She'd taught the deformed child Sylvana Sztamburski the musical interval of a fourth and enough sign language to get her needs met without a tantrum.

If he, Grafton thought, had endured Annie's ordeal, he'd be a gibbering idiot tied to a ring in the wall instead of the man with the keys.

She was charming.

Of course psychopaths knew how to enchant.

But there was something wrong with the syllogism: Psychopaths are charming, Annie is charming, therefore Annie is a psychopath.

Or, hell, it was just stupid.

Grafton sighed.

On the wall facing his desk was the portrait of an old man in mutton chop whiskers who had been the second director of the Northfield State Hospital: one of Grafton's predecessors, Dr. Winston Highgate. Highgate had left behind him a diagnostic protocol that someone with a sense of humor had posted beneath his picture. A man's legacy. It summarized the principal reasons for commitment to Northfield State Hospital for the year ending July 31, 1877.

Looking at it every day for three years, Grafton had memorized the list, and would recite portions of it to himself in the tedium of staff meetings, like a catechism: anxiety, anger, apoplexy, abuse, approaching matrimony, avarice, business troubles, chorea, consulting fortune teller, climacteric, congenital idiot, congestion of brain, domestic troubles, diabetes, disappointed affections, dissipation, diphtheria, death of a child, mother, parents, brother, sister, friends, dyspepsia, deafmute, drowning of child, mother, parents, brother, sister, friend, embolism, epilepsy, eryphilis, excessive study, excitement, exhaustion from travelling, excommunication, fright, fear of starving, fever, finance, grief, heredity, hysteria, injury to head, intemperance, masturbation, overwork, religious excitement, sexual excess, sunstroke, syphilis, typhoid, worry.

He added to the *n*'s: *no place else to go.*

A new day was dawning in the science of the mind. Grafton thought of himself as one of its avatars. Yet, as they entered the second decade of the twentieth century, a census of the wards might yield much the same quaint diagnostic criteria.

Epilepsy.

Of course, medical science understood it to be a physical disease. But most clinicians still tied the falling sickness to an underlying mental, or even moral, disorder.

Could a woman kill her family in the course of a grand mal seizure?

Grafton thought a woman would be too busy.

But again, Annie's interest in Lucy Valenta's baby rose to trouble him. What if she were an epileptic *and* a psychopath?

He must gently lead Annie Leary to remember and speak about what had happened. She must lay it out for him to analyze.

Analysis was the new psychiatric craze.

But by now her memory was deeply repressed.

Hypnosis?

Something of a carnival trick. He didn't trust it.

Perhaps he could interview the sheriff and gain access to the legal records. The idea of playing detective amused him a little.

These things took time.

Meanwhile, his phone was ringing. "Yes," said Grafton into the mouthpiece, thinking "No."

CHAPTER TWENTY-EIGHT

WHEN WILL ALLEN put in his call to the superintendent of the Northfield State Hospital, he wondered whether to introduce himself as a disgraceful husband or a disgraceful priest.

Will wasn't sure which he was. Confusion was a product of what Joe Haggerty called his system of delusions. Haggerty dabbled in the new science of psychology, so helpful to parish priests and men who had to deal with the archbishop.

How much did the superintendent already know about him? he wondered.

Finally he skipped a polite introduction, but spoke diffidently into the phone. "I'm inquiring into the welfare of a patient called Lucy Valenta, or, ah, perhaps Mrs. Allen."

There was silence. Perhaps the line had gone down. Should he rattle the switch hook, or would that make things worse?

"Doctor?" he tried again. "I'm wondering if I might visit her."

The silence continued, but Will sensed a presence at the other end of the connection.

He closed his eyes on the room, the better to concentrate, but the room continued to press its claim on him. He was in an alcove off the chilly cell in the funeral home where his mother's body lay. He had twined his own rosary around her fingers; the brown beads asserted a masculine pragmatism foreign to her nature. She'd have hated that. He'd taken the rosary back. His stomach lurched at the touch of her cold, stiffening hands.

The undertaker's wife had offered a set of pretty crystals. No doubt they had spares. He'd stepped back, unable to repeat the

202

gesture, or any other. The undertaker's wife slipped the beads around his mother's fingers and raised an eyebrow in his direction. He nodded, *yes, you can close the casket.*

"May I make a phone call?" He couldn't help being abrupt. Likely the undertaker was used to that. He'd gestured toward the alcove.

The small town funeral parlor was also a furniture store, and the little niche was an office that served both businesses. It was papered in advertising circulars that whispered of domesticity and—that recurring theme—a simpler life. He found himself unconsciously shopping, as the operator put through the call. Shopping for a new identity, becoming in reverie a man who might own a suite of Stickley furniture.

He closed his eyes and pressed a hand against them. He was worn out. He dropped into a chair at the undertaker's desk, silence lengthening. "Are you there?" he said softly into the mouthpiece of the phone.

There was an audible breath from the receiver at last: words. "Am I speaking to Mr. Allen?" the superintendent asked.

"Ah, yes."

Then came a sentence Will had heard twice in the last week, once from Haggerty, once from his uncle, the archbishop: "Man, what are you thinking?"

Will Allen had kept trying to answer the question. He had his integrity. But he could not do so here, next to his mother's coffin. "I mean," he ventured, "is Lucy very ill?"

There was a gathering of energy over the phone wires. But the superintendent, when he responded, had become controlled, bureaucratic. "Mrs. Allen is unable to receive visitors at present."

"I see, of course, when—?"

The line went definitively dead.

The undertaker was standing in the doorway again. No doubt these calls were expensive. Will Allen had never paid a bill, personally, in his life. He handled financial transactions by stuffing an envelope with more bills than could possibly be required and shoving it over. People never complained.

"I will be putting your mother's body on the 10:00 a.m. train, Father," the undertaker said. He took off his white, clinical apron, and hung it by the door. He took a green eyeshade from the same hook and put it on. "O'Halloran's is prepared to receive her on the other end, and they'll plan the wake for the Cathedral."

Of course. For a priest's mother, every cleric in the diocese would show up. For the archbishop's sister.

"You'll be accompanying the body, I presume?"

"I, ah, no. I have a bit of business in town. I'll be going back this evening."

Cannon Falls was five miles from the Northfield Asylum.

He'd walk it.

•

At his end, David Grafton clutched the phone. Anger could make him voluble, but fury buried itself in some deep stillness. He raised his eyes to Nurse Passmore. Something had called her from next door. Had he shouted? Had he whispered? "It's the husband," he breathed, a hand over the mouthpiece, though, to his regret, he'd intemperately broken the connection. "He wants to visit."

Nurse Passmore stood silent.

•

In the end, Will Allen hadn't walked to the asylum. His polished black shoes weren't up to the job. He'd begged a lift from the sheriff's office. Once again, he needed the confiding presence of a manly man. The sheriff already knew the worst of it. He was an old friend of Will's father, had known Will from boyhood. He belonged to the Knights of Columbus.

"We'll just sit up on the hill, there, Billie," Wally Norton said. "They walk outside at one o'clock, after lunch. Everyone's used to my car and we won't draw attention. You can look your fill of her, and then I'll take you to the train station."

CHAPTER TWENTY-EIGHT

The sheriff was an experienced, compassionate man, and who didn't love Billie?

They parked on the drive just above Men's Detached. Will could watch the rag-tag procession of inmates pass below. It cheered him to see Lucy in the midst of her friends. Surely she was at peace. She was laughing and walking hand in hand with a grotesque little dwarf. She'd gained weight...

No.

No.

Will's eyes filled with the tears of his own tender drama.

He looked at the sheriff, who knew the worst of everything. Now this.

"It happens all the time," the sheriff said. "The kind of men who work there."

But Will was an only child. He had no idea how to calculate the duration of a woman's pregnancy. He was counting now, in panic, the brown beads he'd just taken from his mother's hand.

CHAPTER TWENTY-NINE

"Excuse me, sir."

It was a week later when the tall blond girl, from the new class at Anchor Hospital, roused David Grafton from his correspondence. She wore a grill of pleated lace on her head like a Belgian peasant. "I wanted to report that a gentleman is here inquiring for Miss Valenta."

Christ, had the husband dared to disobey him?

"Mrs. Allen," Grafton corrected sharply. He returned a yellow newspaper clipping to a file marked *Leary*. He glanced truculently at the young nurse.

"I'm sorry, sir. The gentleman asked for Lucy Valenta." The blond girl shifted her shoulders in a demi-shrug. Almost insolent.

"Yes, yes."

If the husband dared show his face here, Grafton required a word with him.

The superintendent rose from his desk and went to the window, which gave him an easy view of people arriving.

There was a handsome Bentley parked out there. A uniformed chauffeur was standing beside it, drumming his fingers on the hood. With the chauffeur stood a man in black clericals, foreign looking. He was gesticulating like an Italian. Grafton noted the Roman collar.

"He wants to speak to you after he visits Mrs. Allen, sir."

"He will not see Mrs. Allen. He will see me."

But no, no, this could not be the husband.

The chauffeur was handing a stout old man, clothed in black, out of the Bentley. The gold of an episcopal cross gleamed on his chest.

Grafton frowned. "Whom shall I be speaking to?" he asked the student.

She read it carefully off a visiting card: "His Excellency Paul Gregory Donovan, Archbishop of St Paul."

"Well." Grafton bit his lip. "Give me a moment, please."

The young nurse began to back out the door. "No!" he called her back. "Order a coffee service, Nurse Torgesson."

CHAPTER THIRTY: LUCY

THE ARCHBISHOP OF St. Paul holds out his fat little hand, weighed down with a gold seal ring. I remember from my years at St. Joseph's Academy, where we were carefully instructed in Catholic protocol, that I am required not to shake his hand but to kiss the ring.

My response back then had been, "You're joking?" Czech Catholics are different from Irish Catholics. Hand-kissing is not in our line.

I decide to play dumb on this occasion. Although I believe you gain a string of indulgences from kissing a bishop's ring. For an archbishop you can probably ransom a soul from purgatory.

I think about Papa and reconsider my strategy.

Perhaps Papa is in purgatory. It's a cold and cheerless place where lonely souls circle dreaming of God and raisin cake and (Papa) meeting Michelangelo Buonarroti.

Therefore, I force myself to nuzzle the cold, precious metal and to press the tips of thin-skinned episcopal fingers. I smell rosewater. The nails are immaculately manicured and buffed.

Papa always said you could tell a gentleman by his finger-nails. Here, then, is definitely a gentleman. I raise my eyes toward what I imagine will be the usual pompous containment of the powerful. But the archbishop's eyes are watery blue and set, each one, in a wreath of smile wrinkles. His face is white and red and babyish. He looks like one of the *putti* in Papa's book on the Sistine Chapel.

Against my will, I am drawn to him.

The archbishop says something in Latin which I discern to

208

be a blessing. Then he says, "Miss Valenta, Dr. Grafton tells me you are well enough to leave the grounds. Perhaps we might take a ride into Faribault and have lunch at the hotel. Would you like that?"

He's talking to me as he might to an eight-year-old, but I let that go, as Annie would. He doesn't know me after all, beyond the bare facts that I am a whore, a madwoman, a thief, an hysteric, and in the family way by one of his priests.

Where have they put *my* ring? I had a ring.

"Would you like to take a ride with Patrick and me?"

Who is Patrick?

I look past the archbishop's shoulder to the long windows that overlook the drive.

I see a man in a khaki uniform who looks like a soldier.

I see another man in a black suit who looks like a priest. I check to make sure it isn't Will. I've never seen Will in a Roman collar. I have only Mrs. Lerner's word that she ironed them for him. But this is a dark man talking nineteen to the dozen with his hands.

Sylvie would love him.

The archbishop shifts and follows my eyes. "That's Father Sebastiano. He's my secretary. And the man in uniform is Patrick, my chauffeur."

The idea of being driven across the countryside by a chauffeur attracts me, but I say "No, thank you."

The thought of riding around with a priest makes me queasy.

"Perhaps another time," says the archbishop. "I don't like automobiles myself," he goes on. "The scenery goes by in a blur, and there is so much noise and a bad smell."

Patrick must drive something like Will.

We have taken seats, now, in the visitor's parlor, on two matching plush chairs. I nod. I will give nothing away.

"I understand you are an artist, Miss Valenta."

I do not any longer like to be called "Mrs. Allen," not since that visiting day. But the archbishop's use of my maiden name twists a knife in the part of my gut not occupied by the baby. "I draw," I say. I try not to sound sullen.

"And do you paint?"

Where to begin?

Paint is expensive, canvas is expensive. And just now I am obsessed with the play of light and graphite on white paper. Or ink. Or charcoal. But especially pencil. This is fortunate because the asylum can, when it chooses, provide pencils.

"I would love to see your work."

Really. I flush a little, thinking about my nude studies of Will.

The archbishop gently raises this very issue, that is, the Will issue. "Father Allen tells me that he met you in an art class at the St. Paul Academy of Art and Design, when he was on his recent, er, sabbatical."

I drop my eyes and remain dumb in all senses of the word.

"I believe Father Allen was interested in drawing," the archbishop muses, as though to an inward listener. "And rather good at it."

•

Believe what you want, I think to myself.

I, too, had believed that Will was a serious student. A beginner, but talented. What is this "sabbatical" business? Will did tell me he was on some kind of leave-of-absence from his regular work. I assumed it was a vacation, such as rich people take whenever they choose. Will had the sheen of wealth, you couldn't miss it.

We met at the beginning of term. I was still in that period of excitement when my eyes were in love with everything I saw, with the sunflowers set out for us on the table, with the gradations of light on a pheasant's tail and the very idea of translating them into black and white. I was in love with every instructor, with the ceramicist, Miss Gideon, and with the young man at the next easel: that was Will.

Now I know that the art school made a lot of money from

the tuition of men like Will, dilettantes in the community who wanted to take drawing classes.

Especially those classes which displayed the human body in all its attitudes. In my inexperience, I had taken Will to be a serious fellow student. Maybe he was. He had talked about "finding himself," a luxury of the well-to-do. But the charcoal renderings on his block of white butcher paper were competent.

Perhaps he was just a rich boy—well, a rich priest—who wanted to draw naked ladies.

I imagine these ladies passing in procession before the archbishop's little *putti* face. His lips straighten into a tight line.

Well, the archbishop is nice, but he's Irish.

They don't see things the way we do, Papa had explained to me, as I'd made the transition from our Czech community in New Prague to the Irish in St. Paul.

We Czechs are earthy and take life as it comes. The Irish are dirty-minded, I had come to think.

I cast down my eyes before the archbishop.

I think about the line of Sylvie's spine as I observe it when I help the aides guide her naked out of the tub on bath night. I've heard them call her an ugly little thing, but that pure line defines her in my eyes. That architecture: this is the way I see the women on the wards, whatever is hung on them in the way of smocks, gray dresses, fat. They are lines, planes, dips, hollows. All of it singing.

Sometimes, looking out at the world, I'm so grateful for an artist's eyes that those eyes fill with tears as if I believed in God, like Annie does.

Mrs. Lerner just about finished God for me.

I feel a malicious urge to hurt the kind archbishop, with his innocent baby gaze and the way he turns down his rosebud mouth as though I've offered him turnips on a spoon. He gives me my opening.

"You were a model at the school, I believe," he says.

He is quite the believer.

I shake my head vehemently, *No.*

If I were mean, I would reveal how much his priest liked to look at my breasts, how uncomfortable that made me. Will demoted me from geometric angles to something else: whore. Maybe I would go on to tell Paul Gregory Donovan about riding around in Will's car, the gin and soda on the road to Decorah.

A priest. Even after cooling off on 4 North, I can barely get my mind around what Mrs. Lerner told me.

I decide, like some kind of witch in a fairytale, to spare the archbishop. However, I raise my eyes boldly to his. "We all modeled for each other, sir, all of the students."

I am supposed to call him "Your Excellency," I know, but I deprive him. He might be a good man, but I am only going to let him be a man.

Donovan puts his little white fingers together and asks, "Father Allen as well? He—modeled?"

Of course he is dying to ask if we took off our clothes, but I'm not going to give him the satisfaction. Everyone, even Nurse Malloy, wants to know about this. The answer, which I guard for my own amusement, would be "no." The male students, with their precious Life Class, had a professional model, we women had our sunflowers and dead rabbits. In class together, we bared no more than a pulse at the throat.

Those puritanical rules made no sense to me, after my experience in the mortuary and Papa's studio. But I was willing to draw my quota of rabbits if that's what it took to go to New York after Wanda.

The archbishop leans back in his chair. He has turned even whiter than when he came in.

Clearly he is not an art lover.

He opens his waistcoat and reaches in the direction of his heart. I'm afraid his mental pictures are giving him an angina attack, but he merely strokes the golden legs of Jesus on a pectoral cross.

Several minutes pass in this way. It's a little like having a session with Dr. Grafton. Then Paul Gregory Donovan closes his eyes, opens them, and says, "Miss Valenta, I've come here to offer you an apology."

I pat my belly, a habit I'm getting into. Practice for calming the baby. If I can somehow manage to keep the baby.

"Father Allen did a terrible thing to you, and he will pay the ultimate penalty."

What? Are they going to execute him?

"He is trying to make it right, though, of course, he cannot. Not completely. I only trust God in his mercy will bring grace out of what you've gone through." A breath. A sigh. "Father Allen confided to me you were a virgin when this, this happened." The little blue eyes close again.

Lord, what kind of inquisition have they put Will through, to get that piece of data?

"When he married me," I say demurely. *Where have they put my ring?*

Now the archbishop looks at me sharply. "Miss Valenta. Father Allen could not marry you. He is a priest of God."

"He did, though," I assert. I feel like an obnoxious schoolgirl.

"What did he think he was doing?" the archbishop asks.

Is he asking me? Himself? Jesus?—whose legs he still has hold of. Maybe it's a rhetorical question.

"He told me"—I continue in the role of bright pupil—"that a man and woman bestow the sacrament of matrimony on each other." I ferret around in my store of catechism. "It's like Baptism of Desire. Even if there is no witness, no ceremony. But we did have a ceremony, in Iowa."

Unceremonious as it had been. The judge reeling drunk.

Again the archbishop shuts his eyes. Fine lines appear and then disappear on his forehead.

He opens his eyes, takes some spectacles from his waistcoat pocket, and puts them on. He doesn't look more serious, he looks like a baby with spectacles. "Miss Valenta, Father Allen could not marry you. There is what we call a canonical impediment. You were raised a Catholic girl. Surely you understand that."

Is he trying to put the blame on me now?

Well, I was expecting it.

Though he has a point. In retrospect, how could I have believed Will? How could I not have seen the Roman collars Mrs. Lerner ironed?

I, who see everything.

Miss Valenta, how could you be so dim?

Because I wanted to believe Will. He was handsome and had beautiful hands. He wore that artistic, open-collared shirt that showed the fine bones of his neck. I had no idea why he didn't wear a cravat. Cross my heart. I didn't know that till Mrs. Lerner thrust her money and her story at me.

I shake my head, then I nod. Feeling dizzy.

Focus, Lucy.

I feel it is safe, as well as truthful, to say, "I didn't know he was a priest. Not till Mrs. Lerner told me. The housekeeper."

The archbishop lets that sit. His lips move a little, praying or ruminating. "Whatever. The burden of this sin is Father Allen's. He was the elder, the priest, the seducer. And worse, when he tired of you, he put you away here to cover his crime."

His last sentence is a slap. That's a mean way to put it.

I want to cry when I think of Will tiring of me. Is it possible this baby-faced man is trying to hurt me?

I almost start to make excuses for Will. Well, I *did* scream and cry a lot. There was that reel of red thread I stole the time Mrs. Lerner took me to the Ben Franklin, there was the night I went joyriding with the hired boy from the Erikson farm, who ripped my dress. Call that crazy.

The archbishop goes on: "Dr. Grafton has just told me that you are not so much mentally ill as depressed and anxious."

This diagnosis is news to me. Good news. I have achieved *neurosis.*

"Father Allen deeply repents his crime. He has discovered in himself a vocation to the cloister. He will be joining the Benedictine monks at St. Conlith's." The cleric's glance lifted from me and reared away to the landscape outside. "I imagine he will spend the rest of his days in manual labor and penitence."

A cackle rises to my lips and I force it down. Hysteria.

What have they done to Will? I think about Abelard and the millstones. I'm quite well-read, especially now that they let me go to the library with Annie.

I stifle my laughter and nod humbly.

"He will be taking a vow of poverty. Before a man does this, he must make something like a will. I want you to know that Father Allen intends to provide adequately for you and the child. For your medical needs and for a place to live and plenty of money to live on. He's giving you his family farm in Nerstrand."

"Mrs. Lerner already gave me five hundred dollars," I say. I don't need Will's blood money, or the judgmental eyes of the Cannon Valley. I have Mrs. Lerner's blood money.

The mention of my princely sum makes the archbishop smile. "You say that now, Miss Valenta, but the world is a cruel place, I must tell you."

I wonder if he knows as much as I do about that.

"Father Allen *owes* you his legacy, Miss Valenta." The archbishop speaks over my objection. "And further, the Archdiocese has a fund..."

How would he have completed that sentence, I wonder to this day: "...for women like you," "for cases like this..."?

How many of us can there be?

It takes about two minutes for my pride to burn off. A vision takes over my mind: *my* farm, *our* farm, Annie, Baby, the studio. *Draw, Lucy, draw, and don't waste time.*

Legal fees.

"I want you to know that I stand ready to help you in any way I can," the archbishop winds up.

Really?

"I need a good lawyer." This comes quickly to my lips.

He looks at me keenly, startled. The baby lips become petulant. Maybe he thinks I'm going to sue him. But, "I'm sure you think so," he says in a silky voice.

"You need a lawyer to get out of here."

"But Dr. Grafton tells me he is ready to release you, if you have a place to go and people to take care of you. We will see that you do. But I'm sure you understand our assistance is—ah—contingent upon your silence. You must not go to law, or to the newspapers."

Whatever, I think. "It's not for me, the lawyer. There are lots of people here who don't belong."

The archbishop looks at me as if I were as feeble-minded as Sylvie. "We can't save the whole world, Miss Valenta."

"One person. Two." I feel as if I'm bargaining for souls like some saint in an old morality play.

The archbishop folds his small hands prayerfully. "I'll do what I can. Of course I know a number of attorneys. And, if you wish, I'll hear your confession while I'm here."

But I say, no thank you.

CHAPTER THIRTY-ONE

DAVID GRAFTON HAD gotten in the habit of finishing up the work, his tie loose, in Nurse Passmore's office, going over the day's insights, the day's expenditures, the frequent perturbations. Often he longed to put his feet up on her hassock, but he knew he must not do this in the presence of a lady, even a lady whom he thought about in the guise of a maiden aunt. Kindly, if severe.

Grafton was the only child of an intelligent woman. The focus of several aunts. He felt at ease in the company of his nurses. Men had hardened him, or perhaps war had hardened them all together. But now, three years after the Armistice, he was recovering his pleasure in female presence. At least in the presence of someone soothing, but smart and rigorous, rather like his Auntie India.

"It did Lucy Valenta a world of good to talk to the archbishop," he reported to the Director of Nursing at the end of that day. She had taken the small, armless, rocking chair opposite him in the alcove overlooking her garden. His aunts had preferred such chairs for knitting, and he imagined Nurse Passmore busy with her needles. To sit with an attentive, knitting woman relaxed a man as evening came on.

But Nurse Passmore's hands remained folded in her lap. They were, he observed, twisted with new knots of arthritis.

He tended to notice women most easily in a clinical presentation. He had not fully recovered his interest in their sexuality, though he dutifully worked on it.

He had been, in retrospect, half-formed, repressed (the new Freudian word), when he went to war. His sexual experiences in the battle zone had been traumatic: how often did one use that word in relation to male experience? But one frequently could.

Well, in his newfound optimism, given the brisk challenge of Mercy Winstead, Grafton felt he might regain his ground.

He continued: "Miss Valenta was smiling from ear to ear." He patted his pockets for his pipe. "I wasn't at all sure of that decision…"

"You mean to let the archbishop see her?" Olivia Passmore asked.

"Yes. But I liked the man." *Against my will*, he thought, but did not say. He'd had his fill of clerics at the moment. He knew that Nurse Passmore was a respectable churchgoer, so he decided not to tell her all that he knew about Will Allen. "The father of Lucy's child…ah, he seems to be some relation to Donovan. He wants to make amends, the archbishop, I mean."

"A financial settlement, I hope?" the nurse inquired. She knew that Archbishop Donovan had a reputation for holiness. Such men were often unlikely to grasp a woman's vulnerability. They might even consider vulnerability to be a sacred condition. Like pregnancy.

"That might be too much to hope for. This is a Puritan country, and people think that the mentally ill are immoral, that they bring it on themselves," the superintendent continued.

"Sometimes people do bring it on themselves, of course." Nurse Passmore liked to separate the sheep from the goats.

"Toronto was the same." Though Canadians, Grafton thought, were more likely to blame insanity on some aspect of provincial inferiority. It came to the same thing in the end. Insane people are not *nice*. Not like us. " I wonder if some day we won't discover that mental illness is a kind of brain disease, like a rare cancer of some sort."

Nurse Passmore shook her head rather dismissively.

Grafton felt hurt. This was his pet theory.

Nurse Passmore went on: "Are you thinking about Mrs. Leary? The epilepsy?"

"Yes, certainly. But Lucy Valenta will do as well. Hereditary susceptibility, bad genes. And finally, brain disease."

The superintendent reconsidered his own words for a moment. Was he merely saying she was foreign? A Czech? Not like him, an Anglo-Saxon?

Nurse Passmore said nothing.

He corrected his own analysis. "To be fair, she's been treated horribly—raped, if I may use so blunt a word. A man led her astray and offered a charade of marriage. She has no one to confide in, and when she breaks down, she's called a whore, a thief. A creature of disordered appetites."

"Well, I've seen no sign of those. She's a pert girl, and talented." (If a bit of a show-off, Olivia Passmore thought).

Grafton remembered again his Aunt India, who had been headmistress of a girls' academy. Olivia Passmore had led a team of combat nurses and did not blink at a glimpse of the carnal world.

"Besides, talent"—Grafton took that up in preference to *disordered appetites*—"is always suspect. One's a little different, and the bullies circle…" Here he was thinking of himself. Playing the piano all too well.

Here, he was thinking of his mother.

Olivia Passmore's thoughts rose as though to meet his in the air: women, in particular, must not be talented. She herself had braved the taunting circles. Until she'd learned to shut down, bury her essential self—Lolly, she'd been called, then. She'd buttoned herself into a respectable life. It had taken effort. She inhabited that life fully now, and could barely remember the wild heart of Lolly.

"You know, on the Somme," Grafton continued, " I saw *animals* go insane. Horses. Dogs. Once a fox, running back and forth on a field strung with barbed wire. And animals cannot be accused of immorality. Therefore…"

Nurse Passmore became more quiet. The reference to France

alerted her. She knew that something had happened to David Grafton in the war. Blighted his spirit.

She knew he longed to speak of it, but dared not. She knew this because she, herself, suffered the consequences of her own war service and her own reticence.

To be wounded made you weak. But without the wound there could be no compassion.

But suffering did not make you holy. The wound did not guarantee an open heart. Often it shut you down and made you cruel. What made a person take one path and not another? *Reticence* protected the privacy in which a suffering person debated such questions. Some days it took all her powers of concentration to stay on the high road.

She knew that David Grafton struggled as well. She wanted to help him, she wanted to warn him.

"You seem very far away," David Grafton said to her.

But, how dare he take that psychiatric tone!

"The human spirit can only be pressed so far," she offered noncommittally.

"Do you think that's true of everyone, Nurse? Or are some individuals more finely spun?"

She shrugged. She could not imagine herself, really, being pressed too far. Lolly might have been, but Olivia never. "Going back to Mrs. Leary: what she saw—or did—put her into a catatonic trance. Erased her memory," said Nurse Passmore rather severely.

"So…?"

"What happens if she gets it back?" She felt she needed to caution the superintendent about his intended course of *analysis*. He wanted to get the poor woman to tell her story: "the talking-cure," as the Freudians called it. She feared it.

Grafton should know better, since he was not eager to tell his own story (though maybe he was).

Nor was she (*though, if only…*)

220

"I'm sure I do not have to remind you, Doctor,"—she settled on a stern approach—"that a psychotic episode like the one that brought Mrs. Leary here damages the brain like the kick of a horse. Do we want to awaken her to a second kick?"

She had overstepped a boundary, but Grafton didn't seem disturbed by her frankness. He pulled out his tobacco pouch and tapped flakes into the bowl of his pipe. "What I'm wondering is, was there a genuine psychotic break, or a grand mal seizure?"

"I'm sure I don't know, sir." The nurse clasped and unclasped her hands. "Bit of both perhaps? We have to think of the family. The children. What people say happened."

"We should ring Nathan Wells at the U. He's the man on epilepsy. Wish I had more time." Pulls on the pipe punctuated these short sentences, and the male business of getting it going.

Nurse Passmore tried on *we*. Perhaps she could search the incoming journals at least. She could ask the new young nurses what they were learning about brain disease. That would take some humility. As much humility as David Grafton was offering her.

CHAPTER THIRTY-TWO

"It could be my child she's carrying," Will Allen whispered to Joe Haggerty.

To Haggerty's ear, Allen sounded more proud than penitent. *Pathological narcissist*, he judged.

The two priests were vesting in the sacristy of the cathedral, alone for the moment before the sinks and spare silver-plated brushes. Haggerty's red hair was neatly furrowed with combing. His black vestment was embroidered in green and silver for Ordinary Time, and the emerald silk at the collar suited his complexion.

He met Will's eyes in the mirror.

"So?" he said ruthlessly. "Leave her alone, Billie."

•

Will Allen had begun thinking about what it might take to apply for laicization, the complicated exit from priesthood. Complicated because of the indelible mark on the soul.

He opened a can of pomade that lay on the counter and applied a little to his hair, golden brown and riding up in a wave toward the bald spot he would no longer comb over. His uncle, the archbishop, had proposed the monastic tonsure for him in any case. It had seemed a good idea at the time, to immerse himself in a cloistered community where women couldn't set foot on seventy miles of holy ground.

But that was before he'd sat in the sheriff's car and watched Lucy drift down the drive, her apron a sail, her body a boat.... He loved her. He realized that now.

They could buy a small house in, say, Ohio, and a suite of Stickley furniture.

"Man, your capacity for delusion is beyond the pale," Haggerty hissed.

The man always seemed to read his mind.

An altar boy knocked and entered the room.

The boy cleared his throat. They could hear the cathedral organist roving over the notes of the Gregorian chant that would, so the text proposed, lead his mother into paradise.

Laicization. He would be, as the common expression had it, "defrocked." No one in Ohio need know.

The Irish, his mother, would call him "a spoiled priest."

But his mother was dead. He was about to conduct her funeral mass.

He seemed to feel again the archbishop's hand on his head: *You are a priest forever.* He remembered the sweet smell of holy chrism.

The altar boy helped him into a black silk vestment flecked with gold that made him think of a starling. He followed Haggerty out onto the altar. There were a thousand people out there in the cathedral, a thousand candles. Will felt the triumphant swell of energy that always came to him when he officiated.

He loved being a priest.

Despite the struggle with celibacy—looking ahead down the years as he counted the pews between himself and his mother's coffin where it lay in the bronze doorway half a city block away—despite the struggle he knew he'd fail over and over as long as he lived—that aside, Will loved being a priest.

He loved it, despite the hours, the venomous housekeepers, the invitations to too many rich meals, being stoned to death with pebbles in the nuns' confessional, the silly dressing up—an altar boy handed him the brass aspergillum, with which he'd sprinkle holy water on the coffin—you had to enjoy it and bear with all the foolery for the honor of a priestly vocation. For the power to turn bread and wine into the body and blood of Christ, no matter what a sinner you were personally.

Will knew himself to be a sinner, but he believed in the Transubstantiation.

In the room behind them, the altar boys were lighting incense. Sweet, choking smoke drifted out to his station next to the altar. Will liked scent. He thought of Lucy's hair. He heard the senior boys admonishing the new ones—*don't play with fire*—then a young one scuttled out, swinging the censor.

For the power, with a lifted hand, to save souls from hell, where the worm never dies. The power to bless. And curse.

Though how often was that invoked these days?

He'd brought his uncle close to it.

The power to drive out demons.

Exorcism. That's what Lucy would have gotten in the old days. It was a perfect cure for female hysteria.

Lucy.

The littlest altar boy, his face solemn now, took his place ahead of Haggerty, swinging the censor. The little flame inside the brass thurible flared up dangerously.

Where the worm never dies.

What worm might that be?

An enormous whoosh and crack filled the cathedral as hundreds of congregants rose and simultaneously kicked forward their kneelers. The first twenty rows were full of priests, and the masculine voices reached Will's ear before the lighter voices of the choir nuns became audible: *In paradisum, deducat te angeli.* May the angels conduct you into heaven.

He turned to the archbishop's throne, where the chubby old man sat in all the glory his saintly heart despised. His mother's brother. His uncle. Will bowed before the throne. The archbishop, eyes closed in prayer or agony, failed to acknowledge the gesture.

He walked across the cold white marble of the altar steps. His mother's casket began its long journey toward him, carried by six brother priests.

CHAPTER THIRTY-THREE: LUCY

I'M BACK ON the ward, puffed up with my baby, my good prognosis, my cigar box full of hundred dollar bills and my farm in Cannon Valley. Maybe god-in-his-mercy does work in mysterious ways.

On my way back from the visitors' parlor, I passed below Annie on the porch off 1 North. They've given her this space to work with Sylvie and sing out of when she feels the need. It overlooks the back walk and a silent woods.

"Call to her in Czech," Annie caroled down to me. She's teaching Sylvie to say "Honey."

My well of Papa's language, so lovingly dammed up, has started to fill again. "*Jak se máš, miláčku?*" I shouted up.

Of course Sylvie couldn't hear, so far away.

I watched Annie hold Sylvie under her chin and say the word I'd just offered her, and then the English word *honey*. Sylvie understands what we're doing, but she learns words slowly. Annie made up a sign to go with the new word.

Annie has endless patience for this sort of thing.

She has a book on finger-spelling Nurse Mercy gave her. Sylvie can't get the knack of letters yet, but Annie and I are teaching her our new tongue of private endearment and secret-sharing.

I smiled and smiled, wending my way home like a normal person.

CHAPTER THIRTY-FOUR: ANNIE

I BELIEVE DR. Grafton and I share a similar world view: I often find an answering glint in his pale eyes when he lets me look into them. In deference to my *seizure disorder*, he darkens the room and himself.

I haven't had a decent mirror for years, but I imagine that my brown eyes no longer have that soulful glint I remember last time I looked: that gaze of a girlchild departing her beloved family to take her place in a benevolent world. My eyes probably tell a different story now, a cultivated story of "nobody lives here."

Grafton's eyes go empty like that.

Lucy laughs when I say such things.

"Look into my eyes," I tell her.

She is only too happy to do so.

I turn down my inner light. "Eyes of a psychopath," I tease.

Sometimes she gets testy with me and scolds in her indulgent, innocent way. "I love to look into your eyes. I see your soul," she'll say, the sentimental girl.

"Not now you don't. I know how to hide it."

She'll sketch my face anyway and light my eyes with her pencil, no easy task, I imagine. I will look at her drawings and see she has refuted me, my parlor trick.

Or she has told the lie of the pencil, the artist. She has imposed upon the paper what she wants to believe.

Or maybe my eyes are never dark to her.

Lucy is so inexperienced that she thinks Will Allen is unusual in the world of men. Here she is babbling about the kindness of the Archbishop of St. Paul, as if he didn't have an agenda.

Lucy is going to be slow to accept the nature of the world. Her innocence is unassailable. I have a dream that I will be able to protect it, that I will somehow find a way to cocoon her in the safety of a house, a garden, a normal life.

Most people *are* innocent, and that's how humanity gets by. If everyone knew what I know, we'd stand around wringing our hands in the backrooms, unable to groom or reproduce.

We'd be madhouse inmates, in other words.

Well, I live in a madhouse, but I long ago ceased to be an inmate. When you see terrible things, there remains the option of acquiring a philosophical position. Otherwise, you'll be shut up forever in your own screaming mind. You'd be surprised how many people who live here in the Northfield State Hospital and Finishing School have chosen option one. Some of their coping strategies are not what I'd choose, some are dead foolish, but they give the thinker a precious element of freedom.

Here's what I believe: you are as sane as you are free. Step one: accept things as they are, however bleak. Step two: love the world. You can always find a little something to care for, be it a particular tree, or a Sylvie, or the lilies carved over the windows in the dorm on 4 North. Dust carefully. Think about how somebody took the time. Step three: stay busy.

There's a woman on 2 North. Her name is Marcelle Trotter. Her job is washing the bodies of the dead. She always has a clientele. This is an institution with hundreds of patients. She goes all over. Nobody knows the Northfield Asylum like Marcelle Trotter. She visits Men's Detached, Feebleminded, Infirm, Geriatric. She knows the tunnels and the kitchens. She knows the morgue. She's had experience I can only imagine.

There are things I have to spare myself.

Lucy would love to have Marcelle's job, what with unlimited access to the human body and those planes and angles Lucy admires. Lucy would like nothing better than to draw dead bodies laid out on slabs day after day.

But I hope to save her from that sort of thing.

To summarize, Marcelle has accepted things as they are. She has found something to love, be it something nonresponsive. She puts her heart and soul into this service. Her lips move in prayer as she washes the dead. I've seen her in action, though I look away. I've seen Marcelle unravel the spirits, say, of a suicide, as she lies tangled up in the knots of her death. Combing it all out, washing as gently as a grandmother, swaddling it up in a clean sheet.

She's not very crazy, Marcelle, that I've noticed.

I could say that about a lot of people here.

They are not necessarily good people, though. Some are sane and evil. But many are good. And many, good and evil, stay here because they have no place else to go.

As for the bad ones, it's best to have them where you can keep your eye on them, I guess. But they cause a lot of damage to patient and staff alike. Probably they should be in prison.

Since many people in prison belong in an asylum, we could all swap at no loss to the government.

I think Grafton is good.

I think he learned, in that war they had, to see things as they are and then he decided to be kind. What he saw separated him from other run-of-the-mill folk. He will never tell about what happened to him, lest he mar the innocence of others. Scripture says *He who injures the innocence of these little ones, it were best for him to have a millstone put around his neck and be cast into the sea.*

I used to take issue with Jesus on that text. I'd think, *get on with it.* Innocence is a luxury. The millstone seemed a little too stern.

But now, since I've met Lucy, I've decided that people are something like greenhouse plants (the greenhouse being one of my special duties). You can't put the seedlings right into the ground. You have to harden them off. Get them used to being in the world.

There are a lot of people in this institution who haven't been properly hardened off. So, when I say I want to protect Lucy's innocence, I don't mean I want to keep her in the greenhouse. She's acclimating on schedule. Her roots are strong—she had that good papa. Whatever kind of maniac bastard Will was, god-in-his-mercy will bring some good out of it.

That's our new joke, since Lucy met the archbishop. God-in-his-mercy will bring me some warm socks. God-in-his-mercy will let us have real coffee today.

I don't believe in that kind of God. I don't believe in God the Father, God the Son, etc. Maybe I don't even believe in God the Person.

I believe *bright morning stars are rising.*

My father was a Holy Ghost preacher: did I say that already? His story was about a God of air and breath. Rising and converging. I could tell you the Hebrew word for it, which I ran into somewhere, but enough of my book-learning.

Anyway, it's become a secret word for me, that I say over and over when I am assailed.

That's my father's concept: *assailed.* He believed we are circled round with Principalities and Powers, aiming to destroy us.

The evidence is on his side.

He believed even more passionately in an angel host, hovering to protect us. When I think about all the stir and danger in the air of this room where I am talking to Dr. Grafton, I get chills.

I close my eyes and say my god-word.

Dr. Grafton has begun to question me about my children. It troubles him, I think, that I am flippant and evasive on the topic.

He thinks I might be a psychopath. It's hard to tell, because the essence of being a psychopath is disguise.

Frankly, I'm worried about that diagnosis, too. Maybe I'm

just fooling myself with the bravado of sanity. That's why I joke with Lucy: *eyes of a psychopath*.

I fend off; I say my god-word.

It's wise to be suspicious. Maybe nothing in my mind is real. Once again, the evidence abounds. Mrs. Haugen believes she belongs to the royal line of Britain. Harriet Macey sits all day with her hoarded stubs of pencil doing complicated mathematical equations that she thinks will save her from hell.

None of that seems real to me, but who am I to say? It seems real to Mrs. Haugen and Miss Macey.

My children aren't real to me. As I've told you again and again, Dr. Grafton, I remember nothing after the midwife said "You have a girl, Annie."

He offers me a cigarette, but I decline. I liked the ones I rolled myself, but I don't indulge the urge anymore. It's my sacrifice for Lucy's child, who must never play with matches.

I think there's a place in my mind where I could look for Samuel and the children, but I'm terrified of what else I might find there. I'm afraid of the grief or shame that would rise up to drown me. So I do not open that door.

Even I am not hardened off enough to do that.

So I will amend my first principle: Accept things as they are, no matter how bleak, unless you can't stand it.

We have a lot of time here in the asylum to work out our philosophical positions. I will keep worrying this one. It doesn't yet, I'm sure, cover all the possibilities.

But Dr. Grafton, you should understand that this dark humor I project about myself as a murderess is my way of hanging on.

I watch you playing a similar game, as do the older nurses. The young nurses haven't caught on yet. When they begin to develop a sense of bleak, black irony, I know their skins will have gotten thick enough to survive here.

To me this means they will be safe to befriend.

It's staff-in-their-mercy who control our access to real coffee, among other things, so I'm happy to contribute to their education. Like the archbishop, I have an agenda. I'm in it for myself, to an extent. I'm in it for the coffee.

I allow myself to think seriously about leaving here.

I think about leaving here with Lucy. To get ourselves released or to escape.

These visions of freedom upset my system of checks and balances. I control them. Even joy has to be tamped down.

But Lucy is flush with money and her farm and she thinks she can get us both out.

I am not insane. I have to keep saying this with confidence. But there is a spot of doubt on the landscape of my brain.

What if all they said about me in that courtroom, before I had the falling fit, is true: that I'm a psychopath, that I killed my husband and children? Let's just admit the possibility.

They haven't been to visit. Where are they, if not dead?

If someone killed them, why not me?

But mostly I avoid that thought in any palpable form. It's the doorway to a Crazy Hole. If you step into a Crazy Hole you can fall down it forever. It almost happened to me on 4 North.

I can't risk it again. The second time, you're finished. I've seen that happen.

Yet somewhere near the entrance to the Crazy Hole, that treacherous piece of ground, lie my memories of Julia, the boys, the apocalypse.

I want them, my memories, even the apocalypse, if it tells me something about what's real. That's why I crawl closer to the edge, let Dr. Grafton creep along beside me.

Last year I fetched up the memory of Julia's name. My oldest daughter. She was, what? five years old?

Julia—the name—came into my mind one day. The name pinned itself to a waif made of smoke, floating through my daydreams.

The boys are still out of my ken. If a memory comes to you softly, the way a butterfly emerges from its chrysalis, you're safe.

If you break into that chrysalis, or pull out the wet butterfly and toss it off the porch of 4 North (I saw a nurse do this once), you will have a bad result.

You have to focus. That's what I tell Lucy.

When Dr. Grafton does his work with me—he calls it "analysis"—he leaves the door open. Nurse Passmore is in her corner office, absorbed in her paper work. I know she's rather deaf and won't be able to hear us. But she's aware of what goes on. Nurse Passmore is our chaperone.

Dr. Grafton is afraid a patient might accuse him of rape or something.

What a blunt word, rape. Not a word I ever used outside. We never talked about such things. Here, you wouldn't believe what hanky-panky people get up to. Accept reality, no matter how bleak.

Dr. Grafton is going to ask me to lie down on his daybed. This is embarrassing. No wonder he leaves the door open. Nurse Passmore is a suspicious biddy. She trusts no one.

She was in that war of theirs as well.

"Analysis" is a new form of healing they pioneered in, I believe, Vienna. You lie on the couch and drowse. At least that works for me. Dr. Grafton leads you closer and closer to the Crazy Hole.

Then, if you're smart, you'll fall asleep.

CHAPTER THIRTY-FIVE: LUCY

I HAVE NEW duties in the guest parlors! They call this "transitional assignment." It means I have some hope of getting out. They're training me to be a housemaid or a cleaner or some such vocation.

I have other plans. I will *hire* housemaids and cleaners, and paint in the studio Annie and I will make out of the dairy barn office.

Meanwhile, I lift my long skirt and pin it behind me like a tail. I drop an apron over my cotton slip. The slip has pockets sewn from waistband to the modest ruffle. The pockets contain my passbook from the bank, a light sketching book and several short pencils. So precious are these items to me that I remove them from my body only to sleep, and then I lift my thin horsehair mattress and tuck them under me.

In my housewifely costume, I salt and sweep the oriental carpets, dust the furniture, and spend happy moments looking out the window. There are few visitors in the morning, but those who do arrive are of the most amusing variety. So far today I've greeted a deputy sheriff, a former patient who's lonely and wants to be readmitted, and a small boy with a kitten to give away.

It's easy for me to switch from skivvy to parlor maid. I simply unpin my tail and pat my hair. I seat the visitors on the handsome chairs I've already polished and report to Matron with the visiting card on a silver plate. I try to give a very good impression of our institution. I am proud that I have been selected for this trustee job because I speak well and have good manners, thanks to papa and the nuns at St. Joseph's Academy.

233

But soon I will have a house of my own.

None of the visitors so far today has presented cards. As for the small boy, I petted his kitten and sent him to the barns behind Men's Detached. They are always looking for mousers. The police officer went to visit with Nurse Passmore and I don't know what they said to each other.

People come up the drive in pony traps and automobiles. Cabs, Ford cars, and the occasional fancy model, the kind Will drove. It's a Ford that's arriving just now. A flock of chickens scatters before it.

I have plenty of time to loose my tail and arrange my skirts. I shake my apron out over Baby and put on my most respectable expression. Two men come up the steps and ring. One is short and a bit stout, with a pugnacious look. His underlip retracts like a bulldog's and his face is set in a scowl. Energy radiates from him. He can barely stand quietly on the stoop. He peers at me over his horn rims as I open the door. I'm afraid he will put his foot through the crack before I invite him in.

Behind him, I see a tall, vague fellow in a homburg, which he quickly removes. The bold man wears rough tweeds. The vague man is dressed like an undertaker or an attorney.

My heart begins to race.

Surely this is the lawyer we've requested through the Patient's Council!

The asylum pretends, at least, to be sensitive to the legal rights of inmates. Of course, we seldom wake up sufficiently to ask for any rights, nor do we have usually have private funds to pay for help.

I stroke my pocket and the outline of my bank book for courage.

Nobody was moving on our request for legal help, so last Friday Annie snuck down to the kitchen and used the phone. I had to tell her how to dial Central and make her connection to that Erik Strommer. He's the editor at the *St. Paul Dispatch* who's been answering her letters for a few years now.

I think it was the recreation therapist on 4 North who first sent him her essays. He published a few. She keeps copies pasted into her scrap book, which she's let me read. They're about odd things that happen around the place—we've no shortage of material, there—and philosophical observations from her unique point of view.

Nothing too personal, but then Annie says she can't remember anything personal. She's been working on a story about Sylvie, I know. They let her clack away on the library typewriter.

Next time she wants to send along some of my illustrations. We are going to be famous, as well as rich.

But I must keep my fantasies under control.

The pugnacious man puts his card in my hand. Yes! Here is a man who comes when he's called.

"We have an appointment with Dr. David Grafton," Erik Strommer says. He charges across the threshold, the man in black trails behind. That man offers me a card with deeper engraving: *Joseph Fell Fielding, Esquire*, it says. I know what "esquire" means, and my heart flips over.

I go for my silver plate and clip off toward Matron.

But Grafton is already coming through the swinging double doors. No doubt he has been on the lookout from his office or heard the Ford cough up the drive.

"Gentlemen!" he greets.

There are handshakes and the establishing of rapport. I try to slide back into my familiar curtains.

But Grafton is looking at me with raised eyebrows. "May I present Mrs. Allen," he says to the visitors, "...who is professionally known as Miss Lucy Valenta."

Clearly he wants these visitors to know I am Somebody. But I am not to be brought into the circle as yet. Grafton leads the men into the west parlor. His next command removes me from the drama. "I wonder if you'd be good enough to ask Nurse Passmore to join us, and order refreshments, Mrs. Allen."

I offer a little parlor maid's curtsy.

Grafton smiles. Probably he was good at charades in school. "Coffee," Strommer barks. A man's man. To Fielding: "You?" Fielding asks for water.

Nurse Passmore is already making her entrance. Refreshments will follow. I slide backwards with my retractable feather duster and think about cleaning the chandelier. That task will bring me close to the parlor transom.

But Nurse Passmore is onto me. "You may go to collation, Mrs. Allen."

It's a command. I have a weak personality. I obey it.

CHAPTER THIRTY-SIX

CRUSADING NEWSMAN, DAVID Grafton thought. It was a diagnosis of sorts.

He handed Erik Strommer a cup of coffee—strong, black—in one of Nurse Passmore's fragile porcelain cups. He watched the cup disappear in Strommer's big hand, a hand that could nail a chicken coop together, Grafton thought.

Overburdened Public Defender, he judged Joseph Fell Fielding. The man was gaunt and ill-looking, with dry graying hair and dandruff in his eyebrows.

Grafton had to categorize people quickly and, often, he feared, inaccurately. Still, he had to do it. He justified this to himself by asking not what David Grafton thought of an individual but whom did that individual take himself to be? What role had he chosen?

Crusading Newsman accompanied by *Overburdened Public Defender*, he decided.

They had come to see Annie Leary. They had demanded, in fact, to see Annie Leary. Grafton had required that they confer with him first, lest they upset the delicate balance of her analysis.

They understood, or pretended to.

Later, presumably, they would crusade and defend.

This quest of theirs—he had mentioned to Nurse Passmore in the pantry, where they had withdrawn to sort out the cream and sugar—might be dangerous for public relations. It might be harmful, even catastrophic for Mrs. Leary's mental health.

Or it might be exactly the opposite. It might draw the Legislature's attention to the underfunding at Northfield State Hospital. It might reopen Mrs. Leary's legal case and perhaps help her to gain additional liberty—permanent status on 1 North, for example, even parole into the neighboring village a few afternoons a week. Freedom from the ever-shadowing nurses.

He suspected Mrs. Leary had a dream of living more independently, but he doubted it could come to pass. She would never be strong enough. There was the matter of financial support.

With so much at stake, both Grafton and the Director of Nursing were on high alert.

Strommer got right to the point. "I'm interested in your patient, a Mrs. Annie Leary. Did you know she's been doing some writing for me? We've published seven or eight of her articles in the *Pioneer Press.*"

"Of course."

They were good pieces, Grafton knew. Not what you'd expect: perhaps humorous vignettes from the madhouse. The sort of things nurses and doctors might write. Annie wrote philosophical pieces, or essays on nature or literature. When she wrote about the patients, they spoke as sensibly as the inhabitants of any boarding house.

In fact, when Grafton had read her essays for the first time, back in '19, they'd ignited his desire to work with her. Her prose didn't match her diagnosis. Not only did they seem the work of a competent, normal woman, they were, to the best of his judgment, original and—well, perhaps *wise* was the word.

"What do you think of her writing?" The superintendent smiled in his cool, self-deprecating way. "I'm not the best judge."

"Damn good," said Strommer, "or I wouldn't print them. She writes poetry, too, but I don't get that." His small, bright eyes darted left and right.

"Hmmm. I had no idea," Grafton said.

The attorney, Fielding, broke in. His voice was high-pitched and lacked self-assurance. "So many creative people have mental problems," he ventured.

Strommer wasn't interested in that line of thinking. "Listen, she told me she wants to get out of here. What are her chances?"

The superintendent whistled through his teeth. "Well, I hadn't thought about going that far. We've been hoping to move her down another floor…"

"I've no idea what that means. Is she sane or not?"

Nurse Passmore had pulled her skirts around her and seated herself on the plushy sofa. Grafton cued her with a look and she commenced her practiced speech on mental illness. "We often have that question, about our loved one, or"—she glanced coyly at the superintendent—"our colleagues at work. Or our own selves. But sanity is on a kind of continuum, you see. And, for some patients, it comes and goes. Mrs. Leary has been stable for a long time, but—"

"Is she dangerous to the community?" Strommer cut in. He seemed to have no interest in subtle distinctions.

"Well, there again…" Grafton began. He disliked the sound of his own voice; it came out sounding evasive. "And there is the problem of her legal status."

"In the prison system, she'd likely be paroled by now," the attorney put in with unexpected vigor. "Most murderers kill only once, and make model prisoners after that. Although—"

"Although, hmm," said Grafton, thinking about the troubling details of the crime. But he said only, "She remembers nothing of what happened on the day in question. Are you aware that she has, in fact, a neurological disease called psychomotor epilepsy?"

It was Strommer's turn to say, "Of course." He pointed to the man in black. "This is the fellow who got her off, remember, off the murder charge back in '13. It wasn't all that hard to do, since she had a falling fit in court and, after that, went catatonic on them."

"It *was* hard to do." Fielding came to the defense of his work. "You have no idea how difficult it is to prove a case of not-guilty-by-reason-of-insanity."

Strommer argued, "In the case of a woman, frankly, it must be easier because we don't like to believe that women can be violent, especially against their families."

Grafton sniffed and exchanged a look with the Director of Nursing. In his own line of work, family was the very crucible of insanity, especially for women. "We just don't know," he said.

Nurse Passmore addressed the attorney. "If someone kills in a fit of madness and then recovers his sanity, does the law resume a claim on him?" She shielded the case of Annie Leary behind the encompassing male pronoun.

Fielding clicked his tongue against a gap in his front teeth. "Assuming the madness was real—and that is hard to prove *post hoc*—there is no question of *moral* guilt. I'm sure we agree about that. But legally, it would be a challenge to return such a person to the community."

Grafton's concentration ran aground on the phrase "we agree." He had seen many shades of mental illness. People went crazy for a variety of reasons; some of them had an element of choice, as Nurse Passmore would quickly point out: drug addiction, say, or syphilitic insanity.

But that was not the case with Mrs. Leary. Grafton steepled his fingers.

He had a hypothesis, but he wasn't sure it was ripe for discussion. He hesitated to trust these men.

On the other hand, they might be Annie Leary's best hope.

He decided to risk it. "Frankly, I doubt that Mrs. Leary murdered anyone. I'm exploring with her, in analysis, a possibility: that it was—I don't know, a terrible accident—something enacted in what we call a fugue state. She remembers nothing, as I said. She can say little in her own defense."

"But the prosecution argued their case well," said Strommer. He leaned forward. "She tied her children to three kitchen chairs and set fire to the house. That argues planning and intention."

Grafton sighed. He had puzzled over the lurid newspaper

accounts. But of course, one couldn't trust them. "I wonder, could it have been, somehow, the husband?"

The lawyer reminded them that this possibility had been explored at trial.

Strommer cut through the debate. "Are you suggesting that the woman you know, your patient, isn't capable of such an action?" This was what he had come to hear.

"A psychiatrist would never put it that way," said Nurse Passmore, as if she feared the superintendent would, in a weary moment, shake his head, or nod.

Strommer barged on. "Because that's what I think. The woman whose writing I've published could not have done that deed."

Grafton looked up ruefully. He had looked down. He brushed a lock of hair away from his forehead. He found Erik Strommer intimidating in his blunt singleness of purpose. Grafton's own purposes had to be many-faceted. "There is such a thing as the psychopathic personality," he said carefully. He didn't like to find himself arguing against Annie Leary. "A psychopath can fool even"—*you*, he had been about to say. But that would be rude. "Any of us," he finished, sounding lame to himself.

"And you think Mrs. Leary has such a disorder?" Strommer asked.

Grafton added sugar to his coffee. Thank God for silverware to play with.

People who saw things in black and white were particularly difficult for him to deal with intellectually.

Still, he called the word *No* back from his lips. Nine-and-a-half times out of ten, Grafton, thought he could sniff out a psychopath. But there was a territory in his mind where reality was up for grabs.

No Man's Land.

"Let me be clear," Strommer began.

Grafton could not suppress a sigh.

"You do understand, Mrs. Leary has asked me to investigate the case for her. She is seeking legal assistance," said Strommer.

"The obvious choice was Fielding, here, because he's already on her side."

The lawyer nodded with some reticence, as though not entirely sure of his side.

"You are working *pro bono*, Mr. Fielding?" Grafton asked. It was too bad, but he had to be thinking about money all the time.

Fielding shuffled his worn shoes on the floor. "Well, I would, of course. But my associate tells me that Mrs. Leary is able to pay a retainer. Did you know she called Mr. Strommer on the phone?"

"She says a friend is putting up the money," said Strommer.

"Well, well." Grafton shot another glance at Nurse Passmore, who returned a prim look. The phone. How had Annie Leary managed that?

Strommer pushed back his coffee cup with a bump. Olivia Passmore reached for her china with a protective hand. "Let me just take this out of your way."

"I'm anxious to meet the woman," the editor said pointedly.

Grafton sat in silence.

He made up his mind. "That will not be possible today. Mrs. Leary has had no visitors for seven years. Any reference to her past, or her married life, ah, upsets her. It would be much too much to put her through without careful therapeutic preparation."

"But she asked me to come," Strommer said.

"I'm sure you understand," said Grafton.

"I'm sure I don't," said Strommer.

Grafton put on his most charming, psychopathic smile. "Please trust me to have the good of my patient at heart."

"I guess I must," Strommer said. He moved to rise. He had places to go. He would be back. "You have an impressive reputation."

"My reputation?" Grafton was surprised to discover that the crusading journalist had researched his work in the world.

The man's next remark confirmed that. "Well, I admire what you're doing with the women here. I'd like to run a story on it, actually. Though tell me something: aren't there seventy men next door? Wouldn't they be more interesting?"

"What makes you say so?" Grafton asked. He shifted in his chair; he had felt the tap of Miss Passmore's little black boot under the table.

Strommer huffed. "I, well, women: it's all hysterics and wetting their pants, right?"

"We have a lot of pants-wetting all over the place. And hysteria is a common diagnosis for *men*, since the war."

"Imagine that," said Strommer.

Nurse Passmore's own cup chinked against its saucer. She, for her part, definitively rose. They were dismissed.

David Grafton walked them to the door. Olivia Passmore opened it. Heat and light rolled in over the Turkey carpets.

"You fought on the British side, I understand?" the editor asked, passing through. He slapped a flat cap on his head.

"It looked like a good team," Grafton said.

"Invalided out or what?"

Grafton suspected the journalist already knew the answer to that, so he looked directly into his eyes as he said, "I had a war neurosis."

Strommer was embarrassed, as Grafton had intended him to be. Honesty was a forceful weapon.

"Shell shock?" Strommer offered.

"It requires neither shells nor shock," Grafton replied.

"Well, heh."

Grafton retaliated. "Did you serve?"

"I? Oh, no, asthma."

The superintendent smiled graciously.

Olivia Passmore claimed the high ground, like everyone's missionary aunt. "We are not all called." She made that little shooing motion, scarcely perceptible.

CHAPTER THIRTY-SEVEN: LUCY

WE ARE AT collation in the solarium on 2 North. I vibrate with so much excitement I think I can feel the bench we're sitting on begin to shake. I slide off and walk over to the coffee urns, which are full of healthful grain beverage. I know that Annie will follow and I can whisper everything I know about Joseph Fell Fielding's conference with the superintendent. Which is nothing but the bare fact.

Annie walks over to the windows as if she needs sun and I trot behind her. They are open. We lean out. A scrim of dust rises on the road where an auto has just disappeared.

When Annie leans back in, her face is drained of color. She clutches me, one hand on the baby. "Oh my God, Lucy, we have to run away."

I give her a little push, as though we are up to some girlish play. Nurse Dolan is watching, and so are all the women gobbling tomato jam.

I think for a moment about what it would mean to run away. I'm not used to being the practical one. I pat my bankbook.

But, "What's the matter?" I ask. We turn back to the window and look at the view. It seems to me we're as close as can be to getting out of here by some direct legal route. So why run away? Get ourselves both back in Seclusion?

She repeats the name of the attorney I seem to have hired: "Fielding. He's the lawyer who represented me in the courtroom."

"Well, good, you remember him." Surely Fielding's the best choice.

Annie stares ahead as if checking for lights in a dark hall. "Yes, I do. I do remember him." Her tone is cautious. "It startled me, is all. The name. I felt…"

When she looks into space like that, I'm always afraid she's going to have a falling fit. *You felt a memory*, I think, *like the paw of a cat*. I know how that goes with her.

It makes me shiver, as if someone's walking on my grave.

She corrects herself, girl on a bicycle going over a bump. "After laundry," she says, "let's take some stuff down to the fishing cabin."

This is an old building by the lake where the male trustees stow their rods and reels. The cabin's on the edge of a woods that could provide cover for a run to the road. "Your best sketches, my notebooks."

"Maybe a change of underwear," I say, moving into the practical role. "Some bread and cheese."

"Your bankbook."

I begin to breathe easier. The frantic look in her eyes has faded, and I think she has begun to play with me. We both love these boy adventure games, which never get past the planning stage.

Well, dreams begin in play. We send up her idea like one of those whiffleballs they give us at recreation now the weather's good.

See if the gods bat it back. Game on.

Playing or planning, I foresee problems. "What if somebody sees us?"

Annie has lately been released from the attention of her two nurses, and Dr. Grafton has given us considerable measure of what they call "parole." That means we just sign out at the main desk and walk the grounds at will. No more locked ward.

Yet I feel eyes on us.

Because there are always eyes on us.

Nurse Dolan's at the moment. We have been standing a long time at the window, listening to birdsong. "Everything all right over there, ladies?" she calls.

"Yes'm." Annie.

She answers me. "Everyone is so tired on laundry day. Even the nurses take naps. We can stuff a lot in our pockets, not attract attention."

"What if the men find our things when they go fishing?"

"You are the what-if girl. Then they get to look at your dirty pictures."

I grasp her shoulders with my two hands and make her meet my eyes. "Are we really going to do this?" It's my turn to be frightened. I realize I've grown used to the security of Northfield. The *asylum*. I have my studio. I'm six-and-a-half months pregnant.

She has a way of running the palm of her hand up her face and shoving the bangs up to attention. "Let's call it a contingency plan. Maybe those men from the city can help us, maybe they let all hell loose." She shrugs.

Hell is her department.

I say, "If Dr. Grafton lets you talk to that reporter, maybe you could slip him our papers. I don't want them to get ruined, down by the lake."

She's thinking about this. "I don't want him to read my notebooks."

"I'll paint a skull-and-crossbones on the package."

"You read too many adventure stories."

Nurse Malloy calls out, "Ladies, we're having social time here." She doesn't mind our "particular friendship," which is the official term for Annie-and-me. But there are community virtues we are called to practice.

"This is an adventure story." I try that idea out.

"Not exactly," Annie says. She puts her arm around my waist and pulls me back toward the collation table. Nurse Malloy doesn't care if we love each other.

CHAPTER THIRTY-EIGHT

NURSE PASSMORE RETURNED to her office to deal with the paperwork. It had been a long day; she has less and less patience dealing with powerful men. Smoking and intimidating each other, leaving the remains of their cigars on her china plates.

She picked up her reticule, ready to go upstairs to bed. Then she put it down. Upstairs, there would be only a candle. Here she has the gaslight. She locks her desk drawer, a new habit, and withdraws to her rocker. She relishes the warmth of her office, the light, the knitted throw and the chance for a few moments with her photo album.

This guilty pleasure inevitably soothed her. She could bring the trials of the day before a panel of women.

She turned the album pages slowly, sometimes reaching out a finger to caress the line of a girl's cheek. Here were the V.A.D.'s from Le Havre. Marianne Le Pac, Monica Derry, Rachel Nimitz, Sheilah—McGinnis? McCarthy? Elizabeth Wellington Demarais. Ruth Scrivitz. She named the women softly, formally, as she had called them forth at their graduation ceremony: Monica Anne Derry, Sheilah Mary—there, it was, McCoy.

Sheilah Mary McCoy had been the first to die. "To fall," as they said.

The men, at least, were "numbered among the fallen." As if they had tripped on stones.

Nurse Passmore spared a thought for the language of war memorials. Women were rarely included. Nurses did not fall. They "tragically perished in the course of performing their duties." On the run.

By the end of the war, Nurse Passmore had written that sentence so many times, under such pressure, that she had schooled herself not to register the name of the deceased, nor call the face into her imagination.

Now, at leisure, she gave each woman her moment, those who died and those who survived.

Elizabeth Wellington Demarais. She had stepped on a mine, carrying groceries.

Rachel Nimitz, who slipped gold rings in her ears the minute her nurse's veil came off. Went to town. She was still in an army sanitarium.

Marianne Le Pac, Superintendent of Nurses at Boston Women's and Children's.

Monica Derry, seduced and abandoned.

Before her panel of nurses this evening, she evaluated Dr. Grafton: *It was brave of him to speak of his war neurosis.*

"The revelation did not, of course, surprise us." Miss Passmore spoke for all the nurses. They'd seen plenty of combat fatigue, suffered it. It explained the man's odd reticence. He was a burnt-out house, rebuilt from the rubble. Didn't trust himself.

Some might judge him harshly. Some in the medical establishment (those who had not served) believed that only weak men suffered shell shock. Olivia Passmore and her nurses did not share that view.

What's surprising, she confided to the pages of her album, is the timing of the admission. Had it been strategic?

Certainly it had stopped Strommer in his tracks.

Though she thought that, on the whole, they could count on Strommer and Fielding.

Preemptive? For surely the journalist had his own sources of background information.

Intuitive? A gesture of instinctive trust.

Unconscious?

In any case, Dr. Grafton understood trauma from personal experience.

Olivia Passmore was grateful to have her suspicions confirmed. She had been wary of his intervention on Annie Leary, the experimental "analysis." But perhaps his own suffering would guide him better than all his books in German. His vulnerability.

The Director of Nursing liked Annie Leary and had hopes for her. The girl reminded her of one of the V.A.D.'s, Miss Winifred Atkinson, from Glasgow.

Another one who'd perished in the course of performing her duties.

Winnie.

That funny old way of photographing the war nurses, with their eyes lifted up to heaven like saints in ecstasy. This was how the men liked to see them.

The men liked to see the nurses other ways as well, of course. She had intercepted the vulgar postcards they passed round. How confusing for everyone: one of those German alienists called it the Madonna-Whore Complex.

But most of the nurses were neither madonna nor whore, they were just ordinary girls. She ran her finger along the line in the photo where Winnie's blond curly hair escaped the veil. An ordinary girl.

CHAPTER THIRTY-NINE

"Don't make me remember," Annie Leary said. She opened her eyes, just when Grafton thought she'd gone to sleep again. "It's not a good thing to do."

Grafton sat back in his chair. He quieted his breathing. "I'm sorry," he said finally. He knew she was right. He had to honor her self-awareness.

"I'll remember when it's time. I promise." Her smile was almost coquettish. He knew she liked him: *transference*. It was a healthy stage.

He liked her: *counter-transference*. He'd better be careful, keep his perspective.

He'd wanted to mend her, like dropped porcelain, something precious.

Transference and countertransference were the great topics of psychiatric residency. Being a little in love with a patient was good for therapy, so long as you used *love* as a keen instrument of inquiry, under surgical control at all times.

Was that even possible? He must believe it was.

She was vulnerable.

She needed his objectivity.

Besides, she was in love with Lucy Valenta.

David Grafton thought it prudent to conjure up in imagination the charmingly rounded and petite form of Mercy Winstead.

Not too much of her form. She was a lady. But she was a permitted object of affection. And he was (was he not?) a normal male. He felt a rush of energy: *reinforcement*.

Annie Leary had closed her eyes again. She reminded him now of his sisters in their sleep.

"Is it time for me to go?" she said, still resting.

"Past time." The glass was run. Grafton checked it against the watch in his waistcoat pocket. He'd never adopted the battlefield fad of the wristwatch.

Or cigarettes. He noticed again the nicotine stains on Annie's fingers.

"You're back to smoking."

"Now I ask Miss Winstead for a light," she said.

"That's good."

"I'm going to stop again for Sylvie's sake. She shouldn't imitate me."

"I should say not."

"Though Dr. Jessen-Haight says it's good for us."

"Dr. Jessen-Haight is wrong."

We are so often wrong, Grafton thought. When you study the history of medicine, we are so often wrong. And with so much at stake. One could cause so much suffering. Unleash so much pain.

If one lost one's objectivity.

PART THREE:
VIEWS OF APOCALYPSE

CHAPTER FORTY: NORAH

NORAH RENFREW, ONCE of County Cavan, has been storing this fire inside her for quite some time.

She sits on the floor in a corner of the library. Everyone else is asleep, or tied down, or under a dose of chloral. Many of the night nurses are asleep, or gossiping quietly with each other in the light of their oil lamps.

The watchman, a trustee from Men's Detached, passes while Norah hides quietly under the library table.

Though people have called her feebleminded all her life, Norah is canny. She knows that the watchman will now descend the stairs through the kitchens and enter the tunnel.

He will walk down the hall toward the morgue.

He will go in, placing his lantern on a marble slab.

He will meet Miss Dorothy Olson, an adventurous student nurse, who is waiting there.

The morgue is a chilly and uncomfortable place to pursue their affections, but Nurse Olson will have brought a blanket. It's private, at least when Norah is not spying. Norah knows the watchman will not return for a few hours.

She loves to wander the halls while everyone sleeps. It reminds her of being a normal woman in a normal home. Once she lived in a place as beautiful as this. It, too, had a library, shelves of books, window seats. She was not, of course, the mistress of the house, but the kitchen maid.

But, wandering at night then as she does now, she could pretend. Mr. Thomas, who in daylight had called her a stupid Irish slut, met her there one night as she sat in the library staring like a dog at the books she could not read.

She thought about her baby. Where had they taken it?

That woman on 2 North is having a baby.

It makes Norah jealous. She remembers an infant's warm weight on her breast, the curling flower fingers.

They should not have taken away her baby.

She has that woman's gold ring in her bathrobe pocket. Finders keepers. Well, she stole it. She slips it on her finger.

Norah strikes one of the long sulphur matches she's taken from the tin slot on the wall of the kitchen. Usually, when the urge to light fires comes over her, she does it in the kitchen sink. Then she douses the fire with water from the bucket and slips the burned match into its proper bowl of sand.

Fire is dangerous, Norah, says one of the voices in her mind. *You must never play with it.*

Another voice says *burn*.

Why did they take my baby?

Norah watches the flame eat sulphur, lick the wood stick and go out. She lights another, calmly listening to the voices in her head. Always this dialogue.

She tries the fresh flame on a page of the book she has in front of her.

I could have learned to read, she thinks.

The children of the big house had their cloth books with pictures of cows and ducklings. Sometimes she would pick them up from the nursery floor when she wandered at night. She'd pretend the letters meant something to her. Once—she just couldn't help it—she'd taken one of the cloth books and brought it up to the room she shared with three other girls who had come all the way from Cavan here, to the prairie.

"One a-penny, two-a-penny, hot cross buns," she'd read to Mary and Sadie.

Sadie—she was so mean—shrieked with laughter. "Aw God,

you silly girl. You've memorized it. That one says 'The friendly cow, all red and white, I love with all my heart.'"

Mary had said, more kindly, "You're both daft. It says 'Three blind mice.'"

The book Norah has in her hands now is made of paper, not cloth.

A page corner feels the flame, curls, browns and gutters out.

This fire is a tame thing, after all, she tells the caution-voice in her mind.

She rips out the page and crumples it, strikes another match and touches it to the paper.

It blooms! At first, the fire is small and personal. The little blaze warms her hands. She feeds it pages. Fire is good.

Fire cleanses the landscape. The house where she was kitchen maid was in Fort Ramsey, Minnesota, on the edge of the prairie. Sometimes the prairie would burn in a lightning strike, and afterwards, an explosion of wild flowers would erupt out of fecund stubble and everything would be new and fresh.

Norah longs for this rebirth.

On a small scale.

But the fire takes on a life of its own. It is no longer her creature. It ascends the cotton curtain drifting in a light evening breeze. It slides up the fabric to the corner of the window, where wallpaper has begun to uncurl. The wallpaper seems greedy for its consummation.

This is not to Norah's liking.

Perhaps she should call somebody.

No, she will get in trouble with Matron. They will tie her to the bed.

She watches entranced as the fire claims things. It glides along the polished floor. The fire seems almost an extension of her own powers—they are limited, but fire is infinite. How far can she go? She has never tried herself.

But she decides to run away, opening a door into the hall.

Fire needs to breathe. It claims the draft, and then a kind of whirlwind. It becomes insatiable.

Norah hears the tinkling of many Chinese wind-chimes, ringing together. The library windows are breaking.

She runs. Matron must not know she has done this. But now her nightdress is afire and her lungs fill with suffocating fumes.

Things turn on you. She runs, and everything begins to be engulfed.

CARMIE

On her silver horse, Carmie still and forever leaps...

But no, she wakens in the bed she shares with Max. Sounds drift through the open window, an owl hoots. The moon is up and bright.

No. Max is not home. He's on night duty at the asylum, of course. Carmie longs to lie back and claim the protection of his breath. She has learned to calm herself that way, breathe with him, and lull herself to sleep.

It will be impossible to sleep. The dream has filled her with jubilation and a sense of adventure. She has been called: a low whicker.

She must get down to the stable. Hand over hand. Pulling her legs along.

Jubilation and danger. The sky to the west is reddening with— can it be?—fire.

LUCY

There is a stirring in our bed pile.

The baby turns inside me.

Annie takes back arms that have circled me all night. She sits up and reaches down toward Sylvie, curled by our feet. Sylvie is crying and wiggling. In the moonlight I watch Annie lift Sylvie's chin and say as loudly as she dares, for others are sleeping around us, "Honey, use the chamber pot."

But Sylvie is headstrong. She hates to use the chamber pot when the moon is full, light streaming in the windows. Any woman in the ward can see her squat over it, and this offends Sylvie's modesty.

Not that we aren't all squatting and farting and knocking over our tin pots in an anvil chorus every night. The sound of the night watch at Northfield Asylum is the sound of a stream of urine hitting a metal pail.

Sylvie wants to go to the lavatory.

She knows the way.

Nurse Cupcake, back there in the lamplight, knows that she knows the way. We are on the sleeping porch, and behind the porch is the night ward, and Nurse Cupcake's desk.

I sit up and look for our nurse-protector. It worries me a little when Sylvie goes off alone, though I know she's perfectly competent.

I am practicing to be a mother.

Now that I'm awake and the baby inside is stirring, I don't think I can go back to sleep. Annie, though, has a gift for slumber, her arms around me again. I am wakeful but I am content.

Perhaps I did go to sleep, for now the sun is coming up. I see a red glow at the windows.

But how can that be? Our windows face west. That's why Annie likes to go down to 1 North for her morning carols. The ladies down there don't use the porch for sleeping. It's open on three sides and she can watch the day come on.

Then I hear a rustle, like many dogs running through dry leaves.

Someone begins to whale on the alarm bell by the door with the heavy mallet that hangs next to it.

This is a very realistic fire drill. That's my drowsy thought.

A thunderstorm has come out of nowhere. I hear the crashes.

No, it's gunfire, or an explosion. There are gaslights, kerosene stoves, the lamps the nurses carry.

Nurse Cupcake and the night aide are coming down the aisle of beds, ringing their handbells. "That's right, ladies, all up."

Nurse Cupcake is so serene that I assume there's no big emergency.

Another clap of thunder.

"I want you all in lines." It's Nurse Malloy, now, singing out, in her customary tone of reassurance. "No bathrobes. Holding hands please. Row one is moving toward the fire escape. That's right, ladies. Row two."

We have practiced this exit at least once a month. They slide open the iron gates, we jump into the long dark tube. A nurse always goes first, to clear out spider webs. She whoops as if she were having fun. At the bottom, other nurses help us out into the walled garden.

But we've never done it at night, and Katie Wallblum, usually dependable, balks at the exit. She's afraid of the dark, I could tell them. And no nurse has gone first. They are all busy herding us.

Now the women are beginning to cry and break down, falling over each other, even on this docile ward. Now the aide, Max, is moving among us with his truncheon, poking here, prodding. "I have to use the toilet," says Clara Herzog, in her thick German accent.

"No, no, no, there will be no stopping. Row three," Nurse Cupcake calls. Her voice has an edge now. I feel the first lick of fear.

Behind me, Annie's fingers sink into my shoulders, propel me toward the fire escape. She is whispering in my ear. Her voice is southern, hypnotic, slow, seductive. "You hold Miss Stepchuk's hand, Lucy. Lucy. Here is Mrs. Lieberman."

I feel her thrust the woman in the next bed at me. Mrs. Lieberman's hand convulses on mine.

"Now *go*."

Miss Stepchuk and Mrs. Liebermann drag me between them. We are usually good at following orders. But I strain and try to break away. Where is Annie? Max is suddenly there. I get a slap.

"Go."

I am eased out the side of the building on the lap of a student nurse ("Be careful, she's pregnant"). We whoosh down like partners on a toboggan.

I am screaming and trying to get back in the tube, illogical as that may seem. It's not illogical to me. Other women are coming down. I cry out for Annie, for Sylvie.

Somebody grabs me from behind, and here is the good old camisole with its long sleeves wrapping my arms in place. These people are so organized, even in a fire drill.

They trundle me across the garden, through the open gate, down the drive. "Be careful, careful, she's pregnant."

I trip over something, and they carry me. Men's arms, the smell of Max. Smell of tobacco.

Which reminds me to scream over and over for Annie.

Because I know she has slipped out of the ward toward the lavatories. She has gone after Sylvie.

Fire is roaring out of the windows of 2 North.

ANNIE

The hallway, oh, sweet Jesus, is full of smoke.

I have grabbed, instinctively, a pitcher of water from someone's bedside table. As if I could put the fire out that way.

But my instinct has not played me false. I dump the water over my head and douse my nightgown. I hold my wet collar up around my mouth. We always wear so much superfluous fabric.

Sylvie will not hear me, she will not be able hear me.

I grope my way into the lavatory, where, Jesus, mercy, there is less smoke. Shall I open the window? Will that kill us or help us? There is a row of ten stalls, and over each one, a suspended tank.

How can I get to that water? Is there a way to save us if I can get to that water? Flood the place? My mind is not at its rational best.

I am screaming, "Sylvie! Sylvie!" I am calling in English and Czech. She will not hear me. I begin to sing at the top of my alto voice, "*Shout O Glory for I shall mount above the skies…*"

I hear her voice come in on a drone. She is in one of the stalls.

"Sylvie"—but she will not be able to make out the words. "Soak your nightie in the toilet!"

I lose her sounding of the bass tonic. "Sylvie, sing!" But she cannot hear me. I wail out the minor third, then the fifth.

She sings back. She loves that progression of sound.

I sing, "*When I hear the trumpet sound in that morning!*"

Something, somewhere, explodes.

And then a plank in reason breaks.

DAVID GRAFTON

I watch Annie's seizure begin.

No, it's something else. Her eyes are shocked open as though the power to blink has been taken away.

We have slid through the floor—I think—riding the cross timbers of the second floor lavatory toward Nurse Passmore's office. Our floor, which used to be the ceiling, is stable, but fire is erupting all around us. 3 North, which has now become our roof, groans above us.

No pain. Nothing broken.

Or, maybe.

We've fallen onto our backs. I spring up—there's only a slight twinge from my ankle—and I try to lift Annie.

Triage. I'll come back for Mortimer, then Wilson. The concussion of the guns.

But Annie begins to arch backward, falling.

I have to leave you, I'm going for Wilson. Sparks come down and little fires are catching. Tame, flirtatious fires.

I think I can see the full moon overhead through a ruined window. I force my mind into the present. It's the kind of night when men batten down, terrified of being ordered into No Man's Land. *Barbed wire in the moonlight, sacks of cloth hanging from it.*

Must get away from here.

We are all going to die.

I reach into Annie's swaddling of wet night clothes and lift her to her feet. She totters. I catch her under the arms and hold her upright. I look into her eyes. There is roaring all around us.

Can I get her out?

She focuses on my face. She is struggling out of her fugue. "Why aren't we killed?" she asks.

We are going to be. The windows are becoming a lattice of fire. I hear a tinkling sound. I think again of angels and the sounds they might make if I believed in angels.

"Damned if I know," I pant. "Are you hurt?"

I realize that she's not looking at me anymore, but into some other world.

She is gone, regressed, in the claw of memory.

Recollection can be state-dependent (I lecture). You cannot remember, sober, what you learned drunk. Nor what you learned under fire when the guns go still. You have to get drunk again, or traumatized again, to know what you knew...

"Sam!" she says to me.

Gone.

"I tied them to the chairs," she says.

I keep a hold on her. She clings to me.

"Why?" I ask. *I know how to be sane. I know how to treat a patient in psychotic break. I know how to tear myself out of my own irrelevant war.*

I must follow her, now, even though fire is lapping around the walls of Nurse Passmore's office. Neither of us has a choice.

From somewhere comes a sound like axes smashing windows.

Can there be an exit?

I don't know where we are. In the building. In my mind.

The claw tightens around us both.

"I had my aura. I knew I was going down," Annie tells me urgently. I try to pull her forward. Her crazy eyes bore into mine, but it is not me she sees. "I didn't want them to wander into the woods, or hurt themselves at the stove. Oh, Samuel, the fire. I think Julia got out of her ropes, I think she dropped the oil lamp."

Annie breaks from my grasp and tries to get away. The hallway is ablaze. She is on business of her own. This has all happened before. The past is reaching out for us, a fire-shaped creature.

I hear the mumble of the guns.

I catch her nightgown and drag her toward me.

"Sam, get them out." She struggles. "I can't, I can't haul myself back."

Her back arches and her head drops over my arm like the skull of a broken doll. Now the spastic motion starts in earnest.

I can lift Carruthers, he is light. I can drag Wilson.

Nurse Passmore is coming with her lamp. My sergeant is coming. Max is coming. He whistles a tune. "Stay back!" I shout. "I can't get you all out."

I lose my grip on Annie. She slides out of my arms. Her hands clutch. She is trying to pull herself by will power alone out of the seizure.

I know this cannot be done. As she lets go, I lower her gently to the floor. I turn away and struggle toward the only opening in the fire. I crash into the corner of Nurse Passmore's desk. It weighs maybe seventy pounds. Her photo albums fall as I lift it with my madman's strength. Photographs of white-veiled women scatter through the air. They burst into flame.

I heave the desk over my head through the flaming squares where the windows used to be. I turn back for the fallen. There is a moment of perfect stillness. The flames cringe.

Into that stillness I leap, carrying Annie Leary.

A woman rides to meet us on a white stallion.

•

In the end, thanks to the distinguished action of all concerned— read Erik Strommer's newspaper—*there were few casualties: a night watchman, a student nurse, an illiterate Irish patient, and one as-yet-unidentified male person from among many in Northfield who'd rushed in to hand inmates out the windows. When all those patients were safe, smoke overcame the anonymous hero, and he fell back into the inferno.*

When his body was recovered, no marks of identity remained.

The public went wild for the anonymous hero. Erik Strommer does not like to think of himself as a sensationalist, but he follows up with an interview of Nurse Passmore.

She had noticed a fellow hanging around the day before, in a nondescript car, on the hill above the asylum. He was not one of the familiar voyeurs from town.

Sad as it seems, she told the *Pioneer Press*, sometimes the families of patients patrol the grounds, hoping to catch a glimpse of their loved one. Maybe the man fell asleep in his car and wakened to the crisis. Hurried to intervene.

It was a hired car and they were trying to trace it, Strommer reported on the third day. No identification in the vehicle, except a generic set of brown rosary beads wrapped around the stick shift.

Then some first-hand observers started talking about a woman on a white horse who had ridden out of the blaze. Like the Angel of Mons. That story claimed the popular imagination.

But by the fourth day, the asylum fire went below the fold. No further information forthcoming.

At the Chancery, they were slow to miss Father Will Allen, because he'd set out for St. Conlith's Abbey after giving away his own flashy car. It took a while for the abbot to contact the archbishop. Many would-be monks disappeared on the way to their cloistered vocation.

So Will Allen's brother priests were slow to put it together, to mourn, to remember him as a hero.

In the end, they thought it best to keep the funeral mass private.

CHAPTER FORTY-ONE: LUCY

IT's A WHITE room, with a white bed, a wicker bed table, a clear glass pitcher and a water tumbler. The floor is polished wood. There are cotton curtains at the window, lifting gently in the breeze, and outside, the men are cutting the first hay in the west field. Somebody's private room on the asylum grounds.

I love these elemental shades. White on white.

I like to draw with pencils because they let me see the world plain. "Draw, Lucy, draw Lucy and don't waste time." If I used color these days, I think my head would burst.

Perhaps it was not the skill of drawing Papa wanted for me above all, but the skill of seeing things plain. Which I have been slow to learn.

I don't read a lot, not like Annie, but I have gone over the journals of the painter Manet. He told the story of his wife's death this way: "All the time she was dying I could not stop drawing her face."

Some might think this heartless, but an artist would know the man was doing his best. He kept trying to connect her to the white and dark spaces of his design. Keeping her with him—yes, we have to try that. He was drawing her into the world, as we do over and over for those we love, as I am drawing Annie.

At the same time he traced the progress of her leaving.

If you love somebody, you go as far as you can into the passage with them.

And so, there is the scratch of my pencil, and outside, song sparrows quarreling over their nesting plan.

Dr. Grafton comes in without knocking, as doctors will. He is in his white coat, and I am grateful. He does not interrupt the design by which I hold Annie in the world.

He stands next to her bed. His good hand reaches for his pocket watch. His other arm is in a sling. He lays the watch on the pillow, lifts her wrist and takes her pulse.

She has been lying like that for two weeks, and the lines of her body are becoming indistinct. There's a concave hollow over her hip bones, where the white sheet dips.

When Grafton turns to me, his face is full of sadness.

Why does he care so much?

I'm sorry, my instinct is to be a little suspicious of anyone coming near us.

"Do you think she's going to wake up?" I can't help asking.

"Yes. Yes, I do."

"Maybe if we let Sylvie come in."

Grafton turns back to watching the rise and fall of Annie's breath. He sighs. "Perhaps." He's remembering, I know, how Sylvie shimmied down the brass drainpipe outside the lavatory before the floor ever caved in. She hid out in the woods like the wild animal she is until the firemen found her curled up on the roof of the icehouse.

I understand then Grafton's sorrow. He's not afraid Annie's going to die. He's afraid she's never going to be sane again.

I'd begged him to tell me what she said up there in the fire, and he did. He wanted to check it out against what I knew.

But this was nothing I'd heard from her before. There were the names, each one an invocation: Julia, Devon, Tim.

Each child a fire memory.

Dr. Grafton and I try to make sense of her, what brought her to this bed, now that she is so far from making sense of herself.

We think she was alone in the cabin. We think Samuel was

off somewhere. She got her aura, and the tingling feeling along her left arm that signals a seizure. What could she do? She didn't want the children to see her that way, and, above all, she didn't want them to wander off into the woods or down to the river. So she tied them to the kitchen chairs and went into the lambing pen, where she could confine her own thrashing. And then a kerosene lamp somehow hit the floor and everything went up in flames. Samuel came back from wherever he was and tried to get them, but—what?

The house fell on him, I guess. As houses will.

How could anyone have blamed her, unconscious in the lambing jug? The injustice outrages me.

Well, country people. She'd always been different. She was alive, the children and Samuel were dead. It made a story. It fit the facts of her elusive ways.

Nobody knew about the falling sickness, because, of course, she'd have kept that to herself. When it manifested at the trial, it confirmed folks' suspicions that she was a dangerous imbecile. That's what country people think about epileptics, anyway.

Not in the city.

Oh, Annie, get well! Let's run away to a very big city. We'll sleep in our own bed with Sylvie and our new little one and hold each other in the world.

Nurse Edith Malloy comes in with two cups of tea, trailed by Max. He takes up his daily station against the wall, like a guard dog. I sketch him in. His tattoos are all torn and streaked with healing scars.

It was Max, of course, who got Annie and Dr. Grafton out, walking in there on his hands, for all I know.

Dr. Grafton has locked onto a different, impossible story he needs to believe. No one could have lifted that desk. Could they?

I don't want to stop drawing. But Nurse Malloy says, "Now, little mother, we need to stay hydrated."

Grafton says to Nurse Malloy, looking again at Annie, "Now that she's got her memories back, she'll either regress severely or incorporate the new knowledge into her system of reference. Or maybe she'll forget it all again."

Max, at his station, nods wisely.

Nurse Malloy purses her lips over this clinical insight and we all look at Annie, calmly breathing. There's a red slash next to her ear, mended with black thread. The yellow hair around it is shaved away.

I see something like a shift in density where Annie's eyelashes brush her cheek.

I realize she is playing possum.

Incorporating the new knowledge into her frame of reference. Smiling a little in tender mockery.

Resting.

CHAPTER FORTY-TWO: ANNIE

I DIVE INTO water element, indigo light.

I surface into brightness and air.

"D" is for "dolphin." There's a picture in my children's book—the only book they have. The dolphin has a bottle-nose and a smile figured right into the anatomy of its face.

I track a school of them, diving and arcing into the light. These are the fins of the god I follow just now. It says in Job: *Ask the animals and they will tell you.*

I'm swimming as deep as I've ever gone into the ocean of my body. I've crossed the line between woman and fish, woman and blind anemone waving from the rock. I travel into the rock, woman and rock: *all being is epiphany and gift.*

The great advantage of epilepsy is that you can enter many rooms most people never dream of. You fall through layers of light as casually as other people wake and sleep.

Now I'm swimming out beyond the seizure and the sickness. I'm going to swim till I drown or I bring back the Word.

My father's voice: "Girl. Girl, where are you? Bring back the Word. Bring it on back!"

He'd yell and weep over me, his longing so intense I could hear the pulse. I would come home on it as to a bell sounding in the ocean. He wanted me, whole and well, and he wanted, also, God.

A lot of wanting.

Would he have known the dolphin for who she was?

Maybe. He was a smart man, but not so smart that it clouded his vision.

Lucy sits here day after day, holding my hand. She puts the sponge to my lips and she knows I drink. She is tracking me.

I will wake up.

I will bring back my own.

CHAPTER FORTY-THREE: ANNIE

OF COURSE WE are not going to live happily ever after on the Cannon Valley farm. Our stay here is temporary. We've already spoken to an agent about the sale. We've pensioned off Mrs. Lerner. I never even had to see her. Erik Strommer and the lawyer are hard on their quest. The archbishop has sent in reinforcements. We've cleaned out the bedroom where Will's mother died. Dr. Grafton has found us two student nurses from the hospital to look after things.

After us.

Because I know he is still wary. I am still pregnant. Annie still has epilepsy. We still wear our asylum dresses because we don't want to go into town for fabric. Besides, neither of us knows the new fashions.

Maybe we can get one of our nurses to bring us a pattern book.

Annie's never run a sewing machine, but she's good with her needle and thread. And we knit up things for the baby out of Mrs. Lerner's old wool.

Dr. Grafton brings Sylvie out on the weekends, trying to determine: Can she live outside the institution? He makes the same rule for her that we will have about the new baby: Annie must never be alone with a child. What if she falls? (Though she never will, never again.)

Annie will always need a Nurse Cupcake around. Thanks to Will and the archbishop, we can afford it. Money makes everything possible or impossible.

We have what Grafton calls a rational plan.

I thought it would be hard to live near town, but this is a good house when there is no Will in it, no Will's mother, no Mrs. Lerner. It's ours. Every window is like the frame of a painting, looking out on field, forest and the huge thrashing barn. That high prairie light.

The same as Annie dove for her memories, I burn through mine.

We have, at present, a mixed relationship with fire. I incinerate Will's papers, Will's old school books, till Dr. Grafton catches me at it.

Dangerous, he judges, testing the smoke on the wind. He returns with a couple of the paroled men and they clean out Will's life.

Now I set up my easel and organize the sketchbooks Grafton rescued from the fishing shack. Annie's journals go on a bare shelf. She sits nearby with her own fresh paper, inkwell and pointed pens. She is writing the story of her life with Samuel, who was a good enough man, though improvident. She is writing the story of Julia, Devon and Tim. She's writing them back to the world in case she forgets again, though I doubt she will.

It's brave work.

The family she's calling home is not exactly the family she lost. We agree, debating the point in our madhouse dresses: that is not how art works.

Annie weeps for her babies, but she holds, in her journal, the transformed children.

She has her arms full, that girl.

And Dr. Grafton takes it all in, making notes. I think he's writing a monograph.

He knows a place where we can live, in England, where he himself recuperated from the war. He knows doctors we can depend on and a good grocer and lending library. A place in London called Bloomsbury.

Or is he dreaming? I've learned to live in the present moment.

In this glowing summer. It stretches over our valley like a translucent skin.

EPILOGUE: ANNIE 1985

WE'RE FAMOUS, AND you are dead.

But I'm moving toward you, in the boat of my life.

What I hate about dying is the loss of words.

I like words. I like telling stories. But now, in this millrace, I am almost as mute as Sylvie was. "Insults to the brain," I hear my doctor say.

This makes me smile. I suppose she means strokes, *transient ischemic attacks*. The things doctors know about.

For my part, I know the inner landscape of the brain, passage after passage. I glide like a child in socks along the prefrontal cortex, slide down the banister of that treacherous temporal lobe.

Some people are vain about their muscles, others about their generative organs. I am at play in the rooms of my brain. It has offered me so much diversion over the course of a long life.

Still, I do not trust it. It is not *me*. The body is a house my life has played in, and I love to tell its stories.

Though now I can't speak the words.

Things come to me in images, like those of a motion picture or the annoying television they sometimes wheel in for me to watch. They think I'm bored, which couldn't be farther from the truth.

Long ago, I lost seven years of my life and I'm still on the trail of those days. Recollection has been the amusement of my elder years.

When my granddaughters bring me their newborns, I feel

that rush of images: the way Julia curled her long toes as she fed, Devon's blond hair, how it grew in a whorl from the back of his head. I see Samuel in my great-grandson's eyes.

Don't bother to correct me. I know these grandchildren are not precisely related to me. They are your line, Lucy.

Yet were we not washed` together in the blood of this world?

I think now in pictures, as you must have done. As our great-granddaughter, Mary, does. "Draw, Mary, and don't waste time," I used to say to her, when I had words.

When I had words, and legs, and my own automobile, I would often take the children to the Minneapolis Art Institute, where your work hangs in the "regional arts" room. Some of them, anyway. Your sketches of the farm and the faces of Dr. Grafton and Nurse Mercy. Of Sylvie. Of me.

There was your self-portrait I loaned to the museum for some exhibition, but I needed it back. It hangs on the wall, now, at the foot of my bed.

I think I can still see it, or do I know it so well it's taken an independent existence behind my eyes, in that inner landscape I visit more easily than the outer world?

I mind the day in September when you sketched it, looking into the mirror in our bedroom, because I begged you to. A few days before the baby, Nina, came.

People used to interview me about our life, physicians, scholars, art historians. I enjoyed the conversations.

I always left off telling the story in the early autumn of 1921, with the heat shimmering on the wheat bales, tomatoes warm on their vines. Nobody ever pushed me past that, they thought it would break my heart.

But really, it was just too personal.

Death has this in common with sexual union: the unstringing of sense from intellect, body from bone. Everything drifting away. Becoming.

I remember how your eyelids fluttered, whitening, opened.

Your eyes held mine. I tried to come along with you: why does the body not permit that transgression? It seems like a simple passage, to flow out on the river of spirit, two together, and wash over the earth.

I was kneeling beside you, soaked in your blood. It seemed as though we had both given birth, as if you had blood enough for all of us, me, the baby.

And then you didn't have blood enough for yourself. Your skin went damp under my hands, the hair at your temples sprang into curls. I held your gaze: "Focus, Lucy."

We will be together forever. We will flow into some natural thing, maybe a cedar. Not two trees behind the house, reaching eternally for each other. One tree.

My body failed to make its journey, but our spirits held on tight.

Not for a single minute have you ever been absent from me.

In the Vedic tradition, I've read, it's the moments of intensity, of illumination, of heroic action—call it love—that survive physical death. The rest of the story slips away. But love wakes up to new landscape, new combinations of experience. Maybe we'll not be people. That's a relief. We'll be birdsong, two mule deer on the ridge. That cedar.

Though I drift now in the twilight where stories dissolve. *Did this happen?* I wonder when I break through. *This*—what I call my life?

Perhaps I'm the dream of a housemaid or a merchant's wife, a flight of someone's imagination between first light and the day's occupations.

I am eight years old, enjoying a few weeks of school. Six weeks of it, maybe, before a falling fit will turn me into a freak in the teacher's eyes or the Holy Ghost will oppress my father and we'll load the wagons and move. There is a girl called Angela Hanson who sits ahead of me in a row of the brighter young children (and the slower old children, and a boy who speaks only Swedish). I covet her place, one chair before mine. I covet her yellow silk ribbons, and the braiding of her brown hair, a style I've never seen before that now I know to call French plaiting. I covet her lunch pail, which is not a lard can but some store-bought tin box with a painting on it of an owl and a cat in a sailboat. I covet, I desire, I envy what these outward signs signify, Angela Hanson's normal life.

The churches say that envy is a sin. I disagree. I call it *motivating*. I am eight years old and I want a house with a large kitchen and a mother who sits by the stove braiding some fancy French hair-do and tying silk ribbons, no brothers and sisters clamoring around. No falling fits.

I want it so badly that somehow I call this picture into being. I become that mother. Julia toddles around on the pine floor. Her slippery baby hair runs through my fingers, wetted down and licked into braids.

But I have strayed from the thought that perhaps none of it happened. With good reason, I mistrust my own mind. Maybe it lied to me from the beginning. Perhaps I am Angela Hanson, sitting at her window counting cross-stitch. She watches the preacher's family load a wagon, spilling little boys and kitchen items, heading out for the horizon Angela Hanson longs for. Into which she sinks the tooth of her desire.

Why should I be in this story, and not some other one? I spin out the idea, bored with my death bed.

David Grafton, for example, made up a story about rescuing me from the asylum fire, and he believed every word of it, no matter how illogical. His story wiped out some other story in his mind, where he failed to save someone. Which version was true? Don't ask me, I had passed out at the time. An unreliable narrator.

But when I play with stories, other lives I might have lived, passion asserts its claim to what is deep and truly mine. I am not permitted violent emotions. Love: I feel it as a weight, like the slow brass bob of a pendulum, that swings me back into the world: to David Grafton, to Nurse Mercy, to Sylvie, to Nina, to the white clapboard house we moved to on the grounds of the asylum, to the bloodroot and hepatica that drifted in May around the pump in the yard, to Edith Malloy having tea on the porch, to Carmie with the dancing horses she taught Nina to ride. Carmie could walk in braces by the time the baby got her feet under her.

Max made a saddle, like a pasha's elephant seat, for Carmie, to hold her stable on horseback. He'd had to pay that Buell Fricke a fortune for the mare Carmie rode off on, and her stallion who jumped the fence after them. Fricke had won the Lipizzaners in a card game at the German-American Cultural Center. He had no idea what they might be good for. Dancing circus horses.

Carmie couldn't stand to see them languishing in the field. She dragged herself out there, clung to that mane and pulled herself out of a story that was holding her back.

Desire is motivating.

She fell off that first time, a mile from home, and the sheriff caught up with her. Were they going to put her away for thievery? A crippled woman, fussing over some skinny white horses with sores?

Not in Wally Norton's jail! And they had a good laugh when Max stormed in. When he offered to buy the horses off Buell Fricke. They laughed when Fricke named his price, until Max pulled out his bankbook.

Max loved to tell that story. How they came to breed Lipizzaners. Max certainly made back the money he paid Buell Fricke.

Dr. David Grafton and Nurse Mercy married, I think, to give Sylvie and Nina and me a home. I couldn't make it on my own on Will's farm, counting cross-stitch and grieving and looking out the windows. Much less with Sylvie in the picture. They adopted Nina and Sylvie, though I never understood the legal arrangement. But they let me be the mother, braiding Nina's baby hair in the big kitchen of my dreams. Which held me in the world.

Mercy and David loved each other, I know, though they kept to their separate spaces. When Mercy died—in the early Fifties—David couldn't get his footing back. He kept staggering in the traces till his heart stopped, close to the anniversary of her death.

Nina was in charge then, and she had to put Sylvie into private care. I know she still broods about it, but she had no choice. Sylvie remained half wild, maybe three quarters. After David died, she started wetting herself again. Nina couldn't deal with Sylvie, and me, and all that sorrow. We moved from Northfield to St. Paul. We found Sylvie a place nearby. Nina worked her way up in a law office—you could apprentice then—and married, a little later than the fashion, another attorney.

Can you imagine how pleased I was to find myself cocooned in a nest of lawyers?

Max had long ago taught me to drive the back roads of Dakota County, and the city didn't daunt me a bit. In my prime, with the new medications and my Ford car, I reached out to *normal* for all I was worth. The grandchildren and I had a big shepherd dog named Mike who always rode with us. He was trained to anticipate seizures, but I never had another. Sometimes you age out of them.

We went to the park, to the art museum. In the gift shop, they sell my book, illustrated by Janina Lucy Valenta, published by the Minnesota State Historical Society.

We're famous.

I hear Nina say on the phone "She wanders in her mind. She doesn't really know what's going on, or who I am." She's crying.

Oh, baby, I *do*. It's you don't know who you are. Shining.

I wish I could speak. I wish I could sing out the back door.

I wish we could have lived out a long story, Lucy: London,

the smartest girls in town. You've had an exhibition in Bloomsbury. Your asylum drawings are the hit of the 1930s, my stories are published to popular and scientific acclaim. We are richer than God and Sylvie has a parasol trimmed with gold braid.

·

"Sometimes she cries. Her eyes are almost always closed, and I see the tears form on her lids"—Nina says.

But it is Nina who is weeping.

I focus. I become bigger than my longing.

Oh, darling, I become everything.

ACKNOWLEDGMENTS

Thank you to the McManus, O'Reilley and Berrigan great-aunts and elders: Mamie, Sadie, Rose and Kate, whose storytelling gave me a vivid sense of women's lives and secrets in the early 20th century. To their cousin, Captain W. J. Herringer, M.D., Royal Canadian Highlanders, who penciled letters to Rose from a forward dressing station on the Somme. Family history and my own early work in several state hospitals gave me on-the-ground access to institutional lore and memory. This is a work of fiction, however, and no one should feel implicated.

From Northfield, Minnesota, I have borrowed spring ephemerals and a peculiar quality of light, but there was never a state asylum there.

Thank you to Brighthorse for choosing this book and to Jonis Agee and Brent Spencer for seeing it through. To Lisa Bankoff and Bob Miller for encouragement on early drafts. To Clara Summers for help with the Czech language. To Mary Tuel for final proofreading.

Thanks to my family, forever. Thanks especially to my sister, Margaret Plumbo, R.N., C.N.M. for her inspiration all my life.

ABOUT THE AUTHOR

MARY ROSE O'REILLEY was born in Gray County, Texas, and spent her professional life in St. Paul, Minnesota, where, as a college professor, she specialized in poetry, environmental writing, and literary modernism. Her first book of poetry, *Half Wild* (Louisiana State University Press, 2005) won the Walt Whitman Award of the Academy of American Poets. Her second, *Earth, Mercy*, came out from LSU in 2013. She is also the author of five books of nonfiction, including *The Love of Impermanent Things: a Threshold Ecology* and *The Barn at the End of the World: the Apprenticeship of a Quaker, Buddhist Shepherd*, published by Milkweed Editions. Her first nonfiction book, *The Peaceable Classroom* (Heinemann), is a classic in the field of peace and justice studies. *Bright Morning Stars,* her first work of fiction, won the 2016 Brighthorse Prize for the Novel. She lives on an island in Puget Sound, where she's active as a potter and—coming from a line of country fiddlers—in the local music scene.